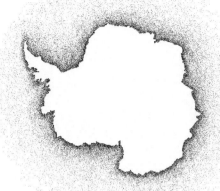

POLAR

T. R. PEARSON

V I K I N G

VIKING

Published by the Penguin Group

Penguin Putnam Inc., 375 Hudson Street, New York, New York, 10014, U.S.A.

Penguin Books Ltd., 80 Strand, London WC2R oRL, England

Penguin Books Australia Ltd, Ringwood, Victoria, Australia

Penguin Books Canada Ltd, 10 Alcorn Avenue, Toronto, Ontario, Canada M4V 3B2

Penguin Books (N.Z.) Ltd, 182–190 Wairau Road, Auckland 10, New Zealand

Penguin Books Ltd, Registered Offices:

Harmondsworth, Middlesex, England

First published in 2002 by Viking Penguin,

a member of Penguin Putnam Inc.

10 9 8 7 6 5 4 3 2 1

PUBLISHER'S NOTE

This is a work of fiction. Names, characters, places, and incidents either are the product of the author's imagination or are used fictitiously, and any resemblance to actual persons, living or dead, business establishments, events, or locales is entirely coincidental.

LIBRARY OF CONGRESS CATALOGING IN PUBLICATION DATA

Pearson, T. R., date.

    Polar / T. R. Pearson.

      p. cm.

      ISBN 0-670-03035-X

      I. Title.

    PS3566.E235 P65 2002

    813'.54—dc21   2001026118

This book is printed on acid-free paper. ∞

Printed in the United States of America

Set in Adobe Garamond Three with Novarese and Caravan Ornaments

Map by Mark Stein Studios

Designed by Carla Bolte

FOR D

A GOOD GIRL TOO

POLAR

THE PACK

There towards the end he got unduly interesting, Clayton did, after sixty-seven years immoderately barren of color and distinction. That's allowing, of course, for judgements, liens and lawful
repossessions as the natural birthright of Clayton's ilk of trash
along with the occasional larceny conviction, biannual drunken
rampage and the odd besotted set-to with an in-law—the strain
of dispute usually touched off by some slattern of a cousin and
contested evermore with a mattock handle or a carpet knife.

Clayton, that is to say, had only indulged in the practices of his
kind until there at the last when he went exceptional on us which
we mark anymore from a Saturday morning in the grocery mart.
Clayton had stopped in for saltines and potted meat, a fresh car-
ton of pouch chew and a twelve-pack of that brand of discounted
beer that tastes like ambitious water and is heavily represented
along the margins of the roadways where the cans and the paste-
board cartons end up and the customers sometimes too.

By all accounts, Clayton had seemed his normal self in the
checkout line—phlegmy, unshaven and fragrant in his ordinary
fashion, wafting anyway his tangy burly leaf and sweat bouquet
with his customary hint of livestock dander and his undertone of

Scope. He visited, it seems, an extended piece of talk on the fellow just behind him in line, that middle Quisenberry with the droopy eye and the jagged fractured bicuspid. To pass the time, Clayton shared with him the particulars of a movie he'd lately seen, a film about a practical nurse and a plumber that proved frankly pornographic.

Clayton had a satellite dish in his side yard, the big sort with the motorized swivel, and he'd paid extra for the bowl to come ornamented with a gaudy airbrushed eagle which he'd grown to regret as a profligacy and a waste. The trouble was that Clayton only ever watched the Satin Channel which he had to point his dish back towards his carshed to receive and pitch it over at an ungainly angle, so nobody saw his eagle who wasn't roosting in his trees.

The Satin Channel offers a twenty-four-hour schedule of triple-X fare which most of us catch only staticky glimpses of every now and again. It's located on the arc between the Congress and the Superstation, but unjamming the signal requires a monthly fee, a declaration, that is, of depravity in the form of a Visa charge. Accordingly, the bulk of us watch that channel only briefly through the snow until our eyes tire or our wives come into the room.

Clayton, however, had never married and, as unadulterated trash, he wasn't given to truck with moral hypocrisy. So Clayton couldn't be bothered to pivot his dish back around for appearance's sake but left it fixed instead on what we all knew for the pornographic transponder. He just sat in his chair with the head-grease stain and the frayed and ruptured armrests and watched without apology or palpable embarrassment the Satin Channel night and day.

Clayton, though, hardly qualified as your standard smut enthusiast. He wasn't the sort to leer at the TV screen with his adenoids on exhibit, a can of beer in one paw and his short arm in the other. Those Satin Channel movies never seemed to work on Clayton in quite the way they were meant to as he was prone to get caught up in the stories, no matter how threadbare and tossed off.

In the hardware once, a pack of us heard him describe a film about a pool boy who'd seduced and bedded a housewife while her husband was out jogging. Clayton had elected to fix upon the peril of the undertaking, and he'd owned up to quaking anxiety once the husband had come home as Clayton was obliged, by genetic inclination, to anticipate bloodletting. Of course, that husband merely kicked off his sneakers and had a go at his wife himself since she had a hand free and a pertinent cavity entirely unemployed which Clayton chose to take for an altogether splendid turn of events, both a triumph of love and a regular marvel of plotting.

"I'd have made that boy a gelding," Clayton told us, saying it sadly as if conceding that he was not so evolved as some people. "Swole up, that thing of his was like this." Clayton's thumb and fingertip fell just shy of meeting about his wrist. "It's a regular wonder he could fit into his trunks."

Clayton seemed to view sex like a man who'd seen an awful lot of the barnyard and was prepared to take for curious, in an academic sort of way, what some creatures see fit to link up and do to each other. He was also afflicted with a healthy dose of rural indelicacy, so Clayton would talk about anything anywhere and loudly.

In the checkout line at the grocery mart he told that Quisenberry how that plumber had squatted before that practical nurse's kitchen cabinet in order to lay a wrench to her drainpipe coupling. It seems her gooseneck was fouled and clotted, and, in his bid to work it loose, that plumber bent in such a way as to cause his trousers to sag below his equator.

3

"Went creeping down his asscrack," Clayton apprised that Quisenberry along with most everybody else who was loitering in the front half of the store.

Somehow the sight of that plumber's backside bestirred that practical nurse with a potency that Clayton suspected uncommon among tradesmen's derrieres, though Clayton allowed, at inordinate volume, that plumber's buttocks had been handsome, and he owned up to the fact that he'd savored them some himself. Not nearly, though, with that practical nurse's strain of enthusiasm, and Clayton told how she'd rubbed her nether gland by shoving a hand up her uniform skirt and had swabbed her lips with her tongue in a show of passionate abandon.

A Dupree just ahead of Clayton fled the line along about then. She went off with a snort, a sack of cake flour and a gallon of whole milk, but Clayton didn't pay her much notice or trouble himself to curb his tone as he was constitutionally immune to indignation and never seemed disposed to suspect it was his manner of palaver that made about town for huffy refugees.

Of course, that Quisenberry wasn't free to retire from Clayton's company as Clayton had specifically singled him out for chat, and local social custom wouldn't allow for him to flee. He was obliged instead to hold his ground and grin while Clayton set about conveying some notion of that plumber's member by hooking, like usual, his index finger roundabout his forearm where it failed by scant inches to meet the tip of his thumb.

They were the pair of them in the express lane which, in the majority of food stores, would have served to hasten and lubricate that Quisenberry's escape. At our grocery mart, however, they like to man the express register with the chattiest and most sluggish employee they have on hand. That particular shift they were going with one of their Tiffanys. Not the dumpy brunette Tiffany who looks more like a Delores or the Tiffany with the ball bearing in her tongue and the tattoos but their blonde beribboned Tiffany who largely lives up to the name.

She's a pretty girl. A high school student. Cocaptain of the drill team. She's been dating for years the son of the Blevins who owns the gravel quarry, and she drags that boy most Sundays to the Baptist sanctuary as recompense for the rest of the week which he spends groping her in his car.

She's pleasant enough at the grocery mart, certainly the most charming of our Tiffanys, and she fills out her apron in a fashion that the men about tend to find thrilling, but she's saddled with a comprehensive ignorance of produce that qualifies her for duty in the express lane. Tiffany can identify iceberg lettuce and carrots without prompting, and she's pretty reliable on celery stalks as well, but every other manner of tuber and green, fungus, legume and globe fruit makes do as mystifying exotica for her.

She has to know just what the item is to punch in the code and weigh it, and her method is to stare through the baggy while she waits for inspiration or word from the customer as to what he's fetched up with the intention to buy. Over time, of course, we've become acquainted with Tiffany's deficiency, so most of us shout out the name of whatever we've got as we hand her our plastic bags, dispensing thereby with the gawking and forging ahead to Tiffany's query.

"What do you do with it?" she evermore wants to know, the operative word here being "evermore."

Tiffany has remarkable recall for anniversaries with her Blevins—the first time they held hands, first kiss, first "I love you," first dry hump in the backseat of his Skylark—and she can remember the clothes she wore every day of the week for the past several years. She's hopelessly incapable of recalling, however, from one minute to the next what a knuckle of ginger root looks like or a parsnip or Swiss chard.

"What do you do with it?" Tiffany will ask a customer buying a rutabaga, and she'll rarely tolerate less than an entire recipe by reply. And even if Tiffany's next rutabaga comes to her straightaway, she'll peer dully through the sacking at the waxy hide. "What do you do with it?" she'll ask.

Tiffany rigorously maintains the glacial express lane pace they seem to prefer at the grocery mart, and the Saturday morning that Quisenberry was suffering Clayton in line, Tiffany had met with cause to be more deliberate even than normal. She was tallying up the purchases of one of our Central American imports, a fellow who'd come up from El Salvador or maybe Guatemala to harvest cabbage and pick apples and nectarines—the type of work the local natives would rather collect subsistence than do.

As his sort has grown common roundabout, the grocery mart stocks anymore a smattering of south-of-the-border produce, and that fellow had laid before Tiffany a sack of cactus paddles, a half pound of shiny green peppers the shape and size of rifle shells, and a bag of tomatillos in their husks. Consequently, Tiffany was even more stymied than normally she would have been since none of what that fellow was hoping to buy looked to her like food exactly. Accordingly, she required not just names for the stuff and instruction in its preparation, but she seemed keen to hear an accounting of why he'd eat such things as well.

Unfortunately, that gentleman's command of English proved to be rather poor while Tiffany, an upland-Virginia public high school enrollee, was but indifferently conversant in the language herself. So he identified his purchases for her as best as he was able, while Tiffany replied to him, in ever increasing volume, "What?"

Clayton, then, enjoyed the leisure to acquaint that middle

Quisenberry with developments in his movie plot at length. It seems the plumber, after a fashion, had taken that practical nurse on her dinette table, once he'd shucked her anyway from her uniform and had let his trousers fall entirely to the floor. Then she'd dropped onto the linoleum to let him thrust at her from behind which was along about when the postman spied them through the front door light.

According to Clayton, he seemed to think that practical nurse in peril, and he responded about as boldly as a mail carrier might. He let himself into the house, that is, and assessed the situation before laying his satchel aside and stepping fully out of his shorts.

"Pretty soon she had one going at either end," Clayton told that Quisenberry and then approximated for him the girth of the postman's member, sliding his thumb and finger towards his elbow where they didn't even threaten to meet.

By then most everybody had congregated at the far side of the store, and they were all of them glaring at Clayton and that pathetic Quisenberry who'd gotten, like folks will, contaminated by proximity and was taken to be fouled by the filth that Clayton was visiting upon him.

"Had her some honkers," Clayton declared. "Nipples as big around as jarlids."

Pushed to his limit, that Quisenberry finally mustered the pluck to speak. "It's some kind of cactus," he shouted at Tiffany. "You boil it and put salt on it."

Apparently, he was loud and wild-eyed enough to startle Tiffany a little. She took anyway that migrant's money without further chat, and, as that fellow sidled down the line to await his change, Clayton dumped his goods onto the belt.

"Then the meter reader come by," Clayton said, and doubtless that Quisenberry was waiting for the suitable forearm measure, but Clayton failed to reach with his thumb and forefinger and

7

neglected, for probably a minute or more, to so much as speak again.

That's when it happened. We're most of us in general agreement about that, but we're fairly fractured as to what exactly transpired. There's a school of thought that Clayton fell prey to the bar-code scanner, that the laser somehow bored clean through his pupils to his brain and fused together a couple of pertinent vessels. Among the *Merck Manual* devotees, spontaneous hemorrhaging is a popular choice, but that Quisenberry has sworn up and down that Clayton never so much as twitched or betrayed in any way that he was suffering some variety of distress. That leaves the considerable faction who subscribe together to the view that Clayton, with all of his vulgar talk and his pornographic pastime, had sorely tried the patience of the Maker who'd seen fit to render him simple, after a fashion, with His wrath.

In any event, Clayton left off with the practical nurse, with her plumber, with her postman, with her meter reader. Instead he stood smiling at Tiffany as she swiped his purchases past the glass and inadvertently double-charged him for his saltines which ordinarily Clayton would have mounted an authentic conniption about. He only stood there grinning, however, until at last he spoke.

"Please, sir, do call me Titus," he said to Tiffany. "Everyone does these days."

Then he handed her a twenty-dollar bill and, shockingly, failed to wait for change. He just took up his sack and stalked out of the grocery mart altogether leaving Tiffany and that Quisenberry to watch him both in silence until he'd climbed into his Fairlane and had rolled out of the lot.

"I thought his name was Claude," Tiffany told that Quisenberry, holding still Clayton's receipt and his folding money and silver in hand.

"Clayton," that Quisenberry informed her as he set down before Tiffany the sack of salad greens his wife had dispatched him to buy.

"Titus?" Tiffany asked him.

That Quisenberry eyed her along her length, from her chest anyway clear up to her hair ribbons. "Sir?" he troubled himself to ask her back.

Then she shook her head, and he shook his head, and together they trafficked in snorts until Tiffany lapsed into study of that Quisenberry's purchase which prompted him to tell her, "Escarole."

———

Nobody saw Clayton for probably a solid week or more thereafter which failed to strike any of us as terribly odd. He fairly lived off of icebox Salisbury steak and that strain of spongy loafbread that's chemically incapable of aging, so it wasn't like he needed to run out every day or two to the store. Furthermore, he had only recently retired for a considerable stretch from view.

The Satin Channel had mounted for the month of February a festival of sorts. To mark the fortieth birthday of Miss Jasmine Love, they had shown all of her movies, both her starring vehicles and those films in which she had played but supporting parts. There were hundreds of them altogether, and Clayton had pretty much watched them all as he was one of Miss Jasmine Love's most devoted fans.

By critical disposition, Clayton was keenly qualified to appreciate Miss Jasmine Love's variety of pornographic method acting. He was equipped to savor, that is, her talent for selling her parts on two fronts at once. She could play, for instance, a persuasive stewardess and, simultaneously, a hopeless slut, a convincing nun saddled with convincing frailties, a suitably tedious congresswoman with an appetite for pages and an earnest news anchor grappling with a weakness for her grips.

She was just the sort of actress to cast a spell on Clayton since she seemed to share with him a genuine passion for those shabby bits of plot that served as prelude to the intercourse. And even once she was naked and suffering the attention of some gentleman or three, Miss Jasmine Love had a way of actually looking interested in the sex. She troubled herself, that is, to glance at her menfriends' faces every now and again so as to convey that they were more to her than merely outsized throbbing members.

Clayton, then, had sprung with March upon us armed with fresh movie plots and had served, consequently, as appreciably more of a conversational trial than normal. So we weren't any of us anxious to see him once he'd slipped again from view, even if he had called a Tiffany "sir" and had claimed for his name "Titus."

It was one of our deputies who finally dropped in on Clayton at length, the only one of that entire bunch who would have. Ray had been circling around toward the blacktop, was coming from a dispute and heading towards a notification of kin. He had smoothed out a spot of acrimony between two cousins over a fencerow and was en route to the home of a woman in town who didn't know she was a widow, a Peagram yet to hear of her husband's carcass out the bypass in his mangled truck.

To the chief's credit, he'd early on recognized Ray as his man for that sort of job. Or maybe instead he'd merely established that Carl and Larry and Walter and Ailene weren't any of them up to that stripe of duty themselves and had given Ray a go essentially in the spirit of last bureaucratic resort.

Ray had hit town, after all, along about when Larry was flaunting his tactlessness. One of those planer mill Caudles had slipped from his bass boat and drowned in the reservoir, and Larry had gotten dispatched to pass the news to his brother who he'd found trimming limbs in his yard.

Now the brother, it seems, was piling the unsacked limbs down by the curbing which violated an ordinance that Larry straightaway acquainted that Caudle with. That Caudle thought the provision a sorry blight on his civic liberties, and he made his opinion known to Larry in a free and salty fashion which served to prompt Larry to write that Caudle up.

In fact, Larry was ripping that Caudle's citation out of his ticket book when he remembered why he'd stopped by in the first place, and he was shoving the thing, by all accounts, at that Caudle as he spoke.

"Elvin come out of his boat somehow."

"Is he all right?"

"No. He's dead."

Larry is thought lucky that Caudle clubbed him with his loppers but the once.

So Ray was certainly the obvious choice because he was the only one untried, but he proved suitable on account of he was Ray—seemly, that is, and possessed of fully functioning ear canals. Ray appeared to know from listening to people what they needed him to say or if, in fact, they required any talk from him at all. He could settle disputes sometimes with just his mitigating presence and deliver dire news with a fitting wince and a suitably downcast glance.

He had a past, Ray did. We never heard the gist of it precisely, but every now and again the chief would up and disgorge a telling nugget. Apparently, Ray had either killed a man or had failed somehow to kill one. He'd either brought about the death of a woman or had neglected to keep one from harm. He'd committed, we'd heard, some manner of violence against his former employer—a sheriff down towards southside in the uplands beyond Roanoke, or he'd declined, we'd heard, in the heat of a set-to to spring to that sheriff's aid.

The only thing we knew for certain was that he'd deputied all over—in Birmingham and Jackson, in Charlotte and in Memphis, down in Mobile and in the wastes just south of Roanoke. Also Ray didn't strike us as nearly so hungry for life as he might have been, which we'd come to take for a settled fact as well.

We didn't know he'd ever been married until a while after he'd come when his former wife showed up one afternoon. He'd arrived in town initially in the company of just his dog. Ray was driving a thirdhand Grand Marquis that looked to be held together by a blend of puckered rust and wishfulness. The chief's wife had found him a rental house off the junction past the airfield, and she'd stopped by with a casserole and a beefy unbetrothed niece before Ray had had time to unpack his sacks and boxes.

Paper sacks, she told us. Liquor cartons. And not a stick of furniture to add to what little had come with the lease for the house. The chief's wife had sniffed about and had satisfied herself that Ray was a practiced bachelor—from his mismatched leisurewear, from his awkward halting manners, from the fact that he seemed to own even less than a settlement's worth of goods.

Then, of course, there was his dog as well, an ancient mongrel named Monroe. She was sullen and unfriendly, greasy, matted and vaporish in a grand and foully intrusive sort of way. She broke treacherous wind, that is to say, with a kind of ceremony. She would still herself and hunker and tauten, and there would come upon her features an expression of devout concentration as if she were running the figures to reconcile the national debt in her head.

The way the chief's wife told it, she and her beefy unbetrothed niece couldn't help but watch that mongrel squatting by the hearth where the planking yielded to masonite beneath Ray's fuel-oil heater. They couldn't decide if she was about to drop dead or recite a holy psalm, but clearly something of moment was afoot. So they watched her, and they waited. They even went together prattleless for a time which caught Ray's notice, and he joined the two of them in study of Monroe until she'd broken the wind that she'd been ushering through her tracts and ducts and went back to shoving her paw in her ear and groaning.

The smell arrived shortly and fairly much seized them with its ghastliness. "We stopped out on the parkway," Ray informed them. "I think she ate a squirrel."

The chief's wife declared Ray a loner and untamable after a fashion which, naturally, served to make Ray a local object of romance. Women with daughters, women with nieces, women with personal desires took to waylaying Ray and favoring him with confections. In the station house, on the street in town, out at his place unannounced they'd ply him with sheet cake and cobbler, banana bread and cookies, and the bold ones who'd driven clean out to his house would study the environs for some clue as to Ray's passions and abiding beliefs, for a hint of his feel for decor and his personal off-duty style.

They got usually just the musty clutter, tapwater if they insisted and polite but strictly measured chat from Ray. The ones who chose to linger and make of themselves impositions were often obliged to endure as well vaporish toxins from Ray's dog.

The local women began to give out that Ray was faulty somehow. In time, the prevailing view held his equipment wasn't functioning, not anyway in the manner that the Lord intended for it to. Furthermore, the women noticed that Ray was wanting in the burly arts. Didn't fish. Didn't hunt. Didn't seem to be given to jawing with fellows about while they loitered on the sidewalks and hocked up phlegm and spit it.

Accordingly, a few of our female wags began calling him a "bachelor gentleman" in a tone that served to render the phrase damning and bunghole specific, and the view that Ray was maybe just a corseted homosexual had begun to take hold a little by the time his ex-wife showed up. Karen, her name was, and she looked for Ray at the station house where she met the chief and Ailene and Carl who pointed her towards the café where Ray was taking lunch while reading what we charitably allow for a newspaper.

They'd grown fond of Ray at the café, Glenola and Ruthie had, because Ray never complained to them about the food. He'd sit in his customary booth by the window, and Ruthie would deliver his iced tea unbidden along with the extra wedges of lemon Ray cut the sugar with. He'd ask after the specials—always either chopped steak or stewed chicken—and he'd mount a show of actually considering them before he'd order the veal cutlet instead which he'd take invariably with snapped beans, sliced bread and applesauce.

They're proud of their food at the café, Ruthie and Glenola are, which is curious since they make none of it themselves. They thaw it, of course. They heat it. They open cans and jars. They work, when need be, twist ties entirely off of sacks, but they never actually cook anything from scratch. They won't even spring for the name brands of the prepared food that they buy, and they're notorious for the watery quality of their succotash and the rawhide toughness of their turkey loaf.

It was no small thing, then, that Ray showed up day after day and didn't complain, especially given that he invariably ordered the veal cutlet—a breaded oval of gray gristle that could have come from a draft goat. He even ate the stuff, or at least more of it than their other customers ate, and Ray tended to be rather artful with his leavings, would shove them about in such a way as to make it look like he'd been fed.

Plainly, the point for Ray was the forty-five minutes he got to spend with the paper and out of earshot of his colleagues back at the station house. He was partial to the fulsome wedding announcements and the stark obituaries, to the breathlessness of the high school sports reports. And he lingered, like most of the rest of us, over the "Heard on the Grapevine" column which is compiled by an anonymous local busybody and serves as a strain of eavesdropping in print.

We know who went shopping for a bedroom suite in Richmond. We know who endured a weekend visit from in-laws. We know who consulted an oral surgeon over a painful gum complaint. And we tend to learn which women about have gotten themselves with child even before the rightful father has been identified and informed, and all of it is managed with the arsenic sweetness of a spinster aunt.

So Ray was eating, after a fashion, and reading when his ex-wife turned up. According to Ruthie, they didn't behave like exes often do, weren't noticeably sharp and brittle with each other. Karen kissed Ray on the cheek and slid directly into his booth, and, when Ruthie came over, Ray introduced them forthrightly—without, that is, any sneering insinuations or sulfurous asides.

Only once Ray had recommended to Karen the veal cutlet and she'd ordered, before he'd finished speaking, the stewed chicken instead did Ruthie believe that they'd, in fact, been joined in matrimony. Then she rushed off to the kitchen to inform Glenola that Ray had not always been gay.

Apparently, they just sat and caught up for a while. Ruthie

would wander in and out of earshot as she refilled their tea, and, the way she told it, Karen was riding up to visit her mother in Greencastle, had taken off from some sort of clerical job she had down in Carolina. According to Ruthie, Karen was at that time dating a real estate agent named Don, but she wasn't, in Ruthie's estimation, serious about him.

They appeared to give out of conversation quicker than most people might, and they sat together for a while in a manner of strained silence before Karen opened her handbag and produced a photograph from it, a snapshot of Ray standing at the seaside holding a child—a little girl with bangs and no teeth to speak of, with water wings on her arms.

"I was going through some things," Karen told Ray by way of accounting for the photo. He left it to lay on the tabletop, contented himself with glancing at it there.

Then she cried, Karen did, trickling at first but gushing pretty lavishly in time. Ray circled around to sit with her on her upholstered bench, supplied her with napkins from the dispenser as he spoke softly into her ear.

Ruthie ventured over with the iced-tea pitcher before Karen had entirely recovered, but Ray waved her off from pouring and asked instead for the check. As Ruthie tallied it up, she glanced at the photo on the Formica tabletop. Ray looked ten years younger, and she hardly recognized him behind his unsightly mustache.

"Cute as a button," Ruthie said of the child, laying the bill on the table.

Ray nodded in Ruthie's direction. Ray informed Ruthie, "She was."

Ray walked Karen to her car and put her in it. He sent her off with one of his better sad little winces and a wave, and two days later we all of us read about that encounter in the paper. About the tears. About the divorce. About the veal cutlet and the stewed chicken. About Don, the real estate agent boyfriend. About Ray and Karen's dead child.

Naturally, we were a few facts and telling particulars short of load. We knew Ray and Karen had been blessed with a daughter and Ray and Karen's daughter had died. We proved content, as a population, to supply the rest of it on our own.

We had her snatched by a marauding infection. We had her kicked in the head by a pony. We had her run over accidentally by a neighbor's minivan. We even had her for a while gunned down by that crazy bastard off in Salem who'd shot up a playschool due to some reversals he had suffered and who'd been given out politely on the nightly newscast as "troubled" and "disturbed."

There was even a version that circulated with a hint of authority to it. A local woman, a Crouse from the slaughterhouse Crouses, knew people who had cousins down by Charlotte, and some one of them had claimed an actual acquaintance with Ray and Karen and had passed along that they'd lost their little girl during Ray's stint in Gastonia. She'd drowned, we were told, in a muddy sump hole of a pond at the bottom of Ray and Karen's lot.

By way of elaboration and narrative color, a few of the women about decided that Ray had neglected to watch her in quite the fashion that he should have due to his depression over the man he'd killed or the woman he'd failed to save, due to his friction with the sheriff he'd not assisted. They were none of them mitigations outright but served as reason enough for pity and helped to render Ray a tragic figure roundabout.

A number of females anyway concluded that Ray was emotionally stymied and not, in fact, a bachelor gentleman after all, so they laid siege to him and fairly badgered him with their sympathy which took the form of cakes and casseroles, scented cards from the five-and-dime and a regular raft of sisterly embraces on the street which, with any encouragement from Ray, would have sweltered and evolved.

Ray stopped, along about that time, in conjunction with Carl a Guidry on the truck route. Ray and Carl were sitting out on the patio at Little Earl's sharing a basket of onion rings when that Guidry sped right past them drifting across the center line. Then she pulled a u-turn just up the road and came back the other way still weaving and racing at ten miles per hour above the posted speed.

"Who is that?" Ray asked Carl who considered the vehicle as he blotted up the last of the onion ring morsels with his damp-ened fingerend.

Carl took up his campaign hat from the bench. "Some woman," he told Ray.

She eased to the shoulder almost before they could switch the beacon on, and Carl—as was his custom—approached the driver's door with his hand on his pistol grip while Ray wandered over to the passenger window to stand. That Guidry was awfully done up for a woman out for a spot of erratic driving. She had her hair piled on top of her head, dangling platinum earrings, pearls, a skirt and hose and heels, a gauzy blouse as well that she'd left un-buttoned to show off her leopard-pattern push-up bra.

"What in God's name are you doing?" Carl asked her and presently added, "Ma'am?"

She didn't even so much as visit upon Carl a glance. "You're Officer Tatum, aren't you?"

Ray nodded.

"My friends call me May."

"I'm talking to you!" Carl smacked his palm on the car roof.

"It's the grief," that Guidry told Ray, laying her fingers to her breastbone for effect. "Sometimes it takes ahold of me, and I do the funniest things. I lost my husband a little while back. I know all about anguish."

Now technically that was not entirely true. In point of fact, that Guidry had lost her ex-husband. He had come up on the short end of a dispute at the penitentiary in Bland. One of his fellow inmates had desired that Guidry's ex-husband's cigarettes and had drummed with a chairleg on that fellow's cranium to claim them.

That Guidry's ex-husband wouldn't even have been in the penitentiary in Bland if he'd not caught that Guidry in bed with an insurance adjuster who'd come out to the house once hailstones had beaten the chrome off of her car. Apparently, that Guidry had told him what she often tells men in the way of a suggestive conversational gambit.

"You know," she'd said, crowding him close as he took Polaroids of her sedan, "I'm an honest-to-God natural blonde. All over."

Like some fellows will, that insurance adjuster had turned her upside down to see. The way we heard it, he was still inspecting that Guidry when her estranged husband happened by and broke, in a snit, all of that gentleman's bones he could lay his brogans to which had earned him his aggravated assault conviction.

In truth, then, that Guidry knew little of anguish except maybe how to inflict it.

"License and registration," Carl said.

"I left my pocketbook back at the house," that Guidry informed Ray. She giggled and tossed her head girlishly. She added, "Silly me." Then she patted her passenger seat. "Hop on in. We'll go get it."

Ray didn't reach for the door handle. Ray failed to move at all, so that Guidry apprised Ray of the extent to which she was personally blonde.

That Guidry scooted in her brief skirt along the seat and reached out to find Ray's hand with her own. "Come on with me. You're just sad. That's all."

Ray indulged in one of his winces and gave a slight shake of his head while Carl peered in at that Guidry fairly prostrate on her car seat and cleared his throat so as to gain her notice. "I've been happier," he volunteered.

She gave a little shriek of disgust as she started her car and veered into the roadway slinging cinders. Ray managed to tell Carl, "Let her go," before he'd fully unholstered his gun.

When the women about still couldn't snare him, they laid it off to "commitment issues'" complicated by Ray's numerous frailties and his guilt over his child. Then he went and hooked up for a while with a female from over in Staunton, a redhead who taught at the college and would come stay with Ray on weekends. She was partial to turquoise jewelry and nearly undetectable makeup, was infuriatingly slender and athletic. It's a wonder she hadn't been done in by the venom in the air.

They only lasted a month or so before Ray took up with a woman, a Negress who had been around before. She worked for the Park Service and had come down from D.C. to investigate some sort of misadventure in the National Forest. That was just after Ray had hired on, and they must have had some truck together while they went around chasing down leads and establishing facts. Kit, her name was, and she grew to be soundly detested by the women about since they could among them just as readily be slender and athletic as they could any of them be black.

She was a handsome woman and accomplished in some manner

of kung fu. She'd fairly thrashed one afternoon a fellow out at the boat landing, one of those sorry Tallys from back in the creases and the hollows, that ilk who sides his house with roof wrap, pitches all of his trash into gullies and figures anything his neighbors haven't bolted down is his. The way we heard it, he ventured a comment that woman found provocative and, to judge by the consequences, at least a trifle irritating. With her shoebottom, it would seem, or maybe instead the heel of her hand, she responded to that Tally by violently renovating his septum for him and relieving him of the few teeth he had left.

By all reports, she was remarkably quick. She was sure and economical. She was, needless to say, a little titillating. Men, after all, like a handsome exotic woman well enough, but we're prepared to adore one trained to leave us in a bloody insensible heap.

So while the females about flagged a little in their zeal for Ray, we men compensated by nursing among us an interest in his love life, most especially those wanton episodes that might involve kung fu.

———

Ray would have surely driven past Clayton's and clean out to the blacktop but for that airbrushed eagle which impressed him as jarring and out of place. In fact, it's a wonder he even noticed it in among the clutter. Clayton lived in the house where his parents had lived and their parents before them, but no blood kin of his, by all indications, had ever picked up the yard.

There were countless lawnmower carcasses, assorted parts and pieces of cars, a pestilential heap of rotting tires, rounds of ancient unsplit firewood, outmoded tractor implements given over to weeds and rust. By the looks of it, all of the appliances Clayton's people had ever replaced had simply been hauled from the house and tossed off the side porch. Cookstoves and air conditioners. Refrigerators and water heaters. The largest privately held assortment of toaster ovens in the Mid-South.

The house itself was one of those rambling frame white-trash plantation structures with rotted columns and missing pickets, sagging sills all around, the bulk of the shutters in with the shrubbery and only traces of paint on the siding. The tin roof was rusted and hopelessly leaky at the seams. The chimney stack looked to be held up by inertia. Clayton had taped sheets of Visqueen over his windows years back against the cold, and he'd punched through them here and there so as to ventilate in summer. That house fairly cried out for a couple of gallons of high test and a match.

Accordingly, it's hard to say just why Ray noticed Clayton's eagle. Ray tended to lay it off to the gaudy novelty of the thing and the fact that he'd never previously known occasion to look upon it because Clayton had been glued to the Satin Channel since back before Ray hired on. Of course, that eagle was hideous as well which contributed to its magnetism, and Ray allowed that he was only maybe forty yards past the house when he put on his brakes and shoved his shifter hard into reverse.

Clayton had swiveled his dish about so that his eagle faced the road. It was a fierce-looking bird with its wings spread and a malevolent glint in its eye, and it clutched some manner of serpent in its talons, a snake that looked remarkably like an oversized fishing worm.

Ray was tempted straightaway to think Clayton had either found Jesus or was dead since watching the Satin Channel was all Ray had ever known him to do. Most of the rest of us had been acquainted with Clayton in his presatellite years, so we were aware he enjoyed an enormous capacity for undirected sloth and used to sit for hours, days even, in a mildewed recliner on his front porch with, for company, a washtub full of ice and three-dollar-a-twelve-pack beer.

For recreation, Clayton had exterminated the last of his mother's hydrangeas by urinating upon them over the porch rail.

Ray pulled in behind Clayton's Fairlane in what passes for Clayton's drive, and he saw that the front door was standing open beyond Clayton's rotted and punctured screen which was a little odd because it was cool—only coming on to May at the time—and even Ray knew Clayton warmed his house with a puny kerosene heater, or warmed anyway his chair with the headgrease stain and the ratty arms.

"Are you in there, Clayton?" Ray called out as he mounted the porch proper, and when he got no reply, he feared that Clayton had met with some manner of mischief, might have been set on by some of his sorry cousins from Clayton's mother's line.

She'd been a Goins from down by Ararat, and her people were notoriously shiftless, the sort who would have to come up in the world to qualify even as riffraff. Ray was prepared to fear a few of them could have broken in on Clayton, might have pummeled him senseless and made off with what they could sell.

"Clayton, it's Ray Tatum. Are you in there?"

Ray lingered at the door and heard what proved to be Clayton around the corner inside. He was humming a hymn. Ray recognized it: "This Is My Father's World."

Ray let himself in which was a matter of wrenching open the swollen screen door, and he found Clayton standing on a quarter-sawn sideboard that he'd shoved up before the fireplace. He was drawing with a sooty hunk of charred wood directly onto the wall. Now that might have struck Ray as alarming if Clayton's house had been a bit finer, but the interior was, if anything, a little less tidy than Clayton's yard.

"Hey," Ray said but failed to raise a nod or even a glance as Clayton declined to interrupt his sketching.

Clayton was outlining freehand an item on the plastered facing of the chimney stack, and Ray allowed that it looked to him there at the first like a skate or a horseshoe crab—a big sweeping flange on the right-hand side tapering down on the left to a narrow hook of a tail.

"What are you up to there, Clayton?"

Clayton still didn't trouble himself to look at Ray but labored instead over the sundry jogs and pocks and irregularities along his outline.

"Clayton!" Ray said it sharply enough to turn Clayton from his sketching. "Are you all right?"

Clayton smiled. According to Ray, it wasn't his normal strain of smirk, and he failed altogether to snort clear his noseholes in his customary fashion as he parted his lips to show Ray his mouthful of sorry neglected teeth.

"I'm well," he said, "thank you."

That was a little out of the way of Clayton's usual response. He ordinarily went with "I guess," supplemented by a grinding shake of his head.

"What's that you're drawing?" Ray peered about the front room as he spoke. He noticed that Clayton's heater was extinguished, and he stepped over to sniff it for fumes. He looked to see if Clayton had gotten into his mother's ancient Drambuie again, but he failed to spy the bottle anywhere about.

"Sort of looks like one of those stingrays."

Clayton kept after his enterprise, not turning, not offering to speak. Ray examined the half-eaten sleeve of saltines on the table by Clayton's chair and passed Clayton's tin of potted meat under his nose.

"Or maybe some kind of crab."

Ray stepped to the kitchen door and scanned around for evidence that Clayton had maybe gotten into the mouse bait. There was just the usual squalor, the customary heap of stoneware and his mother's china service in the sink.

"Did you have some sort of pain? Some kind of complaint?" Ray asked as he closed again on Clayton and drew up before the sideboard.

Clayton was famously in the habit, when he was feeling poorly, of dosing himself from his mother and daddy's medicine chest upstairs. They'd been dead the both of them for nearly a dozen years by then, and what pills and salves and drops were left couldn't have been terribly potent, but Clayton would take them on a whim and mix them freely and in bulk.

"Clayton," Ray said. "Clayton!"

Clayton admired his handiwork, drawing back as best he could to do it. He looked down at Ray and smiled again, once more without the snort. "Please, sir, do call me Titus. Everyone does these days."

"Did you get into the medicine? Titus?"

"I'm well, thank you."

Ray didn't quite know what to do. Clayton didn't strike him as terribly less reasonable than he'd ever been, and Ray could allow that maybe Clayton had given over the Satin Channel and had decided, on a lark, to become artistic and passably genteel. People threw over vice routinely in order to follow the Savior, and Ray was prepared to believe that Clayton might have quit his pornography and fetched up somehow a little wide of the Lord. Who was to say, after all, that drawing with a hunk of charred wood on the wall wasn't a marked improvement over the close study of blue movies?

In shifting about, Ray stepped on some glass that had shattered out of the frame when Clayton had cleared the chimney stack by flinging to the floor a dusty yellowed etching of a bull moose set upon by wolves. Clayton turned at the sharp sound of the glass underfoot. He smiled at Ray and spoke.

"First ice. Skua. Cape pigeon. Petrel." Clayton shifted back around to make a mark on the wall, a puny smudge below his drawing and closer to the mantelpiece. "Fair wind," he said. "The glass is high."

And with that Clayton climbed off the sideboard, dropping his hunk of charred wood to the floor. He crossed to his chair with the greasy headstain and plopped onto the seat where he took up his potted meat tin and chased with his finger after a gelatinous morsel.

"I've got to go see a woman in town," Ray said, "but I'm going to come back by. OK? We'll figure out what's up with you." As Clayton nibbled at a saltine, Ray laid a hand to his shoulder to gain his notice. "All right? You just sit tight."

Clayton moved his head in a fashion that Ray elected to take for a nod, and he was full upon the doorsill, Ray was, before Clayton saw fit to speak.

"It's Melissa now. Sometimes Missy," he said. "Never Angela. Never Denise."

Ray could never quite describe to his satisfaction the chill that shot clear through him. He stopped. He turned. He could never quite say why he didn't sink to the floor.

"What?"

Clayton smiled. Clayton polished off his saltine. Clayton declined to speak.

Ray dialed up the station house and made his excuses which served to dispatch Larry to notify that Peagram in town that her husband was trapped in his truck on the bypass and dead.

Larry noticed as he pulled up that she'd failed to draw her Biscayne all the way into her drive, and, once she'd come to the door, he pointed and told her, "Your tailend's out in the road."

"It quit on me. Dale'll move it. He'll be here any minute."

"Oh," Larry muttered and set about straightaway cobbling up a display of compassion. He shifted a little spit. He looked a little gassy. He shook his head. "I'm doubting it," he said.

THE CAPE

The case had come to Ray by happenstance and on account of simple logistics. He was up in the northwest corner of the county serving a bad-check warrant issued by the superstore out at the interstate junction where they'll cherish each customer and treat him in a chummy sort of way until they get wind of an overdrawn account. Then the papers get filed, and the warrants get issued, and the offenders get scooped up.

Ray had been sent to call on a fellow in a trailer park out by Mint Hill, a Rigby whose check for a chicken cooker had been returned to the superstore. He lived in a tidy little Winnebago with a carport and a redwood deck, and even though Ray was still fairly new at the time, he was acquainted with that Rigby already as a result of all of the other items he'd purchased with bad checks.

That Rigby wasn't necessarily of a criminal disposition but was helpless against his pronounced strain of undue optimism. He would write, that is, wholly worthless checks for merchandise that caught his eye with the conviction that he would come somehow into cash enough to cover them. Not that he had a steady job or any authentic prospects—some plaintiff's judgement in the offing or a solvent relative near death. He was simply sunnier by nature than he had any cause to be.

Most every other business in the tri-county area had cut that Rigby off cold. He was a folding money customer or no customer at all. The superstore, however, demonstrated no corporate memory from check to check, so about once every month and a half that Rigby would get arrested afresh. The ride in the cruiser, the handcuffs, the arraignment at the courthouse—they didn't any of them seem to have much effect upon him. The next month the hired greeter would give him a big hey-howdy at the superstore front door, and that Rigby would come away with a power tool or some small appliance along with his usual stock of baseless hope.

He'd succumbed on this occasion to the potent allure of a vertical chicken roaster. The month before he'd gotten waylaid by an orbital sander and a bread machine just ahead of that, and he'd adored them each in turn for their unique capacities, but he confessed to Ray that he was particularly smitten with his roaster. That Rigby allowed it had more features and rank versatility than any piece of merchandise he'd ever "purchased," he still called it. Of course, he'd said pretty much the same thing about his orbital sander to Carl and had sung to Walter the myriad praises of his bread machine. That Rigby was prone to find retail items extraordinarily stirring.

He had cooked a chicken in his vertical roaster and was pleased to offer a drumstick to Ray who nibbled on it while that Rigby pointed out the assorted features of his cooker. The revolving rack. The grease pan. The temperature control. The suction feet that kept the thing secure upon the counter. The kabob attachment—sold separately—which that Rigby had "purchased" as well.

"What do you think?" he asked of Ray.

"Tasty," Ray told him as he handed that Rigby the warrant.

As far as law enforcement went, it was pleasant enough duty, and Ray and that Rigby were riding to town and trading complaints about the weather when the chief came over the radio to deflect Ray to a call. A woman just west of Mint Hill had phoned up to report that her child had wandered off into the woods.

Those folks were outlanders, Dunns from Ohio. A husband and wife. A boy and that girl. Greg, the father, had been some kind of attorney back in Dayton, and, in the throes of a professional crisis or some manner of spiritual upheaval, he'd convinced his wife that they'd be well served to overhaul their circumstances, had persuaded her somehow that they could stand to give over the splendors of Dayton for a farm in the Blue Ridge foothills and a herd of dairy cows.

Like most people with no cause to know any better, that Dunn initially considered that he was committing a simplification. Over time, of course, he developed a keener understanding of cows which are prone to be more troublesome than even that sort of civilian who has need of a Dayton attorney in the first place. In the common fashion, he'd set out believing cows were big and dumb when, as it turned out, they were dumb first and with a rigor he'd not expected. Then they were big by way of a ponderous complication.

To his credit, it took that Dunn nearly three solid years to become as ill and disenchanted as our homegrown dairymen, but it finally got to where he'd linger with them at the co-op loading dock to complain about his lot in life and actively despise his livestock. The locals presently accepted him roundabout, and we all grew to treat that Dunn about as poorly as we tend to treat each other.

His wife, on the other hand, never so much as threatened to adjust and take. She didn't like the weather. She didn't like the mayflies. She didn't like the public schools. She objected to the wind in the spring and the fall, the snowfall in the winter. She complained that the prevailing local accent was incomprehensible and that people about were hatchet-faced and unsightly. Gloria, her name was, and she drove a Saab sedan that, wherever she went, she parked diagonally across two spaces at once.

In her absence from it, Dayton had become her civic ideal, the sort of remarkable community that our shoddy little township couldn't hope to so much as approach in sophistication and urban allure. Dayton had a ballet, according to Gloria. An art museum. A professional chamber society. Dayton had coffee bars where a woman could buy a no-fat latte on a whim. Dayton had beauty shops run by people actually trained to style hair. Most particularly, Dayton offered a variety of cuisines. Thai and Latin and continental, even a German beer hall. For our part, we had Chinese fast food out at the shopping plaza, but the place was run by a pair of wholly Occidental West Virginians.

That woman was most particularly down on the grocery mart which, in fact, was understandable enough. They ought to hang a sign from the awning over the front doors that reads "For all of your pork chop, cheese food, and white bread needs." There at the grocery mart, they tend to figure for exotic grainy mustards and hot dogs made with beef. That Dunn was always asking after wonton wrappers, fish other than scrod and roughie, rice noodles and mung beans.

The steaks at the grocery mart were never cut thick enough to suit her. The coffee was stale. The bagels were of the dairy case variety. She had a native objection to margarine that bordered on psychosis and a nearly deranged fixation on salad greens. The only legitimate dustup she ever had at the grocery mart, which would be in addition to her snide remarks and her exasperated exhalations, came about on account of that Dunn's uncommon passion for frisée.

She'd noticed a hand-lettered sign taped to the produce bin advertising a special price on curly endive which was usually, experience had taught her, frisée misidentified, just the sort of foul up she'd grown to expect from non-Daytonians. The trouble was that on this occasion there was cabbage in the bin and not frisée or even curly endive, and somehow the very fact of that cabbage where she'd hoped for salad greens caused that woman to surrender her social bearings for a moment.

She set in, that is, with some fairly scalding abuse of the produce man. He's a Royce from out in the valley who retired from a laminating concern, and he took a job in produce at the grocery mart just for something to do. He's nearly deaf which we're all aware of and which that Dunn should have probably noticed since he wears a big oldfangled hearing aid about the size of a deep-sea lure, and he evermore permits the earpiece to dangle free of his ear canal in a display of his utter indifference to conversation.

So that Dunn from Dayton was brandishing a half a head of cabbage and charging that Royce to inform her if it looked like greens to him which he didn't trouble himself to notice her at because he was busy stacking pears and because, as well, he had his ear unplugged. As produce men go, that Royce is a fairly maniacal stacker of fruit. He lays out the stuff in such a way that, no matter where you pluck from, an avalanche is likely to ensue. That Royce is not, consequently, much loved in his professional capacity, and no few of us have stood in cascading fruit and raged openly against him.

It wasn't surprising, then, for shoppers to see that woman shake a cabbage at him and shout across the intervening banana table, "Hey!"

When that Royce failed to turn, when he failed to respond, that woman made a bid to gain his notice by pitching, she chose to call it, her chunk of cabbage at him, and she seemed to mean by "pitch" a dainty sort of harmless toss. Naturally, there were plenty of onlookers about to contradict her. They'd all left off with their shopping in order to spectate, and they saw for themselves that women from Dayton don't, apparently, throw like girls.

By all accounts, except her own, that Dunn hurled her cabbage overhand and on a line, and it caught that Royce pretty squarely in the back of the head. It hit him with a thump and ricocheted into the navel oranges which set about raining onto the floor and served to cushion that Royce as he collapsed upon them in advance of getting covered up by pears.

All in all, it was just the sort of outburst that might have endeared that woman to us if she'd not turned on her fellow customers and berated them as well. The way we heard it, she sputtered and swore and wagged a finger at the onlookers, assured them they couldn't find a proper salad with both hands which we have since decided is probably a localized Ohio expression. She left her cart where it stood, half full of groceries, and stalked out of the store so as to squeal in her Saab out of both of her parking spaces at once.

That Dunn managed to sustain a pretty high pitch of unhappiness after that. She set her mind against adjusting to her new circumstances and getting acclimated, and she doused her husband with misery most every chance she got. That Dunn took to spending the bulk of her time on the telephone with her friends back in Ohio. She would acquaint them with our hayseed exploits and rail against our deficiencies in exchange for news of Dayton soirees and the latest civic enhancements. As a consequence, she wasn't quite so attentive to her children as she might have been. She fed them and kept them clean and got the older one out mornings for the bus, but she'd dial up Dayton come afternoon and leave them to their devices for longer than was probably safe and prudent.

The boy—Matthew Gregory Dunn after his father—would return home from the primary school at three and roam the farm looking for some hapless creature to mutilate or kill outright. His father tried to keep an eye on him, but he had cows to feed and cows to herd and cows to medicate and cows to consume him with percolating aggravation.

The daughter fell under the mother's sway, at least that was the theory about the farm. She was maybe three at the time with beautiful blonde curls and cobalt eyes. Angela they had called her after her mother's mother. Denise after her father's sister who'd sickened as a child and died. She was a strange little girl. She never cried, and she loved the deep woods dearly. Even at three, she hadn't yet bothered to speak.

The farm her father had bought adjoined to the north a couple of hundred acres of untouched old-growth forest. The property had been owned by a local gentleman named Homer Blaine who'd left it to the state for parkland, and they had given the tract his name.

Homer Blaine State Park has a network of trails and an out-of-the-way gravel lot that has proven highly popular with the local youth. We've got countless kids about at that age when they tend to be both hormone-rich and comprehensively parent-afflicted, and they flock to the gravel lot in Homer Blaine State Park for "privacy" they like to call it, a brand of seclusion that usually includes about a dozen dewy-windowed bucking vehicles with half-dressed girls and frantic pimply boys inside.

Tiffany and her Blevins have claimed a special spot in a far corner hard by a buttonbush where they listen to the lite mix station out of Richmond and indulge together in the variety of swelter-

ing negotiation that invariably leaves Tiffany with her blouse un-
buttoned and her brassiere around her neck and that Blevins in
near crippling constipated sexual anguish. Like most of the local
girls, Tiffany has decided to wait for actual intercourse until she
and that Blevins are properly joined in holy matrimony. Like the
bulk of local boys, that Blevins can most weekends barely walk.

Aside from the car lot, however, Homer Blaine State Park
doesn't get an awful lot of traffic. It's far more convenient for
tourists to visit the Shenandoah instead. Regulars at that park,
aside from the teenagers after dark, consist primarily of a grubby
bearded fellow from up by the reservoir who collects drink cans
out of the barrels for the recycling money and a bony woman from
past the gap with an unbridled interest in birds.

She tours most every afternoon along the trails of Homer
Blaine State Park with her binoculars and her field guides and her
corkscrewed walking stick. She'll visit upon anybody she meets
an exhaustive catalog of the various birds she's had the privilege
to see which, as a general rule, will chew up half an hour. She's
probably driven more people out of those woods than the mayflies
and the snakes.

Then there was little Miss Angela Denise Dunn who would en-
ter from the bottom, would pass between strands of her father's
barbed-wire once her mother had met with an absorbing Dayton
communiqué over the phone. A branch cuts through the lower
end of Homer Blaine State Park. It's about two feet wide and
feeds out of a spring up in the rocks, comes tumbling and slosh-
ing down the hillside in a fashion that child found enthralling.
She'd rocked up a little pool for herself where her father, when
she'd go missing, would oftentimes find her with her feet
plunged in while she floated a leaf for a boat.

She had a spot as well up in a stand of hickories where a knot of scraggly laurels had managed to thrive. She'd made for herself a little cave in among the limbs and the leathery leaves, and she would play there with nuthulls for teacups and locust pods for dainty hors d'oeuvres.

She shouldn't have loved the big woods so as there is something distinctly forbidding about the forest, something desolate, something grim and melancholy. Children, we all agreed, are better off in the meadows, are likely to be improved by the sun. If she'd been a child of ours, we decided by unofficial acclimation, we would have had the good sense to keep her out of the forest where even a grown man—under the canopy in the murky filtered light with a rifle in his hand and a pint of Old Crow in his pocket—can get drawn up by the silence, can suffer a penetrating chill.

Carl had found her already twice himself. Walter had turned her up. The chief and Ailene had mounted a search when she'd gone missing once for hours, and they'd finally strayed across her in the red clay gully where rainwater sluices from the lot.

Larry had also been sent once to locate that child, but he'd passed on the way a fellow burning rubbish in his yard without the proper bureaucratic dispensation. By the time that Larry and that gentleman had finished quarreling over the Bill of Rights and Larry had pulled out his book and written a proper citation, that girl was draining a juice box back home at the kitchen dinette.

Ray, in fact, was probably a little overdue for his initiation into the Ohio Dunn experience, but the chief had driven out and been stern with that couple the last time they'd called up for assistance. He'd made it plain that his deputies had better things to do than scour Homer Blaine State Park for that child, and he'd advised particularly Gloria Dunn to see after her with more care, was

37

blunt and flinty with that woman in a fashion that had struck her as positively Daytonian here in a run of country where even the thieves and trash tend to say "sir" and "ma'am."

Once the chief had left off with Ms. Gloria Dunn, had finished with his fulmination, she'd even troubled him to tell her please just where his people were from.

By the time that Ray rolled up with that Rigby, those Dunns were put out with each other. Greg had snatched the cordless phone from his wife and shoved it into his coveralls pocket which had prompted her to apprise Ray, as he climbed out of his cruiser, that she felt isolated and cut off from the civilized world. Ray unlocked that Rigby and permitted Matthew Dunn to play with his handcuffs which that child had to fling aside a ragged chunk of bullfrog to do. Then that Rigby, in keeping with local custom, had a nattering chat with those Dunns. He had met the pair of them previously in the superstore parking lot where Greg had provided him a length of twine for tying his trunklid shut after he'd helped that Rigby load his new gas grill into the bay.

"How long ago did you miss her?" Ray asked.

"Hour and a half?" Greg offered, glancing at his wife. "Two maybe?"

"I don't wear a watch," Gloria Dunn informed Ray. "I mean, around here, what's the point?"

"Checked all of her spots. Went clean up to the lot and back. Nothing."

"She's done this before, right?"

Greg swiveled about to treat his wife to a dose of withering study. "Yeah," he told Ray. "She has."

They all went, even Gloria, across the pasture and through the wire fence, up into the deep woods of Homer Blaine State Park where they separated and fanned out across the slope. Greg and Matthew. Gloria and that Rigby. Ray alone. They called to her, the rest of them, shouted out her name while Ray, for his part, just stood and scanned the forest floor. It was largely barren of undergrowth but for the occasional clump of laurel and rhododendron. It was rocky and riddled with springheads. The ground was spongy underfoot.

The canopy overhead was thick and leafy, choking off the bulk of the sunlight. Toadstools thrived on the forest floor. There was the odd patch of bluegreen moss, the occasional lady slipper poking gaudily from the ground. Tree squirrels chattered overhead. Little birds no bigger than field mice hopped skittishly over the windfall leaves pecking for ants and grubs.

Ray could see them all—the father and son, the wife and that Rigby. He could hear them calling out, could hear the sharp metallic rasp of his handcuff ratchets as Matthew opened and closed the bracelets. He could hear every particular, each winning feature of that Rigby's chicken roaster as that Rigby cataloged them one by one. These were not, Ray knew straightaway, the sort of woods people got lost in. No scrub and brambles much. Easy earshot and clear lines of sight all around. The parking lot was up. The pasture was down. That girl's father should have found her if she was there.

Ray still looked, of course. They all of them looked, back and forth across the breadth of Homer Blaine State Park and up and down over the lifted ground and into the hollows. After maybe forty-five minutes, that little girl's father gave a whoop, and Ray went trotting towards him fully prepared to be mistaken, but it turned out his son had managed somehow to handcuff himself to a spruce.

They covered those woods from end to end and took care to inspect every spot that looked to them the least bit inviting. Mossy patches by the creekbanks. A tangled stand of rhododendron. A slot of a cave in between two rocks where only Matthew Gregory

Dunn would fit. He found inside the grub-infested carcass of a mole which so enchanted him that he could only be extracted at length by a pointed threat of violence from his mother.

She was the first one to tire, the first to propose that their daughter was probably back at the house already, playing likely in the tractor shed or the forbidden loft of the barn. That woman perched on a rock while Ray and her husband went off to inspect beneath a redbud, and she endured for company simultaneously that Rigby and her son.

In his ongoing account of appliances he'd bought at the super-store, that Rigby had arrived at a juicer he'd been disappointed with.

"Thing was about this big," he said as he described it with his arms. "Had to keep it on the dinette."

Gloria Dunn showed that Rigby her upraised foremost finger in a bid to prompt him to allow her to interpose a remark.

"Could you possibly, for the love of Christ, shut up?" She then treated that Rigby to a highly corrosive personal assessment, claimed to have known a fellow like him once back in the suburbs of greater Dayton where some hothead had put an end to his palaver with a gun.

"Turned out it didn't have a proper filter," that Rigby informed her by way of reply. "Those juicer people had left it out of the box."

They all of them departed the woods to look in the farmhouse and the outbuildings. They went down to the cow pond and up to the cement springhead reservoir. They followed the drive clear out to the road. They stood at the mailbox and called for that child. There was nothing on the blacktop as far as they could see but an empty French-fry holster and one soundly compressed blacksnake that Matthew Dunn made a bid to adopt on account of how all of his other dead reptiles had rotted.

Gloria Dunn approached her husband there on the gravel

tongue of the drive. She seemed to have need of a spot of comfort and tender reassurance, and her husband laid an arm about her and tried to draw her to him, but she shoved instead a hand in his coveralls pocket and came out with her phone. She dialed up a friend in Dayton as they walked back towards the house and described to her their present bit of bother which included a rather unsavory piece of talk about that Rigby who troubled himself to inform Ray that he'd rather be getting arraigned.

Ray put in a call to the chief who notified the state police, and then Ray drove around to the gravel lot of Homer Blaine State Park which was vacant but for a puny Datsun pickup with a battered camper shell. The bearded canpicker who owned it was rooting through a refuse barrel.

"Hey here," Ray said, but that grubby fellow stayed hinged over the rim digging through napkins and wrappers and Styrofoam burger containers. Ray jabbed him in the kidney with his fingerend. "I'm talking to you."

That canpicker withdrew from the barrel. He considered Ray. He peered leisurely about the empty lot. He spat. He nodded. "Guess you pretty much have to be."

"How long have you been here?"

He lifted the greasy cap he wore in order to scratch his head. "A while, I guess."

"Seen anybody else?"

"A couple of kids in a Buick." He pointed towards a far shady corner.

"Doing what?"

"You know." He stuck out his cracked and slimy tongue and fluttered it lasciviously enough to inflict upon Ray a twinge. Ray could tell already by then it was the sort of appalling sight that would stay with him no matter how he might try to rout it from his mind.

"Anybody else?"

That canpicker paused, casting back and striking the sort of expression that Ray's dog favored in her vaporish interludes. "People here when I rolled in, seems like."

"What people?"

"A fellow and his wife, I guess. Had one of them vans, you know?" He described with his hands a vehicle about the size of a cinder block. "Wouldn't have one of them goddamn things."

"What were they doing?"

"He was pissing when I come in." That gentleman pointed to a bushy corner of the lot where it seemed reasonable that even a modest and decent fellow might see fit to pee.

"And her?"

He shrugged.

"In the car? Down in the woods? What?"

He shrugged again. "Only seen her after a while."

"Anybody with them? A little girl maybe?"

"Can't say."

"What color was that van?"

"Blue." That fellow fished a generic cigarette out of the flattened pack in his shirt pocket and delicately rounded up the barrel between his thumb and fingerend. "Or green," he added as he shoved the filter between his lips.

Ray walked over to the trailhead at the edge of the woods. He considered the map of Homer Blaine State Park that had been routed into a square of jointed planking and that touched upon the meager attractions of the place. The mountain branch. A white oak grove. An exposed vein of basalt.

Ray could hear them by then. The chief. Walter. Carl. That child's father. They whistled and hooted. They called out her name. Ray detected the sound of that Rigby's voice, lower and distinct from the others. He was speaking approvingly just then of a Teflon waffle iron.

A woman joined Ray at the trailhead. He'd not heard her coming, and she startled him a little. She was wiry and knobby about the joints with her hair bobbed close. She wore a pouch on a strap around her waist with two field guides poking from it. She carried a pair of puny binoculars in one hand, a corkscrewed walking stick in the other.

She pointed with the tip of the thing towards a bird that had lighted on the limb of a spindly maple. The creature was grayish green about the wings and rusty along the belly. Its featherends were mussed where its head swiveled like maybe it had just woken up. As it took to wing and darted towards the upper limbs of a poplar, that woman followed its progress with her stick end.

She watched it until it had skittered about the trunk and out of sight. "*Yank-yank,*" she barked out. "Red-breasted nuthatch," she said.

———

Clayton declined to say anything further no matter what name Ray called him. Clayton sat in his chair with the greasy headstain munching his saltines and dabbing jellied scraps of potted meat out of his nearly depleted tin.

"What is that anyway?" Ray asked Clayton, pointing to the sketch he'd made with his charred stick of wood on the chimney wall, but Clayton didn't seem to hear him and merely nibbled at a cracker.

"Melissa who?" Ray asked him, and, by way of response, Clayton rose from his chair and walked into the kitchen where Ray followed to watch as Clayton drank directly from the tap.

"Are you feeling all right?" Ray wanted to know, and Clayton didn't tell him that he wasn't but simply returned to his chair and dropped onto the seat without bothering to speak at all.

It was as strange in its way as if that Rigby had purchased a Handy Chopper with cash. Clayton didn't ever not talk when he was in proximity to a set of ears to pour palaver into. He'd likely grown accustomed to sitting around at home alone making do with but the odd scrap of intermittent commentary, but in company Clayton was hardly the sort who had need of inquiries to prime him as he was evermore ready with indelicate accounts of cinematic intercourse he'd seen.

So quite conspicuously Clayton was hardly himself, and Ray would have likely called in a doctor if we'd had about town a doctor fit to call. We've only got the one, and his company is notoriously painful. Consequently, since Clayton wasn't spitting up blood or thrashing around on the floor, Ray summoned our local veterinarian instead. Doyle, his name is, and he's sensible and discreet unlike Dr. Lowery, our G.P., who is comprehensively uninformed and garishly opinionated.

Dr. Lowery drives a coral-colored Bel-Air. He wears a Panama hat year-round, suspenders and a belt, two-tone dress shirts he has made special by a tailor in Atlanta, alligator shoes cobbled up to order by a fellow in Baton Rouge. Unfortunately, Dr. Lowery is built pretty much like a six-foot heap of dirt and wouldn't look much worse in flour sacking and flip-flops. He's persuaded, nonetheless, that he's dapper and soundly admired about these parts in spite of his unsuccessful bid for a seat on the county commission when he finished behind not only his half-dozen human rivals but trailed as well a domesticated ferret that had been run on a lark.

In a bid at diagnosis, Ray saw fit to lay his palm to Clayton's forehead, but he'd decided that anything short of a flesh burn would permit him to call the vet which was likely the first disservice to get inflicted upon Clayton though, truth be told, as word got around of Clayton's transformation and the curious strain of Clayton's brand of spontaneous commentary, we weren't any of us terribly keen for Clayton to take a cure. Ray grew to wish he'd carried him to the clinic down the pike, but at the time—and this is what plagued Ray—he did what any of us would have done which was next to nothing whatsoever at all.

Doyle came straight from a cow call just up the branch from Clayton's. He'd gone out to see an Akers who had a couple of failing heifers and a virulent predisposition against the Department of Agriculture. That Akers was convinced that covert operatives of the D. of A., in response to remarks that Akers had made on a phone call to D.C., had come down to contaminate his herd and ensure his financial ruin which, if true, would have been a terrible waste of federal government funds since that Akers had spent his whole adult life ensuring his ruin himself.

He took poor care of his cattle and worse care of what paltry income he had. His TV and couch were both rented at an 18 percent return. That Akers had purchased through the mail shares in a gold mine in Bermuda and had bought from a fellow traveling door to door a hot tub that had collapsed his porch. He routinely upgraded his John Deere even with no land much to work, traded in his truck every eighteen months and took a thrashing for it, and it was that Akers who'd gone to the super flea at the fairgrounds in Culpeper and come home with Stonewall Jackson's wristwatch and a sliver of Moon rock.

So that Akers was widely known about to be a bit of a fool which he compounded by way of galloping paranoia. Along with his bilious pitch of contempt for the Department of Agriculture, he reserved a little venom for the World Bank and the Trilateral Commission which, to hear it from that Akers, kept a dossier on him and fed information to the Japanese.

That Akers's cattle could never just be sick, were always poisoned and contaminated, and once Doyle the veterinarian had discovered the offending parasite, had identified the fungus or put a name to the bacteria, he'd evermore get invited to throw in with speculation as to how exactly the Department of Agriculture had tainted that Akers's forage or managed to infect his water table.

That Akers, for his part, was usually suspicious of covert infiltrators on the ground. "Your coloreds," he tended to call them and generally meant the Emory brothers who were prone to slip out of that Akers's woods to fish in his upper pond. They were both of them retired from the carpet backing plant, wore bib overalls and blazers, identical straw fedoras, and they fished with poles and bobbers, used white bread and drippings for bait.

That Akers had seen once the pair of them peeing together into his pond, had looked on from his collapsed porch as they'd extracted and had drained their ebony delivery systems, he'd decided.

Now there was a time when Doyle would dispute with that Akers over the source of his livestock's complaints, would explain how his cows might have picked up a bug from that Akers's moldy hay or the swampy ditch behind his house that Akers employed for a leach field. It had come at length, however, to be Doyle's practice to shout out "Sons of bitches!" whenever he dosed, injected or otherwise mended one of that Akers's cows. He meant it for a cry of brotherhood and a display of indignation over the plight of one man flogged and hounded by the D. of A. for little more than an abrasive telephone manner.

So Doyle would swab an inflamed udder with antibiotic salve, would shake his head and cry out, "Sons of bitches!" and that Akers straightaway would allow he wished he'd never called D.C.

Then—and this was the point for Doyle—that Akers would lapse into self-pity, and he would mope and pule and moan and rue his wretched lot in life with devotion enough to permit Doyle to slip into his truck or at least get a head of steam up on his way out of the barn leaving that Akers hard pressed to recover his sense of righteous paranoia in time enough to forestall Doyle from racing up the drive.

A radio summons from an authentic deputy merely simplified matters for Doyle as it suggested that he was allied somehow with local law enforcement who that Akers suspected to be in league with the National Guard and the Rotarians who answered directly to FEMA, stooges of the D. of A.

Now Doyle the veterinarian had known occasion to call on Clayton before back when Clayton's goat had eaten the entire cord of a toaster oven which had served to stopper and bind that creature and render him discontent. Apparently, it takes a while for even a talented veterinarian like Doyle to induce a goat to pass a toaster oven cord, and he was out there for a good stretch administering barnyard lubricants while Clayton amused him with plots of triple-X films he'd lately seen which, like most men, Doyle found more diverting than tales of urinary espionage.

One movie Clayton described had been devoted to a woman who was handy about her house, and she'd roped in a strapping girlfriend to help her build a sunroom off her den. They wore brogans and shorts and toolbelts, wore tube tops and yellow hard hats, and their sweat trickled in artful slow motion through the sawdust on their skin.

There was a wiry teenage boy next door who could see them from his bedroom, teenage that is in triple-X years which made him about twenty-eight, but he was suitably gangly and sunken chested, and he looked like he'd cut his hair with a paring knife in a darkened room. He peeked at those girls from his bedroom window, from his back porch, from his yard, and, once they'd gotten stymied because they were too chesty to slip through an access doorway, they spied that boy and invited him over to help them pull electrical wire.

He happily obliged them, naturally enough, and scuttled easily through their crawlspace which those girls were so pleased and gratified by that they decided to thank him with sex, slipped both of them out of their tube tops and out of their denim shorts, flung their hard hats aside and presented themselves to that boy in their toolbelts and boots.

For a gangly pseudo-teenager with no pectoral definition, knobby elbows and abominable hair, that boy proved little shy of miraculously endowed. Clayton apparently didn't even bother with his usual forearm measure but just drew his hands apart as if he were describing a trophy carp. As was his way, Clayton covered the sexual logistics conscientiously, detailed the sawbuck acrobatics, the novel use of channel locks, the bondage achieved with electrical tape and a length of plumb-bob line. Clayton also laid out for Doyle the various features of that sunroom with its Thermopane glass, its five-paddle fan and its slate decking for solar gain.

Doyle might have even gotten stirred and agitated at the time but for the fact that he had his hand plunged into a goat's anus which left him to savor that story a little later alone in the cab of his truck, and apparently Doyle even worked himself into enough of a lather to see fit to swing by his house and visit some ardor on his wife who he knew to be passing her afternoon wallpapering their foyer.

Now while she wasn't sporting a hard hat and wore sneakers instead of boots, she had on shorts and a T-shirt that she'd hacked off at her midriff, and Doyle found her splattered from her ankles up with sizing and with paste. Moreover, she was mightily sick of hanging wallpaper by then and didn't require too awful much in the way of plaintive persuasion from Doyle once he'd done her the service of washing the goat off his hands.

They had a tussle on the floor until Doyle's wife had suffered a drop-cloth burn when they mounted their stepladder after a fashion that OSHA would surely have frowned on which served as prelude to a spot of fornicating by the door where Doyle's wife was clinging to the bright-brass knob for balance when their neighbor shoved a misdirected flyer through their mail slot and then hoisted the flap with his fingers so as to peer about inside, not that he was perverted or lascivious by nature, but he was at loose ends and had come by word that paper was getting hung.

That fellow was an import, a Jessup from all over who'd retired from the army and had bought with his wife a tumbledown house in town which they'd renovated from the basement slab clear up to the roof vents, and that Jessup had grown in the process to fancy himself an authority on most stripes of home improvement and repair. He'd papered the dining room in his house, had papered his puny half bath, had run a decorative band about the parlor walls up by the ceiling, and he had developed and refined along the way a paperhanging technique that he was keen to share with Doyle's wife and so spare her aggravation.

Naturally, Doyle's wife screamed, couldn't help herself really, and Doyle reacted without any palpable forethought to speak of, reached for the knob, that is to say, and jerked open their front door so as to have a look at the sort of creature who'd peek in through a mail slot to watch a fellow having congress with his wife in their front hall. The trouble was that Doyle hadn't bothered to work up any commentary, so he just stood there in their foyer in buff silence with his wife while that Jessup treated the pair of them to a trifling little smirk which seemed somehow to say he'd seen far chestier women in his day and had never run across a punier scepter on a man.

That Jessup pointed towards the grocery flyer on the foyer floor. "Got mixed in with ours."

Doyle had even concocted by then a scrap of excoriation which he'd nearly assembled the spit he required to intone and declare when Doyle's wife invited Doyle to swing shut please their paneled door in wholly uncharacteristically colorful language, sharp and profane and just a bit stirring as best as that Jessup could tell.

Ray was waiting for Doyle on the front porch, was perched on Clayton's dilapidated glider that had thrown a strut and was sitting anymore upon the decking. He rose as Doyle wheeled up the track and parked his truck behind the cruiser, and Doyle was talking already as he traveled the weedy walk and mounted the steps.

"Goat still dead?"

Ray nodded and swung open Clayton's wracked and ratty screen door, ushering Doyle ahead of him into the house where, with his saltines eaten and his potted-meat tin scoured clean, Clayton sat entirely unemployed in his chair with the headgrease stain. He smiled at Doyle, or, more precisely, had been smiling at the chimney stack and shifted about without troubling himself to alter his expression.

Doyle was probably no more than a quarter minute settling on what exactly was wrong, was soaking in still the squalor as he glanced about the room when he noticed a decided lack of orgiastic moaning and a dearth of the manner of viscous backbeat that was as common out at Clayton's as is treacly lite variety mix at the retail shops in town.

"Is the TV broken?" Doyle asked Ray who informed him simply, "Nope."

"Clayton." Doyle closed on him as he talked, drew uncommonly close and considered Clayton's color, parted wide his lids with a finger and thumb and gazed into Clayton's eyes.

"Has he said anything?" Doyle asked Ray while probing with the fingers of both hands at once along Clayton's jowls and neck which Clayton tolerated with the stripe of grin he'd lavished on the chimney.

"He told me to call him Titus."

"Hmm," Doyle said and asked of Ray, "Has he been up and around at all?" Doyle considered Clayton's palms, the backs of his fingers, his nails. He was gentle, thorough, largely wasted—Ray had always thought—on lapdogs and housecats, ponies and cows.

"He was up here when I came in." Ray stepped towards the sideboard before the firebox and slapped at the quartersawn top of the thing with his palm. "Drawing that," he added and pointed out to Doyle Clayton's charcoal outline on the wall. "Ever heard of a skua?"

"Some kind of bird." Doyle joined Ray hard by the sideboard where they considered together Clayton's drawing on the wall. "What is it?"

Ray shrugged and turned to call out, "What the hell is it, Clayton?"

Clayton nodded with near convulsive vigor as he informed Ray, "Well, thank you."

"Ought to go get him examined," Doyle suggested. "Carry him over to Charlottesville and see a real doctor."

Ray nodded but with so precious little in the way of proper resolve that Doyle studied Ray in silence until he'd extracted from him talk. "He knows things," Ray said. "The sort of stuff he's got no cause to know."

And Doyle pointed by way of prompting Ray to confirm it was Clayton he meant and certify that he'd, in actual fact, intended to propose that Clayton had come somehow by a strain of non-pornographic information.

"He told me they call her Melissa these days. Not Angela. Not Denise." Doyle joined with Ray in consideration of Clayton across the way who clawed at an itch on his cheek and grinned towards the mantelpiece. "He's eating and drinking, so how bad off could he be?"

"When exactly have you ever known Clayton not to talk?"

As if goaded and impugned, Clayton suddenly hoisted himself from his chair and crossed over to clamber up onto the quarter-sawn sideboard by the chimney where Ray and Doyle watched him pluck a chunk of charred wood from the mantel and make, with care and deliberation, a sooty mark on the wall. He located it just at a little notch on a nether lobe of his sketch.

"Soldier, he calls me, the owner does," Clayton said to Ray and Doyle. "Erebus. McMurdo. We are landed."

Then he climbed back down and was stalking towards his foul upholstered chair when Doyle intercepted Clayton and gripped him stoutly by the shoulders. He jerked him once or twice as he barked out Clayton's name which seemed to have the effect of provoking from Clayton one morsel further of speech.

"Poor Casey," he said with the brand of wince that Ray was prone to favor. He shook his head and told to Doyle, "Poor boy."

———

They'd not even arrived at the clinic by then, or what passes with Doyle for a clinic which is a house out towards the airfield Doyle has improved and refitted and has supplemented with a couple of trailers out back for boarding cats and dogs. They were still the pack of them frantic in the Sinclair mini-mart lot where they'd stopped in to gas up, make use of the toilet and purchase the flavor of taco chip they'd voted on the interstate to buy—the orange barbecued sort with the spicy smokehouse punch.

They were the Nadlers from Wilkes-Barre on their way to Pensacola on account of how Dud, he had us call him, who was some manner of heat pump salesman, had accepted a week in a Gulf Coast time-share in settlement of a bill. Wendy, Dud's wife, had

campaigned instead for a vacation in Sicily as a means of helping
to render their children, Mia and Mike, more worldly, but she'd
been obliged to settle on what Dud claimed a compromise since
he'd had his sights set, after all, on Miami.

Their children, as it turned out, were hardly the sort that
worldliness would have much helped as they were fundamentally
undomesticated and would have, doubtless, been the same little
beasts no matter where they went since they weren't much interested in the wonders of this earth at large but were only keen instead on the ceaseless torment of each other. They were fighting,
in fact, when Dud pulled his Sable wagon into the Sinclair on account of how Mike, apparently, had seen rummaging in a ditch a
creature he'd taken for a marmoset.

It seems the child had been reading about marmosets in school
and so was in a fit state to misconstrue a groundhog, had in fact
been seeing marmosets pretty much from Harrisburg south. By
way of response, his sister had assured him that he was a fool because there weren't any marmosets in West Virginia which had
prompted her brother to ridicule her since they were in Virginia
instead, a state—he'd learned from his reading—that was filthy
with the things.

His sister saw fit, by way of rejoinder, to douse her brother
with a foamy dollop of spit that he'd taken as cause to uncork a
stream of accomplished profanity as preamble to lunging across
the breadth of that Sable and falling upon her.

They were riding, the pair of them, in the wayback of that
wagon, were stretched out together amidst the luggage on a fluffy
sateen quilt which made, as vehicular venues go, for a cozy
wrestling pit, and they grappled along the highway and down the
interstate ramp, fought on the road to town and were battling
still in the Sinclair lot when their father pulled up to the pump
island and shut off the Sable engine, opened his door to let him-

self out and jaw with the attendant which the Nadlers' dog, a twelve-year-old Lhasa condemned to ride in the back, took for an opportunity to flee.

He scrambled wheezily over the front seatback and flung himself to the pavement, slipped under the car and raced headlong across the Sinclair lot. He ran towards Dale who was coming out to pump the Nadlers' gas, Dale who tends to be a trifle sluggish between the ears and wasn't primed and prepared to entertain a frantic request from that Wilkes-Barre Nadler who shouted out over the roof of his Sable, "Stop him!"

Dale could see a fellow on the walk out by the road, that grubby Sykes who lost his license and smells like he sleeps nights in a cow lot. He could see a surveyor holding a pole up where the Burger King would be, could see a gentleman checking his tire pressure across the way at the Citgo, could see a nasty little dog with rusty eyestains running towards him across the lot along with a boy who was weed-whacking the bank beneath the motor lodge.

Inevitably, Dale paused and scratched and asked that Nadler, "Who?"

That dog was gone by then across the drain trace and up towards the shopping plaza, most particularly in the direction of the Family Dollar Store where he'd detected, we like to think anymore, with one of his well-honed canine senses the presence of Mrs. Ivy Vaughn, a local widow woman with a 1973 Impala and a homicidal streak. In one of those eerie confluences of events that the Entertainment Channel airs breathless documentaries about, that foul little Lhasa scampered across the shopping plaza lot just as Mrs. Ivy Vaughn was leaving the Family Dollar in a snit. She'd had words with the checkout girl who'd charged her more for plastic tumblers than Mrs. Vaughn thought plastic tumblers should be worth.

So she'd stalked out muttering, is by nature a stalker and a mutterer, and she backed her Impala a little heedlessly into the middle of the lot where she felt a bit of a bump beneath her as she shifted into Drive.

Mrs. Ivy Vaughn is not the sort to be terribly inquiring, most especially behind the wheel of her 1973 Impala where she is given, as a matter of course, to tolerating thumps and bumps as she has a personal gift for vehicular mayhem. She has in her day collided with or crushed beneath her tires untold tree squirrels and chipmunks, birds on the roadways guilty of miscalculations, snakes and housecats, deer and opossum, more groundhogs than a fellow could probably count. She hit once the boy who works at the car wash and was directing her into the tracks, ran into a fellow with a paving crew who was perched upon a backhoe at the time, and she swung wide in a turn once and nudged into a gully both a Greevy and the Toro he was mowing the roadside with.

She's known about, consequently, to be blue-haired carnage on wheels, and when Mrs. Ivy Vaughn felt that thump out in the shopping plaza lot, she reacted the way she always does—said, "Oh my," and laid her fingers to her lips.

She looked out to her left, looked out to her right and, since she didn't spy any trouble, she pulled up a little—as is her custom—and ran over the thing again before racing diagonally through the lot and swerving into the street.

For all we know he was dead already as an aging twenty-pound Lhasa isn't likely to hold up terribly well beneath a seventies Chevrolet twice, and anymore we give that incident out as an assisted suicide since we prefer to think he expired before that gang of Nadlers reached him, saw them coming, the four of them, up the drain trace and racing across the lot which is along about when a belted radial sent him to a better place than Wilkes-Barre or Pensacola either one.

They tried to save him nonetheless, carried him at Dale's direction out to Doyle's clinic near the airfield, and Doyle's intern from the veterinary college down in Blacksburg was the one who summoned Doyle to treat a dog that was already dead. It seems those Nadlers, as a quartet, took the news well enough and calculated that they could probably still make Charlotte in time for dinner. They were feeling sufficiently sprightly among them to snipe and chafe and quarrel before they left the clinic proper for their Sable in the lot.

"Do we have marmosets?" Doyle's intern asked him just as Doyle was groping for the words to apprise her that he didn't care to be summoned clean across the county so that he might know the pleasure of pronouncing a dead dog dead.

"Who?"

"Us. Here."

"Marmosets?"

She nodded and Doyle shook his head and grunted in a way that she took for "no" but by which he meant "Sweet merciful Jesus, what in the hell kind of question is that?" Then he drew a breath to calm himself and told her, "Call Ray Tatum."

So Doyle was the one who tempted Ray away from Clayton at last, summoned him to his veterinary clinic near the airfield where they stood the two of them over the corpse of a greasy little dog laid out on a metal table in an examination room with its heartworm chart, its x-ray lightbox, its plucked dead ticks in a pickle jar.

Doyle told Ray the entire story before he handed him the collar—the wretched children, the reckless escape at the Sinclair, welcome death beneath an Impala in the shopping plaza lot.

"Ivy?" Ray asked which brought a nod from Doyle. "I guess her pistol's all notches anymore."

And that's along about when Doyle troubled himself to instruct Ray to look at the tag, not the round one for the vaccination or the oval one for the license but the shiny chrome one in the shape of a bone which was imprinted with a name and stamped with a telephone number.

Ray glanced at the thing, at Doyle. He laid a hand to that canine's carcass and lightly, lovingly even, stroked that creature along his length. "Poor Casey," he said.

Doyle nodded and reached out to ruffle an earflap. He caught Ray's eye. He told to Ray, "Poor boy."

THE SHELF

Now we've got several citizens about who are, in the parlance, special, but we tend not to bother ourselves much on their account. We don't fret about their diets and never ensure that they bathe, aren't inclined to haul them in ourselves to get them scanned and tested. Rather, we just let them run loose and enliven the terrain with their wayward unbridled urges and chemical deficiencies.

We've got your idiots by birth, idiots by numbing intellectual sloth, and idiots by widespread public acclimation. Grover, an Isom from out by the timber works, is probably our most conspicuous natural fool. He sits anymore by the Lynchburg Pike and waves at passing traffic, had to give over his career in yardwork when he couldn't tell flowers from grass and got let go from the timber mill in the wake of a grisly mishap. It seems Grover sawed off the end of his thumb on a dare.

He got goaded, apparently, by a Lund, one of his colleagues at the mill and a prime example of a local dope who's merely thick and lazy. That Lund left school at thirteen to tend to his ailing mother who was afflicted with a galloping enthusiasm for rum and Chesterfields. When her liver finally betrayed her, that boy set about to keep the Lund tradition alive. He sprawls, that is to say, on the settee with his Mountgay and RC and stays foggy pretty much from his cranium to his bunions.

No matter what any of us says to that Lund anymore, no matter how stark a remark, he evermore opens his end of the chat by informing us dully, "Huh?"

The balance of our fools tend to be, unlike that besotted Lund who is curious about nothing whatsoever, feverishly interested in but one thing alone in the manner of that Akers with his dogged fixation on the Department of Agriculture. We've got a woman out towards the National Forest who is nutty over llamas and has been intending for about fifteen years now to buy herself a herd and thereby realize her destiny as an alpaca magnate.

She has actually fenced in a llama lot and built a llama barn and subscribes to all of the llama-tending monthlies. Three or four times a year she drives to llama-herding conventions in her pickup that looks to have rolled off the line back when Edsel Ford was a child. She even flew to Peru once to see firsthand how the natives weave those gaudy little sweaters with the buttons and the stripes.

She's afflicted, however, with a burr on her works that prevents her from purchasing llamas, can only intend to buy them and hope to profit off them in time while she improves her unused llama barn, restrings her rusted fencing, and shares with us her reasons for putting off llamas until the following year when she'll come up with some fresh misgivings we'll hear about as well.

It seems a far-flung friend of hers actually sent her a llama once. It came on a freight truck in a crate, and it was a pup or a cub or a calf, just a puny little thing with spots on its haunches and the cry of a startled woodcock. The driver took lunch at the café in town and left his flatbed parked out front where his cargo snared pedestrians and gathered a healthy crowd as we don't see, in the regular course of events, too awful many llamas about.

Once he'd come out picking his teeth and regretting his entree, he confirmed for us just who that llama was for and sought from us directions, so we pointed him towards the llama barn and the tidy llama corral while we set about working revisions in our opinion of that woman which proved premature since straight-away she turned that llama out.

Her neighbor up the road found it in with his cattle and had her come and fetch it, but once she got it home, she must have merely dispatched it down the road instead since for a month or so thereafter we'd see it every now and again, and it seemed to have fallen in with a run of deer. We'd spy sometimes at a pasture edge feeding on the scrub a buck, a few does, a fawn or two and that gangly speckled llama. The creature is probably running loose still over in the National Forest where it likely serves as a curiosity on the occasional nature jaunt.

For her part, that woman acted like she'd never taken delivery of the thing and went on planning to come by llamas which she would keep and she would shear if not in the coming autumn then the autumn after that. She still rides around town in her rusted truck with its ancient bumper sticker which is weathered and puckered and faded. "Llama Mama," it reads.

Clayton didn't, in fact, fit tidily into one of our lunatic slots since he'd not gone crazy exactly no matter what the Baptists said in regards to Clayton's transformation and their vindictive Savior. He'd only gotten, if anything, uncharacteristically discreet and what we took for unaccountably retiring once we'd heard he'd brought his dish around and shut his TV off. It was a girl who had a cousin who dated a boy who worked for Doyle who injected a dash of wonder into Clayton's situation by broadcasting word she'd come by about that Lhasa from Wilkes-Barre and Clayton's strange precise prognostication.

As a matter of routine, the chances are always pretty good that Mrs. Ivy Vaughn will enjoy about twice a week or so occasion to crush the spark of life out of one of God's own creatures with one of her bias-belted radial tires. Now for Clayton to have foretold just which creature she would kill and for it to have been a lap-dog on its way to Pensacola—a transient pet from Pennsylvania he'd identified by name—instead of just a stray tree squirrel, a blacksnake or opossum, tickled us pretty thoroughly since, as prognostications go, Clayton's was useless and trifling and touched with a hint of arithmetic wonder.

We couldn't, that is, begin to work out how fast a family of four would need to travel in their Sable from their home in Pennsylvania in order to have their canine rendezvous with Mrs. Ivy Vaughn's Impala just as she backed it in a snit out of her Family Dollar slot.

If Clayton had said that the earth was about to be swallowed up in hellfire or a plague was to rage across it or it was doomed to collide with Mars, we wouldn't among us have paid him any notice. We would, however, have probably thronged the shopping plaza lot since, like people everywhere, we're keen these days on inconsequential mayhem, watch shows devoted to videotaped police chases on TV, programs given over to air disasters and marauding carnivorous beasts, and just last year when that weathergirl reporting from a Hampton jetty was snatched microphone, slicker and all into the ocean by a wave, that scrap of footage ran more frequently on the nightly news than their entire assortment of gastric advertisements.

We're a bloodthirsty people but in a detached and impassive sort of way. Our preferred mayhem is inconsequential, that is to say, to us.

Even so, our interest in Clayton would have surely flagged and waned since anybody can get lucky about a Lhasa apso once, but then he went and firmed up his standing as our local surefire mystic by conveying to a fellow a troubling crumb of news about his girlfriend. That boy was from out in the valley on the Allegheny side and wouldn't even have run up on Clayton if he'd not been enterprising. He had a beat up old tank truck that he pumped out septic systems with, and he'd been forestalled by the law from working in the western counties once they'd caught him dumping a load of septic honey in a ditch.

He tended to prey on folks like Clayton, grizzled oldsters for the most part who were spinning out their days in tumbledown houses that they'd lavished with their undivided neglect. That boy would knock on their doors and speak to them earnestly about their septic systems, would wager that they'd not had their tanks pumped out in years if ever at all which he'd let on to be an oversight of magnitude and moment. He'd allow how, for his own part, he'd hate to have his sewage back clear up his drain line and into his kitchen sink.

"Got my truck right here. Won't take twenty minutes."

"How much?"

And that's when he knew he had them. "It's usually seventy-five, but . . ." He'd glance about the premises and mount a show of pity and custodial disapproval. ". . . I can go forty for you," which was the genius of it really, the uninvited charity that invariably worked as a nudge and a provocation and led, more often than not, to flashes of molten misdirected pride.

"I've got money!"

Here that boy would drop his head so as to consider his shoetops and mutter, "I'm not saying that you couldn't . . ." Then he'd usually peek up to find himself abandoned in the doorway, could generally hear his customer inside foraging for bills, three twenties ordinarily that evermore got shoved at him across the threshold, a dignified price that was still shy of retail but more than he'd offered to take.

That fellow's talent for pumping out septic tanks was a little less refined. Sometimes he'd even actually find the things, would dig down and locate the plug and plunge his hose into the sewage, would switch on his pump which had a bad bearing and made a terrific noise, the sort of racket that suited a motor sucking sludge out of the ground. And frequently that boy would even drain those septic tanks a little before he'd yank out the hose and drop in the plug and pronounce those systems scoured.

As Clayton was perched upon his sideboard, he couldn't be bothered to answer his door, but that septic tank boy could hear Clayton laboring through a hymn and let himself on into the house to set in with his line of chat. The looks of the place had persuaded him to anticipate that Clayton would be the usual upland geriatric sort—past caring, that is to say, about being presentable any longer with stubble on his face and shiny thirty-weight hair, with the leavings of a full week's worth of dinners on his shirt.

And while Clayton did prove passably filthy and noticeably untended, he was also—that boy couldn't help but remark—drawing on his chimney stack which served, to that fellow's way of thinking, to render Clayton artistic, meaning his personal squalor was not the result of mere shiftless hygienic sloth but was the consequence instead of Clayton's preoccupation with his muse.

That septic tank boy had come across artistic sorts before, not so much in his professional life but in his personal dalliances. He'd bedded his neighbor up the road who was a potter of sorts and made jugs that were bent and dimpled in such a way as to be useless, wouldn't hold anything but a person's attention for a quarter minute or so. He'd seen fit, nonetheless, to admire those jugs and flatter that woman's talent, and she'd proven helpless against him once his esteem for her had approached her own.

With fit cause, then, that boy had grown to think himself adept in the willful lubrication of your creative sorts, so he stood there in the alcove that makes do for Clayton's foyer and said lowly to Clayton, "Don't mean to interrupt."

Clayton, however, failed to let on that he'd heard him and just kept on with his sketching, pecked at the plaster with a hunk of cinder direct out of the grate, made a mark down towards the nether edge of what that boy took for a blossom, and he let on to be prompted to a spot of appreciative warbling.

"Pretty!" he said.

For his part, Clayton troubled himself to pivot on the sideboard, dropped his hunk of charred wood and bestowed upon that boy a gaze. "Second November," he told him. "Cutting wind. Cruel surface. We are away." Then Clayton climbed off of that quartersawn sideboard, using the drawerknobs for steps, and ambled across the front room to pitch himself into his chair.

"Don't suppose you've got much call to fool with your septic system, a painter fellow like you."

Clayton said nothing straightoff, only gazed, that boy noticed, towards a cobwebby corner where the wall met the ceiling and the crown molding sagged and puckered because the nails had pulled away. That fellow threw in to join with Clayton in imbibing the beauty of the view and remarked on the charming effect of the sun on the nappy cobweb fuzz which seemed to prompt Clayton to smile at that boy. "I'm well, thank you," he said.

"Got my truck outside. Her pump's got some suck on her." That boy pointed a little aimlessly with his nose. "Your tank runs what? Seven hundred gallon?"

Clayton slouched back against his headgrease stain. He picked at a cottony tuft of stuffing available through the upholstery of his frayed and tattered chair arm as he considered the middle distance, as he smiled.

"Don't matter. I can go a thousand, rolling about empty up through here." That boy set in on a tour of Clayton's front room so as to mount a performance of soaking in the threadbare squalor of the place which called on fewer of his thespianic gifts than was normally the case since Clayton's front room was authentically revolting, the sort of digs a hog would probably feel obliged to tidy up.

"Seventy-five a throw most times, but I can go forty for you."

Clayton hardly so much as blinked and failed altogether to seem remotely tempted towards indignation. He just sat in his ratty chair and ignored that boy which served to work his sap up a little given all the bother he'd gone to to admire Clayton's blossom on the wall.

"Want to do this thing or not?"

Clayton watched a little fondly his vacant piece of air, fingered still his ragged tuft of stuffing.

"Hey." That boy closed on Clayton, reached out and jabbed at Clayton's shoulder with his foremost finger. "Hey!"

Only then did Clayton shift his gaze upon that boy and speak. "She's weak," he said, "and that Floyd is such a charmer," which failed to make legitimate sense to that septic tank boy straightaway since it didn't have a thing to do with sewage or the pending transaction between them, but that boy knew a she, as it turned out, and was acquainted as well with a Floyd, so Clayton's remark had soon impressed him as both curious and familiar and called for a spot of mulling on the part of that septic tank boy.

The Floyd he knew sold secondhand cars off a lot down from his house while he figured the she for the creature he'd taken up with the year before, a woman he'd poached from a buddy of his who'd been down at the time with a tumor and had seemed to be threatening to expire before he satisfied his debts. That septic tank boy, apparently, had called upon his buddy so as to wish him well and make a plea for the piece of money that was due him, and he'd run by happenstance into his buddy's fiancée who he'd met with occasion to chat up in the hospital corridor once they'd gotten invited to step outside that semiprivate room while the buddy with the tumor's bunky had his seepy abscess swabbed.

As it turned out, that septic tank boy's buddy's tumor was benign, proved to be comprised predominantly of gristle, but his predicament had set his fiancée to reconsidering her options, and she fell for that septic tank boy in the hospital corridor, went out with him to cement their bond in the cab of that boy's tank truck. That girl even had a house that she allowed him to move into, had a pine bedstead that held her mattress and springs up off the floor, cable TV and city water, proper pots and pans and flatware.

In their full year together, they'd endured a few bumpy interludes. That septic tank boy had gotten found out in a betrayal or two, but with his gift for palaver he'd evermore managed to win that girl of his back. Like most faithless men, he tended towards irrational jealousy and couldn't bear the thought that girl of his might see fit to deceive him in the fashion and with the manner of mates he was given to cheat on her—most particularly Floyd from up the road who that septic tank boy detested.

Floyd was divorced and available, was his own boss and worked out of his home. The cars he sold were arrayed on his front lawn either side of his drive, and he'd strung gaudy plastic pinions from his treelimbs so as to lend a tasteless commercial car-lot atmosphere to the place. He'd been married to a fine woman once, a Dinkins from Norfolk way, a handsome brunette who'd endured him for far longer than he'd rated on account of how Floyd was a devoted layabout and hapless schemer, was evermore sprawling on the sofa hatching some means of evaporating funds and had gotten to where pending ruin hung about him like a musk.

When his wife left, she failed to do Floyd the service of throwing him over for a man but was driven instead by an appetite for ordinary salvation, so Floyd didn't quite know where to direct his bile. He spent, consequently, a half a year on his settee just feeling aimlessly wretched and enlisted anybody who happened onto him to hear how he'd been wronged. It proved difficult, however, for people about to work up sympathy for a man who could rarely muster the gumption to change out of his pajamas and was supporting himself on a rather suspect disability claim.

Floyd had been for a stint employed at the landfill and had gone down with scavenger's elbow.

When that money gave out, Floyd set about selling what goods he could dispense with—an oak buffet and a bedroom suite, a glider and a garden tiller, a utility trailer he'd borrowed in fact from a cousin in the valley, a set of his ex-wife's mother's china she'd seen fit to leave behind. Presently, he got down to where he had little left to him but his car, a V'69 Chevelle that he had overhauled and pampered. With his marriage falling apart and his house dilapidating around him, Floyd had managed still to keep baby oil on the dash of his Chevelle and a dazzling luster on his fender chrome.

Floyd took out an ad in the *Trading Post* and parked his coupe out on his lawn. He got traffic straightaway and entertained a few offers, but he didn't much approve of the quality of the clientele he attracted and was ambivalent anyway about letting go of his Chevelle, so he declined as a matter of course to accept the offers he received until he met up with a fellow who turned out to be tenacious, a retiree from up Connecticut way who lived on a fairway outside Staunton and fondly remembered the ragtop Chevelle he'd driven in his youth.

Naturally, Floyd found him at first an unworthy prospect as well if, for no other reason, than that he was a Yankee. So that fellow would bid on Floyd's Chevelle, and Floyd would turn him down which would prompt him, Floyd noticed, to return a week later with an improved proposition. Pretty soon it was a matter of competitive principle for that fellow from outside Staunton, and he lost sight of the money at stake as he fixed upon the prize which was along about when, in Floyd's case, that the cash came into focus and eroded Floyd's attachment to his coupe.

The whole experience served to edify Floyd in the nature of this world and led him to a fresh formulation of a philosophy for living. He shortly grew to believe, as a matter of faith, that people are prone to be dopes—both at rest and at play but, most particularly, while in the throes of commerce. That's along about when Floyd finally left his couch at home for good and charged into life with the dancing spark and savor of a man firm in his belief that the fruit about is evermore in season.

He fairly overhauled himself, took to wearing shiny suits and sheer socks inside of slippers with no laces. He combed his hair straight back and cemented it down with heavily scented pomade and bought for himself a pinkie ring and a chunky gold-plated bracelet with his name engraved along a tasteless slab on the band. He accumulated at the auto auction a baker's dozen vehicles, assorted sedans for the most part but a pickup truck or two, and he parked them there flanking his drive and hung his plastic pinions, had a sign made designating his vehicles as "luxurious" and "pre-owned." Then he sat around and waited for folks to come along and offer him less money than he could, sadly, see clear to accept.

What with his utter lack of anxiety and studied transactional inertia, Floyd found he could best about anybody in a negotiation since he'd been low and financially desperate already—unfit even for work at the landfill—so he never much worried about what might happen if an offer walked away. People, then, would come and try to buy his cars, and he'd decline to let them until they'd come back at least a time or two. Floyd had confidence. He had swanky clothes and a full head of larded hair which made for more joy in Floyd's life than he'd ever known before.

That septic tank boy's girlfriend had fairly driven her Pinto to pieces. The thing had grown to be compression-poor and severely gasket-weary, and she had a boxbottom flap in her passenger window where the glass had fallen out. Once the hatch latch had failed her and the lid kept popping open as she drove, she set about badgering that septic tank boy and made him to understand that he had some sort of common-law duty to keep her in vehicles. In a bid to oblige her, that septic tank boy went with her down to Floyd's where she became acutely smitten with a little red Pontiac two-door which that septic tank boy made to Floyd a modest offer on that Floyd saw fit to reject without discussion.

It seems that septic tank boy decided straightaway he didn't much care for Floyd who, with his shiny suit and his hairgrease and his fake alligator slippers, gave the impression of a man who was out to show up fellows roundabout. Moreover, he tended to ogle women and investigate them along their reaches, and that septic tank boy caught him feasting unduly upon his girlfriend's figure which peeved him enough to withdraw the offer that Floyd had already declined, and he advised that girl of his to drive her Pinto until it quit.

That boy raced home from Clayton's as best he was able with his half a load of sludge, and he laid plans along the way for the sort of violence he'd visit upon Floyd and cobbled up a spot of commentary to bestow upon his girlfriend which he honed and refined as he traveled across the valley.

Still he was shaken when he rolled in alongside that little red

70

Pontiac in his drive which he decided that Floyd had used as a temptation, had brought over to render his girlfriend frail against his overtures. Naturally, that septic tank boy imagined them naked together inside, and he decided straightaway he'd ruin that cherry red Pontiac while it was handy as preamble to the thrashing he intended to inflict upon Floyd. So he ran the hose end from his tank truck into the window of that coupe and switched on his pump and opened his valve to free his sludge to flow.

The sewage came boiling out of that hose and splashed about that coupe, surged up over the seats and the console, sloshed against the dash and was lapping at the window wells when the paperwork floated out—a tissuey yellow receipt from the DMV and a document from Floyd laying out the terms of the loan that him and the girlfriend had agreed to which was along about when the pump bearing clatter served to draw her outside.

Like any other part of the world, we have our share of domestic disputes when the years or the months or the weeks or the hours of conjugal irritation get vented. Now that septic tank boy and his girlfriend had been pretty peaceful as a couple until the sight of her brand new Pontiac coupe loaded full of sludge served to prompt that girlfriend to an eruption. She let out a scream and fell on that boy with murder in her eyes.

They fought in the yard. They fought in the house. They fought out in the street for a while, screamed at each other while lobbing gobs of sewage back and forth which the county police got called in to interrupt them at. They observed a truce for nearly twenty-four hours before the animosities set in afresh, and they reconvened in the front yard where they doused each other with shit until a deputy rolled up to make of himself an active antagonism which induced them to turn on that fellow and fling some septic gravy his way.

They got invited to pass a few days together in the county

lockup where they screamed at each other through a vent hole in the ceiling as they grew between them notorious in the outside world for the shameless white-trash spectacle they had mounted. It got covered on the local news and in the local papers, was dissected at length and from assorted perspectives in our "Heard on the Grapevine" column as that writer knew people acquainted with folks who'd gotten wind of details, grubby little facts for the most part about that boy and his slutty girlfriend, about their trashy blood relations, about their previous romances, about the shabby unsavory decor of their house.

A correspondent from a news-magazine show even interviewed that couple in jail as there was a lull just then in celebrity deaths and celebrity litigation. Since that septic tank boy and his girlfriend were still irate with each other, they functioned together as dazzlingly tasteless news-magazine show fare, and while that correspondent was interviewing that septic tank boy in his cell, his wife was contradicting him through the air vent in the ceiling which made do to heighten and ratchet up the pitch of that boy's rage.

He laid the blame for the whole business on the head of some upland psychic and even provided that correspondent with directions to Clayton's house which somehow looked on television even homelier than it was, near implausibly trashstrewn and dilapidated.

That correspondent set the scene with a brief bit of chat in front of Clayton's porch and then undertook to inflict Clayton with an interview. He was sitting in his chair with the headgrease stain, was glassy-eyed and sooty, and he failed to respond to that correspondent, didn't even look at her much until she'd fairly given out of questions when Clayton glanced her way and dropped his jaw.

"I'm well, thank you," he said.

It seems a cousin of Clayton's, one of those Goinses on his mother's side, happened to see that show with a buddy of his, and they recognized together that Clayton didn't appear to have much use for his television which caused them to wonder if they could maybe tempt him to yield it up. So they traveled together from Ararat clean up to Clayton's house to find Clayton drawing on his chimney stack. He remained on his quartersawn sideboard while they pilfered through his goods, and he only paused once in his sketching so as to ask them to call him Titus. They left him his bedside radio, a three-way table lamp and his musty upholstered chair, even took his kerosene heater and the dregs of his mother's liqueurs.

As it happened, Larry stopped those fellows south along the bypass where they were traveling at a lawful speed in Clayton's cousin's freighted pickup, but that Goins had mended a fractured taillight with a length of electrical tape which Larry had spied from his spot in the shrubbery alongside the shopping plaza and so had rolled out into the roadway and lit those fellows up.

They had a big lumpy load of Clayton's furnishings piled up in the bed covered over with a couple of blankets and tied down with extension cords which any other of our deputies would have surely quizzed those boys about, invited them at least to account somehow for the swag that they were hauling, but Larry is always a little too deep in the trees to make out the woods.

"Don't know about this light," Larry told that Goins, and then he noticed a spot of grievous wear on that Goins's left rear tire. Larry fished a penny from his pocket to test the depth of the cuppy tread, established that he could see Mr. Lincoln from his nostrils up.

Larry winced. Larry groaned. Larry leaned briefly against Clayton's refrigerator before he informed that Goins, "Guess there's no help for it," and whipped his summons book out.

———

They looked for Angela Denise right up to the time when they decided it seemly to stop, scoured the woods about and patrolled the banks of the streams and the rivers, went on a three-county hoodlum roundup and conducted interrogations in an old warehouse at the railyard that the state police had commandeered. For a month or so they held official briefings every afternoon. A state police captain in his starched grays and his campaign hat would mount a siding platform with a federal bureau agent, and they would each of them read a statement to whatever press was about in advance of entertaining questions they would either decline to answer or respond to with enough shifty circumspection to make a senator blush.

They got tips there at first from assorted locals with corrosive grievances who hoped both to collect the reward for that child that the women's circle had offered—a fairly modest piece of money augmented by a dazzling assortment of baked goods—and make trouble for various citizens about that they'd mounted careers of detesting. Everybody who got picked up and interviewed was fairly paraded to that railyard, driven slowly through town in a state police cruiser for anybody to see, and we're the sort who, once infected with suspicion, are painfully slow to take a cure.

Fortunately, they brought in the sort of people we'd never thought much of anyway. They started out by hauling in fellows about with local police records, that ilk given to casual violence and undue sexual appetites which meant they carted through town an array of Hayslips and a smattering of Blalocks along with that quartet of Parhams who were said to have forced their ardor on a woman—three brothers and a cousin who'd commandeered the favors of a Massey from down the gap.

Soon word got around that there were cold cuts and sodas

available at the railyard and that those fellows the law hauled in were encouraged to dine while they got quizzed which resulted in a healthy influx of wholly voluntary suspects who'd stop by to own up to unsavory urges while they enjoyed a sandwich or two. A couple of them even confessed to crimes that they'd not been found out at which got laid off to the lure of the kosher salami and the Cape Cod kettle chips, but it turned out that we were short on that ilk most likely to snatch a child and then make unspeakable criminal use of the creature. They did turn up, however, two gentlemen from opposite ends of the county who proved independently guilty of unnatural attachments to their yard fowl.

There at the outset, our local police chief was a party to the inquiry, and he would join those fellows up on the siding platform at the briefings and even entertain the odd questions dispatched his way. They were a study, those three men, in distinct law-enforcement types. The chief is blubbery and folksy and his uniform is often stained with ink from his ballpoints and chili from his burgers while that state police captain was trim and tidy and as jolly as your average marine. That federal agent could pretty readily have passed for a tax accountant. The longer they went without finding that child, the smaller the part the chief had to play, and then the state police bowed out, yielding the reins up to the feds, and the agent in charge inflicted upon us what he called "bureau assets."

As it turned out, they had ways of knowing what we were all of us up to at home, what sort of videotapes we rented, what sort of magazines we took, what sort of smut we tapped into on the information superhighway, the manner of goods we saw fit to order discreetly through the mail, and they hauled in a number of us for "conversations" they liked to call them, and then permitted to seep out generally just what those chats had been about.

Accordingly, we learned that the associate pastor lately come to the Methodist church subscribed, in addition to *Guidepost, Gospel Life* and *The Upper Room,* to a bimonthly periodical called *Swank* that he had delivered to a post box in a town down in the valley.

We came by word that a bachelor motor-grader driver from up the ridge wore women's delicates beneath his coveralls which he attempted to insist, while being badgered by that federal agent, was on account of his uncommonly sensitive nether skin. Talk got around that the Ritchies, a couple of white-haired snowbirds originally from somewhere in Wisconsin, didn't actually visit each July their son and daughter-in-law in Fort Wayne but went instead to Antigua to be nudists for a week and meet up with assorted former neighbors from Sheboygan.

We learned as well that the Pratt sisters from over by the airfield were not, in fact, authentic siblings after all, weren't even the vaguest strain of blood relations as it turned out but shared instead, we were made to know, a perverted passion between them. Furthermore, we heard that our local vet and his wife wall-papered naked and were prone to engage in congress once they were good and slathered with paste.

What we didn't come by was word of that little blonde child who had gone missing which, after a while, didn't seem to be much on that federal agent's mind. He proved far more intent on our wholesale reduction as a community, appeared to delight in indicating to us just where we had rotted and soured, those pockets about of lunacy and creeping moral decay. He even brought in Grover for a session, folding chair and all, Grover who passed an hour or two waving at the video camera and owning up to a giddy fascination with trucks.

It was Clayton of all people who finally did that agent in. That was the occasion when Ray and Clayton first made each other's acquaintance as Ray had been sent out to gather up Clayton and carry him to his interview. That special agent's minions, in prying into Clayton's credit history, had noted both his Satin Channel subscription and his taste in videotapes as Clayton, over the years, had ordered a number of fairly damning titles from *Love Socket* to *Jug Island* to *Vulva Patrol* to *Field of Reams*.

Ray tried to prepare Clayton on the way into town for the sorts of questions and insinuations he'd be obliged to weather, but Clayton failed to whimper and twitch and sweat like the folks Ray had carried in before him, most particularly a Boyd from up the gap with an interest in hand puppets which that special agent had taken for troubling and worth inquiring about.

Clayton, for his part, welcomed occasion to talk about his movies and describe in clinical detail the nature of his Satin Channel fare which that special agent had not been personally equipped to anticipate. That fellow's ordinary method was to kick off a chat with a smattering of innocuous inquiries, a few homely unprobing questions intended to put his subjects at ease before he'd loose upon them freshets of his flinty righteousness, would have them to know that he was acquainted with whatever they'd been up to and, accordingly, was fairly awash in virulent contempt.

In fact, that agent was just before shifting with Clayton from arid bureaucrat to his role as federal moral conscience and belittling corrosive scold when Clayton troubled himself to point out to that agent a clerical mistake, a typographical omission on a sheet upon the table that Clayton felt constrained to rectify. It seems the Satin Channel had mounted one of their cinematic festivals. Fleet Week they'd called it, and for seven days they'd shown each evening films with nautical themes or, at the very least, a stimulated sailor or two.

Naturally, Clayton had watched them all, had been most particularly taken with *Down the Hatch* which had featured Ms. Jasmine Love as the bride of a high-powered financier who was ever-more jetting off to pillage far-flung industries and leaving his wife to her own amusements and enthusiams. Chief among them were sailing jaunts about the San Francisco harbor where she sunned herself naked and serviced deckhands in the rigging of her sloop.

Eventually, Clayton troubled himself to acquaint that special agent with the particulars of the plot of *Down the Hatch,* but there at the first he merely made a punctuational adjustment. He took up from the table the sheet that agent had hoped to berate him with, dug a stubby pencil out of the pocket of his shirt and over-hauled with it one of the Fleet Week titles, transformed *Damn the Torpedoes* to *Damn! The Torpedoes!* instead.

He was through, that special agent was, though he didn't know it yet as he wasn't incisive by nature and penetrating but had need to badger Clayton and probe him for some trace of shame. Clayton, for his part, only confessed to a spot of disappointment over a Fleet Week import of Scandinavian extraction, a film about a whaler's wife that Clayton had found rather dreary due both to the subtitles and the hair beneath the starlet's arms.

Otherwise, Clayton comported himself like a man without misgivings, a fellow wholly unacquainted with disgrace, and, when that agent would up and fling at Clayton a sordid movie title, Clayton would respond with a scrupulous description of the plot which served to provoke that special agent to a strain of spitting rage.

The chief and Ray were listening from the far side of a cubicle wall, didn't just happen to be there but had lingered by design as the chief had come to a dim opinion of that special agent's tactics. Ray couldn't ever say what comment exactly finally served to set the chief off. He just seemed to remember that special agent was busy berating Clayton for his want of Christian virtues and his appalling lack of taste when the chief orbited around from the backside of that cubicle wall and brought to an end that fellow's investigation.

He hooked his thumbs on his belt, the chief did, as he considered that special agent, troubled himself to expend some heed on that agent's junior assistants as well—the wiry boy with the cowlicks who operated the video camera, the girl with the runs in her stockings and the lipstick on her teeth who jotted on a notepad incriminating revelations with a shake of her head, most usually with a smirk.

"We'll take it from here," the chief said, and with his tone and with his bearing he conveyed somehow that he had no stomach for that agent anymore. He didn't offer to speak further but just considered that special agent as he snorted up a troublesome gobbet of phlegm while that fellow, for his part, appeared for a moment tempted to commentary before he imbibed and digested the essential nature of the chief's intent, before he recognized that he was getting invited to depart our little town, was being assured of a monumental thrashing if he elected to stay.

While that special agent was mean and petty and contemptuous of people, he wasn't tough in any way that mattered. "Fine," he said, and the chief and Ray both lingered to look on as he gathered his papers and packed up his briefcase, as he led his associates out of the warehouse bay and towards his sedan. He informed the chief that he fully intended to write a candid memo which brought the chief off the platform in such a fashion as to prompt that special agent to make an undignified leap into his car.

"Didn't much care for him," Clayton told Ray and spat onto the rail siding. "No sir, didn't much like that fellow at all."

Ray stopped off with Clayton at Little Earl's where they ate on the patio slab, had little Earl's deep-fried oysters and his sweet white-meal corn dodgers while Clayton shared with Ray the

touching subplot of a Satin Channel movie he'd lately seen, a detour in the thrust of the story devoted to a pair of randy twins,
chesty things who of an evening would make novel use of
squashes which served both to stifle Ray's appetite and drive six
patrons off that slab.

As it turned out, Ray got appointed the "we" who would take
the inquiry from there since Larry and Carl, Walter and Ailene
weren't afflicted among them with an investigative bent. The
chief, for his part, volunteered to help Ray along as best he could,
but Ray had noticed already that the chief was the sort prepared
to abide a mystery, wasn't prone to be troubled and nagged when
motives failed to get laid bare or even when perpetrators went un-
detected. He could be at his ease with the notion that there were
some things he'd never know.

The trouble with that girl who'd disappeared out of Homer
Blaine State Park was that there weren't even facts enough for
Ray to build a theory upon. That child had just gone into the
woods and hadn't come back out again leaving Ray with but a
canpicker, a bird watcher and a couple in a van that had been
green if it wasn't blue instead. So Ray was largely left to wander
the woods and chat up that girl's parents who had neglected
somehow to come to be cemented together in grief.

That girl's father declined, like men will, to discuss his daughter much. Ray stopped off pretty regularly to talk to that Dunn,
would hunt him up at his barn where he'd be tinkering with one
of his milkers or blaspheming one of his cows or maybe just lying
around on a bale of fodder, and Ray would apprise that Dunn of
where he stood with his investigation which tended to be, more
often than not, just where he'd stood before. Then Ray would put
that Dunn through a species of catechism, would ask him a slate
of questions in hopes his memory had been jogged and he could

name for Ray some article of clothing that his daughter had worn or recall if perhaps, instead of the woods, she'd wandered towards the road.

That Dunn, however, hadn't known much to start with and didn't grow forthcoming, would invite Ray to find himself a perch and would tell Ray about his plans, proved to be one of those fellows who was evermore scheming up a change, stayed anxious to be most anything than what he had become. He was— Ray learned in that barn in the course of their unproductive chats—contemplating a shift in avocation from dairyman to orchard keeper, and he'd taken, as was his custom, to reading exhaustively about nectarines which had the virtue of peachy sweetness without the liability of fuzz.

"The grocery mart gets theirs from California," that Dunn informed Ray, saying the name of that state as if it were a province of Communist China. "I'd bet a man around here could probably do a good business in nectarines."

Ray, as it turned out, was acquainted with several fellows in nectarines, most particularly a Wooten whose orchard bordered to the north on trash, a clutch of Meechams and their attachments by marriage who lived in a quartet of rubbishy houses and evermore helped themselves to that Wooten's fruit as soon as it grew ripe. They didn't pick it like decent people weak in the face of luscious fruit, which is to say they didn't slip of an evening into that Wooten's orchard and cart off in their shirttails what nectarines they could eat. These particular Meechams hailed from a considerable line of shiftless sorts, so they picked that Wooten's fruit as if they had been hired by him to do it.

They came with pillowcases and joint compound buckets, coal scuttles and grocery sacks, and they'd harvest just the ripest reddest nectarines they could find no matter how deep in that orchard they were obliged to wander, and they'd keep at it until their containers were full or that Wooten had squeezed off their way a round of number 7 shot.

Naturally, that Wooten would call in the law, but there's not much to be done with trash, no sense among Meechams of a better nature a deputy might appeal to, no moral leverage a fellow might apply. Ray always talked to them nonetheless while Carl and Ailene rarely bothered. Walter, for his part, had a weakness for fruit and would usually buy from those Meechams a couple of pecks of nectarines.

That was the hell of it really. Those Meechams had a stand out by the roadside where they sold to passersby the fruit they'd plundered from that Wooten's orchard, and regular people would buy it up because they asked a sensible price, folks who'd had ample occasion to see the Meecham compound, who knew they didn't own a fruit tree among them, who knew they couldn't even grow grass.

So Ray would go out and talk to those Meechams on that Wooten's behalf, partly to stave off bloodshed as that Wooten had a magnum revolver that he was evermore claiming to be of a mind to speak to those Meechams with, but partly as well so that Ray could put himself in the heady presence of that Meecham brand of congenital mendacity.

As a clan, they were without guilt and shame pretty much from conception, and they were capable of a strain of accomplished unperforated prevarication which Ray, as a student of people, couldn't help much but admire since, while your ordinary sorts are instinctively fearful of getting snared in a lie, those Meechams seemed to feed upon and savor their deceit.

Ray would show up at their produce stand out along the roadside which those Meechams had made of scrap spruce and some sheets of Masonite, and he'd browse among what merchandise those Meechams had on offer which was prone to be nectarines mostly but not nectarines alone. They pilfered as well from a fellow in the bottom who grew melons and pole beans, stole side meat from a gentleman who hung it in his barn to cure and lifted trifles out of the five-and-dime for that ilk of customer likely to be tempted by a charcoal insole or a pocket comb.

Ray, of course, had cause to know that everything they had was swag, and all of those Meechams must have been persuaded that he knew it, but still when Ray would pluck up a nectarine and inquire where it had come from, whatever Meecham was working the stand would point and tell him, "Boy up the road."

The beauty of it, to Ray's way of thinking, was not that there wasn't a boy up the road but that there wasn't even a road much for a fellow to be up. The gravel track that passed before the Meecham compound and climbed the rise ended a quarter mile up the hillside in a clammy locust thicket, just gave out without even so much as a turnaround, and Ray could stand there at that fruit stall and eyeball where that roadway quit.

"Who?" Ray would ask just to try a little the Meecham he'd happened across, and they would all of them—down to the towheaded gradeschool Meecham they called Skunk—fling an arm to point and inform Ray, "Some boy."

It was the self-assured carelessness of it that Ray most appreciated, the indifference to contradiction and patent fact. Those Meechams even made out to believe a little they'd gotten their fruit from a locust thicket, had a sort of viral tenacity where it came to their strain of lies, and Ray would usually apprise them of his opinion that number 7 shot might kill a man if a pellet or two should strike him in his vitals. Those Meechams were hardly the type, however, to fret about being dead which they let on to have decided would be very much like living though without personal property taxes and gnats.

The bulk of Ray's time got devoted to the Wooten who owned that nectarine orchard and who Ray frequently had to talk out of spoiling his life by exterminating a Meecham or two. That Wooten, fortunately, was blessed with an overriding sensible streak that would impose itself upon him once his fury had waned and ebbed, and Ray would sit with that Wooten down at his pack house, perch with him on the steps from where they could oftentimes see a plume of smoke lifting out of the Meecham compound as those Meechams were given to burning bits of rubbish in their yard which was far more convenient for them than picking it up and hauling it off.

At length, that Wooten would invariably get around to cows and confess to Ray he might just up and change careers and keep some, pen them in his orchard and let them get by on windfall fruit and grass.

Ray carried that Wooten along on one of his visits to that Dunn so that they might serve to put each other off of their ambitions. That Wooten could belittle nectarines and orchard keeping in general while that Dunn was qualified to run down cows. All they did, however, was throw in together to grouse about the weather.

———

Gloria, the wife, never called for any prompting, had discovered in the wake of the disappearance of Angela Denise that she was blessed with a natural affinity for grief—not, of course, dignified and private bereavement but that brand of conspicuous mourning that people practice anymore to advertise how very sad they are. That Dunn's despair as a mother became, in fact, an avocation for her once she'd hooked up with a fellow out of Richmond. He was one of the anchors on the weekend news, the strawberry blonde with the rugged features who got dispatched weeknights to school-board meetings and ice-felled power lines.

He was obliged to cover the state fair and touring troupes of senior cloggers, got sent to the mountains to usher in autumn, got sent to the beach to herald spring. He filled in sometimes when the sports guy went off on vacation, did remotes from Libertarian headquarters on Election Night.

Gloria Dunn and her missing daughter served as a godsend for him as that fellow was hoping to get himself hired onto a magazine show since he had already the requisite rugged good looks and the splendid head of hair. All he needed was occasion to exhibit his reporter's nose for tawdry tripe, and the story of a mute little girl gone missing in a virgin forest impressed him straightaway with its inordinate potential. He figured he'd make a tape to ship out by way of résumé in a bid to put his Richmond days behind him.

Now, of course, there had been some TV coverage early on when that child disappeared, and Gloria Dunn had shown up in person on one of the national morning chat shows. She'd had a four-minute segment with the perky hostess between an interview with a fellow who'd written a novel about an orthodontist who was a bit of a sleuth and a cooking demonstration conducted by a licensed dietician. That Dunn had even been invited to return to the set and sample the paprikash that dietician had whipped up with chicken tenders, vegetable spray and yogurt.

When that Dunn's daughter failed to turn up either lost in the forest or as a rotting corpus delicti, newspeople shifted along to fresher instances of anguish and more timely stories of wholesale human despair. Along about then, they had floods in Missouri and wildfires in the Adirondacks. They had a plane that went down for no apparent reason on the coast of California and killed not just all of the passengers but three fellows on a pier who might, with luck, have been elsewhere doing something otherwise. They had drunk professional football players beating up policemen and the senseless slaughter of a Swedish tourist for his Tiempo in Miami. They had an insecticide scare in Texas and an electrocution down in Florida that had seen the condemned man burst into gaudy flames, and, naturally, there were bits of carnage throughout the rest of the world, and every now and again some of that got mentioned as well.

That correspondent with the rugged good looks and the handsome head of strawberry hair was shopping himself in what turned out to be a golden age of crap, and it proved an easy matter for him to enlist that Dunn as an accomplice since she'd been warped already and contaminated by her fleeting brush with fame. Now while that doesn't make exactly for an untempered justification, it does go a ways towards explaining how they saw clear to do what they did, why they were content to add color, they called it, to the story of that lost child.

They had already a mute little girl who'd strayed into the woods, and what they provided by way of supplement was a national outpouring of grief, or at the very least a healthy measure of regional concern. The segment that correspondent taped featured Gloria Dunn in the parking lot of Homer Blaine State Park where she laid a lone rose on a heap of bouquets at the base of the routed park map, sprays of flowers and a half dozen wreaths that strawberry blonde correspondent claimed to have come from folks about who'd gotten touched by that woman's loss.

As it turned out, in fact, that correspondent and his camera operator had borrowed—they called it—those flowers from a graveyard on the Lynchburg Pike and had piled them up at the base of that sign in a fashion they'd found artful and more than a little true to life since it was just the sort of thing that people would have done if they'd bothered to think to do it. We were at the time full in the throes of a national spasm of flower laying, and there were folks all over this country who'd reasoned they couldn't be properly sad unless they'd helped to bury the site of whatever tragedy was handy under mums and roses and lilies and hand-lettered scraps of doggerel.

Most recently, just before that Dunn's child had vanished in the woods, a beloved television actor had perished on a New York City street, a young man who'd played a thoracic surgeon on a prime-time melodrama, a People's Choice winner and a multiple Golden Globe nominee who, as it turned out, was also a thoroughgoing jackass.

He'd been in a taxi on a Midtown cross street in lively dispute with his driver, a Bengali who'd chosen to travel a route that fellow disapproved of, and that actor had set about acquainting that driver with exactly who he was—a People's Choice winner and a multiple Golden Globe nominee who starred in a weekly prime-time show with an appreciable Nielsen share.

That Bengali, however, did not know the leisure to watch much television, and he remained steadfastly unimpressed by that actor's list of credits and his catalog of nominations and outright accolades which served to heighten the pitch of that actor's pique. He flung open the back door and jumped out of that cab in a demonstration of his displeasure just as another taxi was trying to pass them and squeeze up for advantage at the intersection. That actor got pinched between that cab's front grille and his own taxi door, had the life squeezed from him by a gentleman from Mauritania who didn't watch awfully much television himself.

On the twenty-four-hour news channels they ran obituaries of that actor and teary interviews with his colleagues and his former romantic attachments. He was featured in a paid tribute by the American Medical Association because that fellow, though not a

doctor, had winningly played one on TV. The Senate passed a resolution in that actor's honor and endured from the chaplain a
prayer on his behalf which prompted the president, during a joint
news conference with the Russian foreign minister, to reminisce
fondly about an evening he'd passed in that actor's company during a fund-raising soiree at a Laguna Beach estate while, for his
part, the Russian foreign minister had actually had thoracic sur-
gery that he spoke in unsettling detail through an interpreter
about.

That actor, it seems, had collapsed and expired on a manhole
cover just off Seventh Avenue, and his fans set about straightaway—in the spirit of showy bottomless sadness—to piling up
bundles of flowers on top of the thing until the block had to be
closed off and the traffic all rerouted. Then the TV people showed
up so the correspondents might have for a backdrop what they
chose to call a touching display of grief. They interviewed fans
who laid candles and fans who laid trinkets along with various
fans who laid flowers and poems and who waited each for a turn
to speak to a correspondent before hurrying home to tune in their
TVs and watch themselves be sad.

We learned in the following week or so far more about that actor than even his most feverish admirers probably had much yen
to know. We heard about the extra nipple he'd had surgically removed, saw a high school picture of him in his wrestling leotard
and met with occasion to share in the grief of the girl he'd squired
to the junior prom. She lived anymore in Council Bluffs with her
husband and her son and about an extra coed's worth of blubber.
She was pleased to display the prom photographs she'd saved over
the years, her dehydrated corsage and her slinky strapless gown.

A reporter turned up that actor's estranged father in Modesto
where he lived in a shack and nursed a bitterness against the zoning board that had permitted a fellow to open a grocery and gas

mart just beside him, a Pakistani who burnt his vapor lights all night. That gentleman couldn't remember awfully much about his son, though he did make a threat of violence against a Modesto zoning commissioner that the local prosecutor saw fit to swear out a warrant about.

A few of that dead actor's colleagues piped in with glowing tributes to his craft which they could very nearly manage without rancor and without envy, and that actor's sisters held a news conference in the company of their attorney, their agent and their spiritual adviser to identify the various parties in Manhattan who, after anguished deliberation, they'd decided they'd best sue. Their publishing contract forestalled them from fielding questions from reporters, though they did prove pleased to discuss the gentlemen's fragrance that would bear their brother's name and the organization those girls together had founded in his memory devoted to the safety and education of vehicle passengers around the world.

They were selling, as it turned out, a sticker to be placed near car-door pulls, a little square of shiny orange paper with adhesive backing that had Look First! printed on it in seven languages beneath a tiny likeness of that actor. Or rather, the thing read Look First! in fully six of those seven languages since, in point of fact, they'd gotten unreliable Urdu, so that sticker said Look First! mostly but said Jolly Apricot! once as well.

The producers of that medical drama threw together a special episode which accounted for the disappearance of that fellow by sending him to France where an earthquake had given rise to the urgent need for emergency thoracic procedures. They replaced him with an actor known for taking off his shirt in the course of a cola commercial, but before anybody could get too terribly interested in him, a fellow who'd played the mouth harp in a band with four hit singles got found dead at the bottom of a motor hotel pool in Oklahoma. There was the suggestion of foul play or, at the very least, indifferent aquatic skills which proved sufficient to rout that dead actor and his sisters from the airwaves, though their lawyer and their agent and their spiritual adviser caught on as commentators.

So for anybody with an eye towards the national psyche and a finger on the national pulse—a fellow, for instance, like that savvy Richmond correspondent with the rugged good looks and the strawberry blonde head of hair—it was plain that there was a national appetite about for tragedy, most particularly some sort of mishap that was telling of detail and artistic in its TV presentation.

Consequently, when he saw Gloria Dunn on that morning network chat show and heard her speak about her missing child who'd been not only blonde but unaccountably mute as well, that Richmond correspondent must have known straightaway that he'd found a fitting subject, and as he watched that Dunn congratulate the licensed dietician for her tasty no-muss low-fat paprikash, that fellow probably shivered with delight.

The way we heard it, that Richmond correspondent directed Gloria Dunn and actively coached from the woman her performance, would ask her a question and suffer from her an untutored response before wondering if he might be so bold as to tweak her remarks a little. Apparently, he rode her doggedly but with sufficient charm as to tempt her, in time, to invite instruction before she ventured to talk, so that fellow would inquire after some aspect of that Dunn's ordeal and then would tell her how to hold herself and advise her how to sigh, would have her cut her eyes, would have her speak.

The final edit made for six full minutes of remarkable maudlin rubbish. There were shots of that Dunn at the dinette with her husband and her son who'd been scoured clean and combed for the occasion. They prayed over a noodle casserole and beefsteak tomato dinner, and little Matthew—with his hands clasped and his eyes clenched shut and his hair cemented flat with VO5— pleaded for Jesus to let his baby sister come back to them which Gloria Dunn, in fuzzy close-up, managed a moist wistful look about.

Then there was the heap of plundered flowers by the Homer Blaine State Park sign and the walk that Dunn insisted she made daily through the woods. The camera followed her down the trail where she drew up by a comely laurel thicket and recited what she claimed to be a poem that she had written which would have come, we learned later, as a great surprise to Miss Edna St. Vincent Millay.

That Dunn wore on her blouse the likeness of a basswood leaf cut from green chintz with pinking shears, and she gave it out to be the emblem of the society she'd started to help prevent the senseless abduction of little blonde mute children. Then she set about blubbering, and the camera left her to find that correspondent standing with his microphone in a shaft of golden sunlight.

"Police sources tell us," he declared with the strain of earnest gravity that is elusive to all but news correspondents and community theater actors, "that there are no new leads in the disappearance of Angela Denise Dunn." Then the camera tilted back and the picture dissolved on the sun-dappled hardwood canopy.

That piece got snatched up by the magazine show with the lanky blonde full-lipped anchor who had a chat with that Richmond correspondent right there at her faux-mahogany desk. She introduced him as a colleague and an equal and called him nearly by his actual name in a fashion that he had probably only dreamed of back when he was still in school and she was famous already for her three-month defense of her actress/spokesmodel title.

The chief's wife, who needlepoints evenings in front of the TV, called the chief in in time for him to turn on the tape machine, and, come morning, he gathered his staff in his office so that they might watch that segment and inform him just who, for the love of Christ, "police sources" might be.

As it turned out, Ailene was afflicted with a weakness for handsome strawberry blondes. He'd found her out on the way to the café and had bought her a chicken-fried steak, had fairly bewitched her with talk of his career in television and scuttlebutt on all of the celebrated people he had met, most particularly that fellow who'd played the dashing insurance investigator on TV and then had gone on to star in a Hollywood movie about vampires in deepest space where they'd thrived because there wasn't much wood about to serve for stakes.

Once him and Ailene were tight and chummy, he asked after that missing child and learned from Ailene, his police source, that there was nothing new to know which still got Ailene chewed out for being a conduit and an accomplice.

Ray rewound the tape and watched that segment over again, studied the tortured misty expression on that Dunn woman's face and felt vaguely like he'd run across her poetry before. He considered her basswood leaf in chintz and the mutilated tree squirrel that that correspondent had come across off the trail upon a rock which raised the specter, he declared, of black arts and Satanism. Ray, of course, knew it straightaway for the handiwork of the brother who was obliged, after all, to engage himself between prayers for his sister's safe return.

It was the flowers, however, that Ray took particular notice of, most especially a mixed spray of baby's breath, hollyhocks and gladiolus which were featured prominently atop the heap by the Homer Blaine State Park sign. A woman up the pike had sworn out a complaint over a strikingly similar bouquet, a Humphrey who in her golden years had achieved a pitch of irritation that somehow never seemed to flag or threatened to wane.

She stayed ill all of the time and was famous about for swearing out complaints—against her neighbor who had a corgi that barked on occasion at night, against the fellows who mowed the roadside margins and left tractor tread impressions in her ditch, against a boy up the road who was evermore tinkering with his turbocharger.

She'd been shamed, it seems, into laying flowers on the grave of her least sister by a woman she played canasta with about four times a year, a lady who took her own dead sister tulips on her birthday and who'd suggested a failure to do so would have served as some strain of disgrace. The trouble was that Humphrey had never much cared for her various siblings in life, had most particularly detested her brothers who'd come home from service in Korea joined in matrimony, the pair of them, to slutty tramps.

One of them ruined his liver while the other Viceroyed himself to death, and they were hardly in the ground before those wives of theirs had taken in boarders, they called them, fellows put upon for more of an evening than shoving their feet beneath the dinette. And sometimes when that Humphrey would stop by the memorial park just out the pike so as to commune in her fashion with her late husband, Douglas, she would oftentimes have enough bile left over to douse her brothers with since she was not the sort to let the veil of death serve to blunt her contempt.

Now that Humphrey was peeved with her dead sister for having traveled to Nova Scotia which had run contrary to that Humphrey's wishes and advice. It seems that Humphrey had read at the time some damning fact about Nova Scotia which had impressed her as adequate cause for a sensible woman to cancel her trip, but her sister had ignored her and had ventured up there anyway, and, not three years later, she'd been stricken with a crippling nerve disorder caused, that Humphrey had convinced herself, by some Canadian parasite.

As far as she was concerned, her sister had died of acute pigheadedness. In fact, when that Humphrey went out to the graveyard and surveyed her relations, she saw a crop of folks who'd be upright if they had but listened to her—her husband with his bacon and his butterfat, her brothers with their aggravating wives, her sister with her itch to ride a church bus clear up to Cape Breton.

That Humphrey was evermore a bit of a sight out at the memorial gardens. Everybody else would be pulling weeds and clipping fescue off of markers, scouring headstones with Ajax and replacing dead lilies with fresh, while that Humphrey would stand with her handbag at the head of her family plot and pass a quarter hour or more excoriating her relations.

So her canasta buddy must have stung her pretty good to have prompted that Humphrey to invest in flowers for her sister's grave, a bouquet she'd paid a scandalous fifteen dollars for at the florist shop that doubled as a scented taper and greeting card boutique and was evermore choked with Mylar balloons and the stink of sandalwood. Once she'd selected the baby's breath, the hollyhocks and gladiolus, that Humphrey set about resenting her sister for the trouble she'd put her to, not even to mention the galling and wasteful expense which that Humphrey was in a dudgeon about by the time she'd reached the graveyard, so she flung down those flowers with, for commentary, a diatribe.

Her native distrustfulness had led her to take a Polaroid which she offered to Ray once he'd shown up to endure from her news that her bouquet had up and disappeared. She let that picture serve for confirmation of the actual flowers she'd laid and evidence of how little fifteen dollars would purchase anymore, and she suggested Ray start off investigating her brothers' widows' houses—shacks, she told him, separated by a hollow full of trash—and she advised him to announce himself by giving a yip on his siren since they'd probably be servicing boarders when he rolled up.

Ray, of course, did what he always did when it came to that Humphrey's complaints. That is to say, he sat and let her vent her vitriol his way and then made out as if he would undertake an actual inquiry which he never, in truth, much bothered himself to do since he'd noticed early on that Humphrey had no use for resolution and was only in it for the chance to level charges and the sanctioned occasion to snipe.

Ray, then, hadn't actually attempted to track down the bouquet bandit, but the photo of that baby's breath, those hollyhocks and gladiolus, was fresh enough for him at the time to permit Ray to recognize those flowers on the TV at the base of one of the creosote posts that supported the state park sign and just alongside where that grieving Dunn laid her solitary rose. So Ray set about studying those flowers and considering the various wreaths which looked, the most of them, a little weather-worn and sun-bleached, and he invited the chief to pause his tape so that they might consider a frame which gave a pretty fair view of some manner of item studded with buttercups. The thing was in the shape of a heart and had a stenciled sash athwart it.

"What does that say?" Ray asked of the chief and tapped on the TV screen.

The chief studied that sash and labored over the florid script upon it. He drew back from the screen and shrugged at Ray. "We miss you, Daddy," he said.

So Ray drove out to Homer Blaine State Park expecting to confirm a spot of petty theft and an instance of magazine show mendacity, but he discovered by the time he got there that he was already far too late since everything phony in the filming of the segment on that grieving Dunn had been made authentic by the airing of it. Viewers had responded with what passes these days for heartfelt spontaneity, had been moved anyway to imitate what they'd seen on their TVs and so had shown up in force at the state park lot to bury those pilfered flowers under lawfully procured bouquets they'd gotten touched enough to buy.

A newsgirl from a Lynchburg radio station and a Charlottesville cameraman were recording testimony from the citizens about who proved a bit too melancholy for coherent articulation and so prattled on in jagged scraps of senseless fractured chat about children they'd known and children they'd seen and meanness afoot on this earth which could poison and spoil for a little blonde girl an innocent walk in the woods. Some few women had even troubled themselves to drag their daughters along as tokens of their personal fitness for that Dunn's species of grieving since, on any given day with the proper neglect, their girls could vanish too.

A pair of local teens had gotten caught up in the hubbub. Ray recognized them for a couple he'd rousted out of the state park lot before. They were nooners, the two of them, who held down jobs after school and into the night, so they weren't often free to grope each other beneath the cloak of darkness which left them to double up and take their foreplay with their lunch. The boy was a Murphy and that girlfriend of his was a copperhaired slaughterhouse Caudle who wore pinned to her tubetop a basswood leaf in chintz.

She blubbered a little as she told how she felt to that Charlottesville cameraman. Then she smiled and waved and said towards the lens, "Hey, Ricky," which prompted her boyfriend to tell her, "I'm right here."

Naturally, the whole crowd closed on Ray once he'd climbed out of his cruiser—the girl from the Lynchburg radio station, the fellow with the camera, the women with children themselves who might have up and disappeared. They swarmed Ray and pressed him to acquaint them with the clues he'd come across and any telling information he'd accumulated.

For her part, that Dunn hung back and lingered at the edge of the lot over by the Homer Blaine State Park sign and the unruly heap of flowers. She was in the company of a friend, a sleek little woman with highlights and a handbag who'd come out from Dayton to make herself a comfort to that Dunn, and they peered down from the curbing as if it were a palace balcony.

"Ma'am," Ray said to that Dunn as he set about sorting among those bouquets, digging down through the pile in a fashion that Dunn and her girlfriend found unseemly, and they treated Ray to identical Ohio Valley curdled sneers.

"Caught you on TV," Ray told that Dunn as he plucked free the withered baby's breath, the hollyhocks and gladiolus.

"Well," that Dunn said, consulting her fellow Daytonian with a glance, "somebody had to do something," which prompted that friend with the highlights and the handbag to bob her head.

Ray declined to respond to that newsgirl from the Lynchburg radio station who charged over to fling at Ray a faintly inquiring accusation and mounted a bid with her microphone to ream out one of Ray's ear canals as she followed him across the Homer Blaine State Park lot to his cruiser.

They all of them wanted to hear from Ray just what he intended to do to turn up that little Dunn girl and return her to her mother, wanted Ray to tell them how he meant to keep their children safe, and they were gathering about his cruiser and seemed disposed to make trouble for Ray when a sedan rolled into the state park lot and our congressman popped out to console that Dunn and speak of a bill that he intended to sponsor.

The crowed swarmed him, of course, since they'd seen that

gentleman previously on TV and so were primed to think him first a star and a jackal only later.

Ray drove directly to the memorial garden down the Lynch-burg Pike and sought directions to the Humphrey family plot from one of the caretakers there, a Stroup with what, even in these parts, is an uncommon gift for palaver. As he walked Ray down a shaded lane flanked by mausoleums, that Stroup afflicted Ray with his opinion of the weather, or, more precisely, he shared with Ray the entire content of a show he'd watched on television about typhoons.

Naturally, Ray was hoping to shuck that Stroup, but the man proved a human cocklebur, and he stuck with Ray down the hill-side and out into the sun among the low granite markers and the wind-toppled wreaths and clean over to the Humphreys proper where he acquainted Ray with the fact that he had personally known a Humphrey once, not a local Humphrey but a boy from Texas he'd shipped with in the navy.

Ray squared up before that Humphrey's least sister where that Stroup paused as well to contemplate her dates. "Thirty-four." He shook his head. "Awful young."

"Forty-two," Ray said.

"What got her?" that Stroup asked as Ray dropped to the grave that Humphrey's comprehensively dead bouquet.

"Nova Scotia," Ray told him.

As it turned out, that Stroup had known a woman who'd been engaged to a fellow who'd come down himself with a lethal dose of that once.

As they retreated across the hillside towards the shady lane and up to the cemetery gate, that Stroup told Ray how that woman he'd known who'd been engaged to that fellow had worked her first job for the gentleman who'd invented the trouser clasp. "Had him a little office, and she answered his phone and such."

It seems that Stroup had been attached to that woman in a romantic sort well back before he'd ever met his wife, and she'd had down along the small of her back a grainy mole in the shape of a june bug and a scar on her shoulder where, as but a wee child, she'd been bitten by a rat which reminded that Stroup of the time he'd snared a tree squirrel in his glue trap that he was actively holding forth about as Ray wheeled into the street.

THE RANGE

She had come, apparently, from people who were horoscope en-
thusiasts and hopeless premonition devotees, the sort to extract
life instruction from the lay of coffee grounds and distill prophecy
from scents upon the wind. It seems her mother had warded off
ailments with totems made from hair and twigs and her father
had bet his weekly numbers with the guidance of Holy Scripture,
would pitch a Bible onto the settee to see what page it opened to.
Kit, though, had never known much use for the mysteries of this
life, was hardly the sort to traffic in signs and portents, and, as it
turned out, she couldn't muster any charity to speak of for those
misguided sorts among us who did.

"Oh, for fuck's sake!" she told Ray right there out among
people once he'd started in on Clayton and his curious transformation, had embarked upon news of Clayton's shift from pornographic movie maven to the manner of seer equipped to foretell
the fate of transient lapdogs.

They were in the fish house at their favorite table hard beside
their window, the bowed bay one overhung with a stuffed and
lacquered marlin and ringed round with netting and buoys and
fishing bobbers. That window gives onto a view of the valley

across to the bordering Alleghenies where the interstate corridor blinks and sparkles like a string of jewels at night, most particularly the amber vapor lights at the rest stop by Verona which lend those toilets and truck lots and drink machine sheds the look of a gaudy carbuncle.

In fact, the view from the fish house—which is cantilevered off the spine of the ridge out over an actively crumbling vein of basalt—is sufficiently spectacular to very nearly compensate for the cuisine.

The bulk of the seafood arrives at the fish house frozen and pre-breaded, gets hauled up from Norfolk in stout waxy boxes and evermore fails to give much indication on the plate of having lately actually been alive. They do make their own hushpuppies and grate their own cole slaw, shoestring their own unpeeled russet potatoes, and they brew their iced tea fresh—it tastes like—maybe twice a week. There are, then, but modest culinary allurements to the place, and most everybody comes for the jolly nautical atmosphere and the view.

So Ray could hardly be said to have spoiled Kit's meal with talk of Clayton's powers since she was just sopping up cole slaw juice with a wilted French fry at the time and chasing each nibble down with a sip of tepid Riunite. He did serve, however, to put her onto a chink in his appeal. It seems Kit had decided they shared between them a reliable pitch of skepticism and yet there was Ray professing to a sense of what Kit took for unbecoming wonder.

"Sweet Christ, Tatum. Get a goddamn grip."

And pretty much everybody heard her there in the fish house on the ridge though not because she was inordinately loud in the fashion, say, of those Womble sisters who are a bit too old for their ringlets and little too plump for their clothes and prefer to carry on at a volume sufficient to make of themselves distractions, and not even because she had the sort of voice that bored and carried like Russell the telephone man who can vibrate your teeth when he talks. Instead, most everybody heard her because she was the object of special notice, heard her, that is to say, because Ray was white and she was black which served to subject her to a variety of local scrutiny meant to come off as worldly indifference and open-mindedness.

So we tended to study her surreptitiously while pretending that we weren't and cocked an ear whenever she dropped her chin to speak.

She was not, we had noticed, especially polite or even dependably civil but was the sort who tended to give vent to exactly what she thought which, if she'd not been a comely Negress with a talent for kung fu, would have functioned alone to render her exotic as we traffic by custom in a manner of cordial insincerity and are evermore dousing each other with hypocritical palaver. There's a woman, for instance, a Dickerson who lives out past the quarry and comes into town every couple of weeks to visit the liquor store where she buys a half gallon of Everclear and invariably declares in the checkout line that she needs the stuff for a layer cake she's making.

Now we're all of us in that place often enough to have heard her once or twice, but nobody among us has ever charged that Dickerson to describe the sort of confection that might have need of a dose of ethyl alcohol.

The truth is that she drinks the stuff and in remarkable quantity. Moreover, she has a married boyfriend from Manassas who drives down most weekends to help her. He's got an arm that ends at the elbow and a taste for Tampa Nuggets, and we know all about him even though they rarely come out of the house. But we still tolerate from that Dickerson talk about her layer cake and chat her up as if we're actually prepared to believe she bakes which is all in the service of social lubrication.

Kit, however, was not the sort inclined to grease and slicken the way, and there in the fish house as she dredged her shoestring potatoes in her cole slaw seepage, she pressed Ray to share with her how a nasty old upland cracker like Clayton might have come by the power to foretell the fate of a Lhasa from Wilkes-Barre which Ray was struggling still to account for when their waitress, Ashley, fetched up.

The fish-house Ashley who waits tables, as opposed to the fish-house Ashley who seats diners and makes change, is a big-boned girl with an awkward manner and clumsy social skills, but she's strong enough to carry with relative ease a tray freighted with fisherman's platters. As is her custom, however, she arrived table-side when they didn't want anything from her. Kit, most particularly, wasn't looking to get quizzed about the quality of the fish-house cuisine since she knew, even as an outlander, that nobody went there for the food.

So Ashley asked them, "How is everything?" and had very nearly waited for a reply before she'd set about with her recitation of desserts, commencing with the fish-house icebox fudge and the fish-house lemon cream pie. She was advancing, in fact, on her detailed description of the fish-house blueberry crumble when Kit showed to Ashley the palm of her hand and instructed Ashley, "Not now," which constituted an appreciable transgression.

It was as if that Dickerson had started in with her layer cake in the liquor-store line, and some one of us had tapped on her Everclear jug and said, "Hell, sister, we know you drink it."

Ashley had never been sent away with a palm and a "Not now" and no show of counterfeit pleasure over the wretched fish-house food, so she couldn't, in fact, bring herself straightaway to leave but just lingered at a wholesale loss for niceties and prattle until Kit had glared her way and had inquired of Ashley, "What!?"

Naturally, Ashley could only manage to sputter, partly on account of how Kit was sharp with her but mostly on account of how Kit was black. We've few black people about in the uplands, no people much of any dusky hue. There's a black fellow out by Afton who finishes cement and a little nut-colored woman up by the salvage yard in a trailerhome. Mostly because we don't know how else to go about it, we tend to talk to them like they're simple, or at least not the sorts of people we like to think ourselves to be.

Now Kit was not just black and short of fuse but comfortable about it as well, didn't seem at the fish house to care that she was an object of general study, didn't appear even to notice that she'd made Ashley upset which turned out to be Ray's obligation in their partnership, and he smiled at Ashley and made her way ambassadorial overtures.

"I think we'll just have coffee," Ray said, and he was grinning at Ashley still when Kit added by way of enlargement, "And not that Sanka shit."

Now by the time they actually got around to talking about Clayton, most everybody at the fish house was listening in except for the kitchen staff. Them anyway and that Bolick woman who comes Fridays for the shrimp, gets driven over by the Ames girl she hired on as a companion, a lumpy bashful thing who'd thought she had a taste for people and a gracious instinct for domestic care until that Bolick came along to illuminate and contradict her.

Even as a younger woman, that Bolick was prone to be peevish and ill, but here in her golden years she has settled into accomplished sour displeasure which she sustains with an admirable rigor and impeccable thoroughness. She can carp, that is, about her various physical complaints and then shift seamlessly to a searing condemnation of the weather before touching upon her poor opinion of our senior senator and peppering the air with vile assessments of what locals come to hand.

It has grown to be her habit on Friday evenings to complain about the fish-house scampi and fling a barb or two at that Ames girl on the topic of her weight. So that Ames girl flagged their waitress down to take back that Bolick's shrimp and picked at her clams and scallops while mulling career options and entertaining from that Bolick news of the sort of beltless smocks that would very likely flatter her full figure.

Everybody else, however, had an ear towards Ray and Kit and so sopped up telling details of the Wilkes-Barre Lhasa episode, most especially those points that felt to Ray curiously prognosticated, and then he forged on to speak of Clayton's mention of that littlest Dunn who got called Melissa anymore instead of Angela or Denise. Of course, nobody much at the fish house failed to recognize that name as that child was still at the center of a spot of local turmoil. Her shrine anyway on the verges of the Homer Blaine State Park lot was even, three long years after her disappearance, an ongoing attraction of sorts.

Tourists would regularly swing in off the highway to lay flowers, that ilk who didn't mind coming late to a national spasm of grief, and the entire congregation of the Church of the Holy Sepulcher, led by the Reverend Lyman Byrd in his dingy ivory robes, would convene at that heap of flowers for prayer vigils and the manner of High Masses that a former tire retreader who'd been instructed in a dream to build a pole-barn chapel in his backyard near a hollow in a rock, a sort of a dent where the Lord Jesus might have been interred but wasn't, would be likely in the open air and without notes to conduct.

But the trouble out at the state park lot was not with the

preaching per se or with the people who came by to drop off flowers and mount displays of grief. The problem was more in the way of a simmering public-use debate since all of that sermonizing and those exhibitions of bereavement didn't know any regular hours which meant our local rutting teens couldn't often roll into that lot and hope to find themselves alone.

By "teens" of course what's meant here is both actual high school youth along with arrested young adults who live still with their parents and are reluctant to squander what money they make on such as food and rent. By "alone" what's meant is thrown in with a complement of other teens—no Protestant brethren, that is to say, or adults with mums and asters and considered stagy grief.

Naturally, the teenagers had been complaining for a while about the influx of scolds and outlanders to the Homer Blaine State Park lot, but since teenagers complain about everything, nobody paid them any mind until parents about began to meet with occasion to discover their children up to the manner of business they'd previously conducted in the state park lot. A widower, a Ketner, happened onto his Rachel Marie in their side-yard hammock with her jeans unfastened and her blouse untucked. She was in the arms of a pimply pulling guard and high school classmate who was simultaneously massaging that girl in one of her private places and swilling tepid High Life direct from a quart bottle.

Like most parents, that Ketner had hoped to never learn what his daughter was up to those occasions she told him she was out just knocking around with her girlfriends. And she wouldn't, of course, have resorted to that hammock but for the crowds at the state park lot which was true as well of that elder Neal boy who got found out by his brother while in the sprightly throes of a sexual release. That elder Neal was supposed to be at a Methodist Youth Fellowship meeting, but his brother happened onto him in their toolshed out behind their house once he'd heard what sounded to him a hoot owl or a coon, the sort of creature anyway that had no business shut up in their shed. Upon peeking in through the doorcrack and spying his brother clucking and warbling inside, that younger Neal boy—who was only seven—set up an inquisition so as to establish what his brother was fairly yodeling about and if the woman inspecting his belt buckle might, in fact, have set him off.

That elder Neal boy explained that him and his ladyfriend were engaged together in a manner of devotional meditation which his ladyfriend wiped her mouth off and agreed with him about, told that child anyway, "That's right, sugar," as she reached to muss his hair.

She was a Pratt from the beauty shop, a wiry bottle blonde who was older even than the elder Neal boy. She drove a Mustang and had a tiny orchid tattooed on her belly, had a common-law husband with a motorcycle and a string of misdemeanors, had an actual ex in Gum Springs and a taste for the local youth who were apt to come to her along about then to get their hair skinned close as they were collectively antagonizing adults at the time with sanitarium coiffures.

That Pratt is one of those creatures for whom genuine sexual relations can only take place on a mattress or perhaps upon a dinette, and, to qualify for intercourse, both parties need be naked, stripped even of their seed caps and their socks. Otherwise, it all just counts for foreplay and salacious recreation which permits that Pratt to submit boys about to close short-arm inspection and remain still faithful to her common-law spouse.

So she proved hardly the sort likely to be stymied and put off by inquiries from a child. Consequently, once that elder Neal boy had lost a little traction on his account of just how he'd come to praise the Maker by getting his scrotum moistened, that Pratt chimed in with a wholly fabricated rationale which sounded even to that elder Neal boy like church doctrine and fully satisfied his little brother who retired across the yard once he'd sworn not to tell his parents who was worshiping in the toolshed.

True to his word, that little Neal asked casually of his mother if she ever prayed with her nose in his daddy's lap which served, in its way, to put her on the path to revelation.

Fundamentally, then, the problem was that the kids were in plain sight and getting stumbled onto in delicti as opposed to when they were all of them in the state park lot at night and their parents knew precisely where not to go. So it was the grown-ups about who began to organize and agitate and inquire after the sorts of provisions in our local civil code that might touch upon unlicensed shrines on commonwealth property and serve as cause for wrongheaded religious zealots to get routed from a state park lot.

Accordingly, the chief got prompted to relocate that shrine along a pasture edge just up the way from Homer Blaine State Park. Carl and Walter pitched those flowers into the trunk of their cruiser, drove them a quarter mile up the road where they pitched them out again while Larry lingered in the lot to explain the relocation to a couple down from Saginaw who might have even made off unscathed but for the tone the wife took in pressing Larry on the civil libertarian particulars of the thing as it didn't seem lawful and proper to her for them to move a shrine, even a spontaneous and unsanctified heap of rotting flowers.

By way of response, Larry discovered that the address on that woman's husband's license didn't jibe precisely with the address on his Buick registration card on account of they'd moved and he'd been shiftless about getting his license changed which induced Larry to cite him on behalf of the Saginaw DMV.

They had piled those flowers, Carl and Walter, against a locust fencepost that had sprouted with thorny suckers along its length, and they'd attached to one of the stickers a sign made from a manila folder. "Dunn Girl" it read in green Magic Marker with an arrow pointing down.

There was, then, a little more to the case of that missing child than lingering local melancholy and human appetite for mystery. In fact, the most of us had never even laid eyes on that littlest Dunn in life, so we were hardly so personally wrought up as we otherwise might have been. We knew her chiefly from a photograph taken at the superstore that her parents had gotten printed onto flyers, a shot of that girl on a carpeted box with a Christmas scene behind her, a picture of a mantelpiece hung with stockings and a fir tree strung with lights.

Those Dunns had taped their flyers to utility poles and signposts throughout the county where they had weathered and faded and rotted, the most of them, presently away. A scant few had survived under awnings and shed roofs and porticoes in town leaving that child to peek out from behind broadsides from the Rexall and the Shoe Show, from back of hand-lettered ads for castoff sofas, barbells, and seasoned firewood.

Those of us who troubled ourselves anymore to think about that girl tended to conjure her in her Christmas shift and her green and red plaid socks getting snatched up in the half-light beneath the hardwood canopy by some sick and ghastly son of a bitch always from somewhere else—up off the interstate and in from a farflung quarter of the world. We clung still, you see, to the notion that there was business we wouldn't conduct, poisonous scraps of enterprise decidedly beneath us, though we were well equipped to imagine in unsavory detail what a fellow unhindered by a proper sense of damnation might get up to.

So the fish-house patrons were attentive when Ray finally

called her name, told Kit, "Angela," and said to her, "Denise," as prelude to inserting Clayton into the equation which proved enough to tamp and choke down the routine pitch of fish-house murmur until all Ray could hear was the clatter of the fryer baskets in the kitchen, the tinny *ching* of the register bell as the willowy Ashley opened the cash drawer. The patrons set about chatting again only once Ray had glared them into shame, and even then it was but for display and seemly show. They heard the most of what Ray elected to disclose about Clayton, and, needless to say, they heard every syllable of what Kit informed him back.

Ray told her about the curious alteration in Clayton's personality, but, since Kit didn't know Clayton, it didn't mean anything to her, and we'd all heard by then from witnesses out at the grocery mart that Clayton had likely gone a little daft, had given that is a twenty to the comeliest of our Tiffanys and hadn't troubled himself to loiter about for change.

Clayton, though, had always been a trifle dodgy and erratic, and we most of us had neighbors we considered just as loopy as him. However, once Ray had declared that Clayton had given up his movies and had swiveled his airbrushed satellite dish around to face the road, that alarmed the fish-house patrons a little and captured their attention since there were some things in this world we thought we'd never see again and one of them was Clayton's eagle clutching its outsized fishing worm.

Apparently, Ray talked Kit into stopping with him off at Clayton's on their way back to Ray's shabby rental house. Or since she didn't know the roads about, he might have just swung by on his own as she was hardly the sort to get talked into much. At any rate, they ended up at Clayton's which was not as Ray had left it on account of how Clayton's mother's relations had dropped by since Ray's last visit and had unencumbered Clayton of everything that caught their eye. So he had in his front room just his ruptured upholstered chair along with his quartersawn sideboard that had proven altogether too stout for his cousins to lift.

Now Clayton's parlor, of course, had been homely enough fully furnished and lamplit, but with its naked bulb in the ceiling and even the throw rugs spirited away, that room made for a bracing display of domestic desolation. Kit was sniping, in fact, at Ray before they had properly gained the foyer due largely to the re-markable stink of the place. Then she took notice of the gritty floorboards, the dingy puckered paint and the lord of the manor across the way in his tattered grimy chair who was, by that time, sooty from his fingertips clear to his elbow joints.

So Kit probably would have striped Ray further with a vivid spot of talk but for a massive hairball that the doordraft loosed to drift across the floor which was about the size and girth of an adult groundhog, and Kit felt compelled to expend a little scrutiny on it instead.

Ray looked around at the dingy outlines on the wall where the furniture used to be, most particularly the spot Clayton's sizeable Zenith console had occupied, and Ray asked of Clayton, "What happened to your stuff?"

Clayton smiled and rose from his chair. "Please do call me Ti-tus," he informed Ray. "Everyone does these days."

Together Ray and Kit watched him cross towards his chimney stack and mount his sideboard. He'd broken off the pulls by then and was using for steps the open drawers. Clayton took up a hunk of charred pine off the mantelpiece and stood, arms crossed, con-sidering his sketch upon the chimney plaster in an altogether painterly sort of way.

"Did somebody come take it? You give it away? What?"

Clayton applied his charred wood to the outline of his drawing, rerouted an indentation and touched up a knobby jog.

"Clayton," Ray said. "Clayton!" This time he poked Clayton along about the kneejoint which prompted Clayton to shift about and ply Ray with a smile.

"Mutsu and Winesap," he told Ray. "Empire and Delicious. Wasp and windfall come autumn. Sweet blossomscent come spring."

And with that Clayton climbed from his sideboard and returned to his ruptured chair with its exposed stuffing and its prominent headgrease stain while Ray and Kit lingered still by the hearth and watched him settle.

"Mutsu and Winesap?" Kit said while considering Clayton across the way who sat stock still, failed even to scratch himself or expel vapors in the fashion Kit had grown to rely upon from nasty crackers like him. "Empire and Delicious?"

"It's about her," Ray said. "Bound to be."

"Her who?"

"Isn't it? Isn't it!?" Ray fairly shouted at Clayton across the way, Clayton who smiled and nodded at Ray, who assured Ray he was well.

"He knows," Ray said. "Look at him."

"Knows what?"

"It's got something to do with that stingray." Ray indicated the chimney stack with the ridge of his nose, twitched his head towards the sooty sketch upon it which prompted Kit to lend the thing her undiluted attention.

She studied the pocky borders, the outcroppings and indentations, the hollows and rises, the lobe to the right and the whip of a tail to the left, and Kit realized directly she'd known occasion to see that item before.

For Clayton's part, he picked at his ruptured chair arm, worried stuffing in his fingers. He looked up to find Kit watching him, assured her he was well.

———

Likely things would have played out differently if he'd not been dead already, if that Dunn had been still available for Ray to deliver his daughter to. That Dunn had grown, however, distraught in the wake of his daughter's disappearance and had seen call to cause himself to perish more or less by his own hand. His wife, of course, gave him out anymore as a full-blown suicide since she required for her trials and her grieving an impeccable pedigree, but the truth is that Dunn had known some trouble doing himself in.

We'd all heard he was depressed. He'd seen fit, after all, to call on Dr. Lowery who'd broadcast, as is his way, the various details of their consultation and so had clued us all in as to why precisely that Dunn was down and blue. Naturally, the fact that his child had gone missing for what was nearly a year by then made do for an appreciable factor in his distress, but he had cow troubles too and nagging regrets over his shift in careers along with general anxiety fueled by suspicions his life was turning out poorly.

His marriage was not, quite apparently, as happy as it might have been, and the child that he had left was not, in fact, the child he had preferred. Angela Denise had never made herself a bother to him while his son was beginning to practice his unlicensed vivisections with an ardor that seemed to foretell of a future in state facilities. Then there were the cows who'd not, somehow, grown manageable over time but resisted that Dunn more mulishly the better that they knew him, and when he'd snatch one off to the slaughterhouse to make do as an example, the spared ones never let on to be curbed and edified. They just kept knocking down his fencerows, bucking in the milk stalls, defecating blithely in their troughs.

Then there was his income which had gone from lawyerly fees at Daytonian rates to local upland struggling dairyman's wages which qualified him for strains of government charity he'd never previously heard about. He got coupons for cheese and butter and number 10 cans of stewed leathery beef. He got stamps to spend at the grocery store, but his wife was too proud to use them. She did, though, apply the monthly check they received for the up-keep of their son to her long distance bill and her captain's wafers supply. That Dunn got help with his tractor fuel from the county extension office and help with his feed from the state agricultural commission. He even got paid for the milk that he held out from pasteurizing so as to keep the price of the milk that he did process agreeably high.

Having come, though, from a successful law practice in the tony heart of Dayton with a Cape Codder in the suburbs, a string of leased sedans, a generous expense account and a wife making mostly local calls, that Dunn hadn't been obliged in a while to think much about money since whatever he might squander would invariably get replaced. As a dairyman, however, he'd fallen into the practice of weighing his options, would consider at length what he could get by with and what he could do without.

He went for the rusting off-brand of barbed wire as it was cheaper than the dipped. He drove three miles out of his way to buy no-name gas at discount prices, had a rotary antenna on his roof instead of a dish out in his yard. He made special excursions to the day-old bread store in Waynesboro down in the valley, traded off ground chuck and flank steaks for his auto and tractor repairs. He eventually sold his wife's Saab to a doctor in Afton and made her drive instead a Nova which she sniped mercilessly about.

There are some of us who tend to think the tedium is what got that Dunn, the prospect of passing the rest of his days a little short and a trifle strapped, of having to stand in the grocery mart and compare the price of dishwashing powders, of having to make do with Dollywood instead of Paris or Milan, of having to wear Malaysian dungarees, of having to paint his house himself, of having to wonder evermore just what became of his little blonde wisp of a girl. It was all too wearing to contemplate, too grinding to endure, so that Dunn reasoned that it might be just as tolerable to be dead.

At the first, anyway, that's how he went about it—like a man who'd decided he'd settle for death if death happened to come his way. He became, that is to say, careless of his safety and indifferent to his health, most particularly once Ray had served to ruin for him nectarines since he knew he couldn't persevere throughout his life with cattle and he didn't have any appetite for returning to the law.

So he decided it might be a welcome thing to perish, and he went hoping for a while to get snatched away by grisly happenstance. Nobody, however, would run him down or crash into his car. No lightning bolt would strike him, and his heart was hale and sturdy, and nobody would take him for a deer when he wandered through the woods while wearing a snowy white knit cap, his amber coveralls and snorting like a high-strung doe in season.

Accordingly, that Dunn got at last to the place where he guessed he'd have to do the job himself, but it turned out he knew almost as little about mortal bodily harm as he did about cattle keeping. He had a pistol that he planned to turn on himself, but, as he'd not been raised with guns, he'd only bought the thing for prowlers and was a little frightened of it. He'd fired it but twice for practice at a stump out in the yard that he'd pretended was a fellow coming through a window, and the bullet had made, he'd noticed, just a puny hole in the wood which caused him to wonder if that gun was actually potent enough to kill him. He didn't want to linger and writhe in torment, certainly didn't want to survive, and he was likely fearful that a gunshot wound might, in fact, sting a little.

That Dunn, then, was lacking in nerve and resolve where it came to his revolver, and he convinced himself he was worried because his harpy of a wife couldn't collect the insurance he carried if he died by his own hand. So he mounted a bid to end his misery and make it accidental, spent a few days anyway just cocking his revolver in the barn and then flinging it onto the hardpan where it frequently discharged. That Dunn would put himself in what he hoped would prove to be harm's way, would shut his eyes and toss that gun while puckering up his sphincter.

He did kill a chicken and wound a cow and put a few holes in the roof tin, but he didn't personally ever even get so much as grazed which prompted him to rethink his method and shift to antidepressants instead which he took by the fistful without much thought for his wife's insurance claim. By all accounts, he got just sleepy and uncommonly frank, expressed a raft of unvarnished opinions punctuated by spells of dozing.

He had hard things to say about five-grain bread and the defensive play of the Bengals, made withering remarks about the feeble talent of a starlet he'd lately seen in a film, spoke uncharitably of a Pontiac he'd owned as a teenager, allowed he'd like to set fire to the local branch bank and throttle the dope who ran it.

That Dunn considered gassing himself with his pickup which burned rich anyway, but the carshed was too drafty and the passenger cab window had dropped off its lifter down into the door. It was along about then that a boy up the road made do as inspiration by perishing under the weight of a tractor tire. He was a Fouchee who'd climbed off his Farmall to open a pipe gate, and that tractor had jumped out of gear and run him over from behind. Everybody said it was quick and had to figure it was painless. Everybody conceded that Fouchee had never had much luck or sense.

Now that Dunn drove an Allis-Chalmers that was hardly given to slipping gears, so that Dunn had to work up nerve enough to help his tractor crush him which required a month or two of fairly steady contemplation and a few aborted attempts by that Dunn to fling himself under a tire. He eventually settled on a plan that would, to that Dunn's way of reasoning, lay the nature of his fate quite squarely with his God. He located a gentle slope down towards the bottom of his pasture that was just above a gate which he could seem to have been opening, and he figured he'd leave his tractor out of gear and nosed down towards him while he lingered by the gatepost available to get squashed.

By that time, he was cooling a little to the notion of death by his own hand and had halfway decided, it seems, that the Lord had a special purpose for him or otherwise he'd be moldering already from pistol flinging or pills. So it got to where that Dunn would stand before his Allis-Chalmers out of gear as a personal demonstration of his advancing faith in Christ who was looking out for that Dunn, he was tempted to think, and sparing him from death which that Dunn grew entirely convinced of just before he got run over.

That is to say, he'd become nearly as chatty about the books of the Gospel as he'd been just previously about nectarines, and soon enough he was leaving his tractor up above him out of gear both as a show of his profound faith and a consequence of habit. Now the ground down around that gatepost stayed rather boggy from a spring, was usually soft enough anyway to grip and impede a tractor tread, but, as that Dunn became emboldened by his ardor for his Lord, he took to parking higher up the hillside, and one evening he left his Allis-Chalmers sitting on hardpan, a patch of ground his cows had wallowed on and packed relatively smooth.

By then, of course, that Dunn was not much tuned in to his tractor. He was one of those fellows who tended to fix on one thing at a time, and he'd moved along to a wholesale fascination with his Maker, so he didn't remark the sputtering of his Allis-Chalmers engine that served to vibrate and jolt that tractor and yield it up to gravity, sent it creeping anyway down the hillside where that fellow was distracted by his Jesus and the rusty chain he kept his gate shut with.

That Dunn had just loosed that gate and swung it open when he got run over, and, as it turned out, his Lord was smiling on him still, since the ground where he was toppled proved sufficiently soft to receive him. So that rear tractor tire failed to crush him but instead mired him snugly up. He got plugged, that is to say, in the soft earth, fell flat onto his back, and the weight of the tractor mashed him in clear down to sideburn level. Consequently, just his face was left exposed and the toes of his Red Wing boots.

The tractor rolled on down and became ensnared in a clammy locust thicket where it ran for another hour before it gave entirely out of fuel, an hour that Dunn spent trying to squirm himself free of the mud and make a little sense of the rough use he'd endured from his Savior who could, that Dunn resolved, have squeezed the life from him instead.

So he had joy in his heart and chilly seepage in his undershorts, and, since he was just a face and boot toes, no creatures seemed to fear him. A couple of groundhogs happened by and subjected that Dunn to inspection. He got sniffed by a tree squirrel and marked as the territory of a fox. His cattle all traipsed through that gateway and threatened to do him legitimate harm as they were heedless, in the usual way of cows, as to where they put their hooves and upon whom they voided their intestinal tracts. So he yelled at them as best he could with the breath that he could muster which intrigued them as he'd never chastised them from underground before.

That Dunn decided he would get around to feeling blessed retroactively, and, in the meantime, he occupied himself calling out for help and managed thereby to raise his neighbor's hound who proved delighted to find that Dunn convenient for a comprehensive swabbing. She's a friendly girl, that hound is, and well stocked with saliva, and she plopped onto her stomach to tongue that Dunn from his hairline to his chin. At length, she spied a rabbit and chased it into a brambly hedgerow, and that Dunn failed to call out anymore in case she might come back.

He expected his wife to miss him or his son to stray across him, but his wife was busy just then with a drive-time radio interview while his son, who was strictly forbidden from wandering the forest alone, was up in Homer Blaine State Park dissecting woolly worms with a six-penny nail.

By that time, the wife of that Dunn was fairly famous for her grief, and she was evermore sharing with the listening or the viewing public the story of her little girl's tragic disappearance and, most particularly, the wrenching aftermath for her. At heart, that Dunn's topic was routinely the caliber of her personal sadness, the transforming purity of her native bereavement which had spurred her to form her organization for parents of children gone missing and had left her, she liked to say, a touch less kindly than she'd been.

Of course, that Dunn had never been kindly to any degree that could be measured, but as a mother with a daughter gone missing, she'd come by license to be blunt, and there was a world of people about anxious to have her singe and scold them. That's how it seemed anyway since that woman was a bit of a media sensation, in part because she'd come by grief at the just the proper time. A fair number of radio networks had given over music for chat, and the TV was fairly infested with the variety of show that called for people to sit around and harangue each other, the strain of endeavor that Dunn had always been impeccably suited for, and her missing child had blessed her with credentials for an invitation.

She stayed busy, then, as she knew a gift for the sort of inflammatory talk and unvarnished corrosive opinion that was the coin at the time of the chatworld realm. She would invariably start out with the tale of her personal tragedy and then account for her green chintz basswood leaf with talk of her organization that took in donations and helped in some vague way to guard and protect our nation's youth. That Dunn never troubled herself to explain just how exactly since, by then, she had usually moved along to her dudgeon.

As a rule, she'd speak to the desperate troubles of our country today, was adept at inflicting upon most any exchange her personal tirade, would steer talk around to a point which could accommodate a snit, and she'd uncork a searing excoriation. She was down on criminal coddling and simpering bleeding-heart impulses, was of a mind that there was too awful much senseless meanness afoot that she allowed could be best curbed and stanched by public executions. A blow to the crown of the head with a poleax was that woman's method of choice.

She deplored single motherhood and government subsistence which was merely a way, she told it, of paying layabouts for sloth, was opposed to vulgarity on TV and bloodletting in the movies, and she claimed our national moral blight could be reversed through earnest prayer along with a ban on professional wrestling and a moratorium on tattoos. Furthermore, she was never in the market for contradiction or addendum and tended to be, without provocation, starchy and contrary which made her a reliable and welcome source for sparks.

So those urges that had prompted her to pitch, she'd called it, a cabbage in the grocery mart and leave the produce man insensible upon a bed of navel oranges served, at length, to make her a bristling media sensation, most particularly on that manner of national afternoon FM broadcast that features rants and uninformed opinions punctuated by advertisements for hair restorers, breath mints and sedans.

At the time, then, that her husband was flat on his back and earlobe deep in the mud, that woman was having a live and nationally syndicated set-to with both a third-term congressman from Massachusetts and the spiritual adviser of that actor who'd died when he'd stormed out of his cab. They were debating the three of them pop-song lyrics and school vouchers both at once, and although the congressman and the spiritual adviser differed hotly with each other, that Dunn had found a way to disagree with both of them together and to take issue as well with the host whenever he ventured an opinion in a display of her considerable gift for human carbonation.

So that boy of hers was out making worm porridge, and she was busy on her cordless phone and occupied as well with throwing supper together. She'd opened anyway three Banquet dinners and had shoved them into the oven while staving off forays from that spiritual adviser and congressman both at once and troubling herself to dismantle the claims of a caller from Traverse City who seemed deluded as to the pernicious effects of the federal income tax.

For his part, her husband had set about singing a cleanser jingle by then, the one promoting the virtues of the bathroom spray with the lilac scent and the scrubbing bubbles which he warbled and whistled in turn as a means of helping him pass the time.

Nobody came searching the pasture for him or calling to him up by the barn. He thought once he heard his wife out shouting for their boy from the back steps of their house, but he had enough mud in his ear canals to keep him from knowing for sure. Back at the house, his boy asked after him at the supper table once he'd returned from the half bath where he'd washed most of the worm off of his hands. He asked anyway after the chunk of stuffing underneath his daddy's turkey, enlisted his mother to tell him if his daddy was much of a stuffing eater and would be likely to miss his stuffing were he to come in and find it gone.

That boy's mother, of course, wasn't concerned with his daddy's appetite for stuffing and shifted over his entire tinfoil plate of dinner towards her boy which he scoured clean of everything but its succotash and apple Betty before bolting from the table once he'd kissed his mother on the cheek and had left her stained with a blend of spit and gravy.

By that time, that Dunn and her husband weren't what passes these days for close, which means they never loitered in the kitchen to fret together over the mortgage, rarely sat both in the front room of a night to watch TV and didn't even share between them their plantation bed anymore as that Dunn had banished her husband to the guest room down the hall on account of his ceaseless twitching and his intermittent snoring. So once she'd gotten over her irritation at the fact that she'd gone to the trouble to heat his supper and he'd failed to show up to eat it, she pretty much managed to exclude her husband entirely from her thoughts as she was occupied just then with trying to figure how many chintz basswood leaves she'd be obliged to sell to get out of her Nova and back into a Saab.

The muck her husband was mired in had set to hardening a little by then. It was late in September, and we were enduring our first spots of lowland frost, so that Dunn got to be both damp and clammy on his underside and frigid up around his exposed top. He guessed he would die. That's what he went around telling us anyway as he came out of that ordeal with a dreadful jones for talk of his revelation, in the grip of a healthy ridicule for the silly presumptions of men. There he was, a fellow who'd tried to snuff his life with a flung pistol, with a handful of prescription narcotics, with an Allis-Chalmers tractor tire, and the Good Lord had deigned to inflict upon him a respite and a pause so that he might know occasion to reflect upon his folly.

That Dunn decided, understandably, that he would prefer not to be dead, would rather be mobile anyway and free to claw his itches which made do for him at that moment as the precious essence of life. So that Dunn struggled through the night to keep himself awake, warbled out his cleanser jingle so as to drive away those creatures that might be tempted to slip up on him and chew his face.

He was stuck still in the morning when his son came across him, was stiff and cold and chafed and rapturously in love with life, and he heard what he thought was likely a calf come to urinate upon him which turned out to be his boy who vaulted straight into the air when that Dunn told him, "Hey here!" robustly from down in the muck.

Apparently, Matthew Dunn was in the habit most mornings before school of touring the farm in hopes of finding something to mutilate, had grown to prefer a touch of senseless carnage instead of juice at the top of the day. Like most boys his age, he instinctively resented being startled, and, once he'd landed, he jabbed his thumb towards the barn and told his father, "Saw you up there."

They didn't speak for a moment thereafter as Matthew formulated an inquiry, considered his father half submerged and cemented in the frosty mud and managed at last to ask of him, "What are you doing?"

By way of response, that Dunn expounded at appreciable length on his strain of revelation as prelude to dispatching his boy up to the barn after a spade, and, once he'd endured instruction on how to chip his father free, Matthew paused to pass a moment in contemplation of his options, seemed a little torn between liberating his dad and laying his torso open but finally elected to jab that spade beneath his father and lever him loose.

Even by then that Dunn's wife hadn't missed him and hadn't wondered where he was, or had assumed anyway that he was twitching and snoring still upstairs while she was down seeing to Matthew's lunch and packing it by herself which meant stuffing a can of Vienna sausages and a banana into a sack.

Apparently, that Dunn came bursting in with word of his transformation while he rained little nuggets of frosty mud onto the kitchen floor, so his wife responded straightoff with a freshet of abuse as she stalked over to snatch the broom from between the icebox and the wall. She was shoving the thing at her husband when she finally imbibed the news that he had passed the night in the pasture which she took for a deception since he'd permitted her to think that he was in the twin guest bed upstairs.

That fellow had gone overnight from being desperately sad and dissatisfied and more than a little sorry for himself to a giddy intoxication with the blessings of this life which, as is commonly the case, he felt the need to proclaim about at length. He was not married, of course, to a woman cordial to incoming proclamations, and she drove him across the side porch and down into the yard where that Dunn was instructed to fall dead silent and carry their child to school.

Nonetheless, he drew a breath and remarked upon the splendors of the day just as his wife bounced the keys to her Nova off his forehead and then informed him by way of warning as they hit his shoetop, "Here."

We'd never paid much mind to that Dunn before his transformation. To us he was just some fool who'd swapped his billable hours for cows, an outlander who'd failed to intrude much upon us until he up and got overhauled. His wife, of course, was fairly assaulting us by then with her bereavement and her hotheaded social commentary, so we guessed we had things pretty much covered where it came to exposure to Dunns.

That fellow claimed to be transformed, though we couldn't really say transformed from what exactly as we'd not been any of us acquainted previously with his strain of faith. We just came to know that, after a night mired up out under the stars, that Dunn embraced an unbounded enthusiasm for his Lord and Savior which had made him more chipper than any human has a right to be and had rendered him almost virulently helpful. He took it as his newfound Christian duty to aid and assist his fellow man whether or not there was call to speak of for his aid and his assistance, and it got to where he'd loiter about in town just looking for people to help since there wasn't much measurable humankind out on his dairyfarm.

He'd wrestle sacks away from customers in the grocery mart parking lot and situate them on car seats and in trunk bottoms. He'd usher women and elderly men across the main roadway in town and was evermore collecting one of our trio of hitchhikers on the roadside. We had that Tuttle boy who loved his malt liquor and kept getting his license suspended, that girl from the crossroads with the toddler and the scorpion tattoo, and that old arthritic Rutledge who could no longer grip the wheel and who lived with a sister he detested up towards the reservoir.

He'd get the wanderlust and catch a ride into town where he'd dine at the café on the chopped steak, great northern beans and squash. With a wink, he'd tell Glenola and Ruthie that he wasn't only stiff at the joints which they cackled about reliably as they were homely women who didn't between them hear much of that stripe of talk.

That rejuvenated Dunn took to traveling the roads in his pickup and his wife's shabby Nova and would stop for that Tuttle and that girl and that Rutledge whenever he chanced upon them which, ordinarily, they would have been gratified about. The trouble is that Christian virtue usually comes freighted with Christian palaver, and that Dunn was prone to poison his good deeds with ceaseless talk, scraps of approximated Scripture—as he wasn't a Bible reader—and effervescent testimonials to the healing mercies of his Lord.

The short of it is that we were most of us fairly well spent with that Dunn by the time that his Lord and Savior snatched him from us. He was driving at the time north of town on the road that skirts around the quarry, was looking for people in distress who he might plague with his assistance when he came across a car stopped on the cinder shoulder of the southbound lane. That Dunn assumed there was some manner of vehicular complaint, could see the driver fiddling about inside, so he eased over on the northbound shoulder and sprinted headlong into the road.

Now the car he stopped for proved to be a Nissan driven by a Wade, or that girl anyway from Hagerstown who'd wed one of our Wades and had blessed him with a son she'd pulled off the road to have a confab with. It seems that child had taken for amusement to softening up his Cheerios with spit and then stuffing them into the cavities of the seatbelt buckle in the back of his mother's coupe as a protest, apparently, against the snug confinement of his car seat.

He was a big boy who, in the manner of his daddy's people, was prone to be ill and willful, so he'd had countless spells already of clotting up that seatbelt buckle, and he had developed an effective technique for shrinking from his mother's hand whenever she reached across the seatback and tried to swat him. Consequently, she'd wheeled off the road into a cindered pullout so as to unstrap herself and pivot around to threaten her child as she invited him to suck that buckle housing free of Cheerio sludge.

There was, then, distress most certainly though not vehicular by nature which that Dunn couldn't have known from across the road or would have even cared about since what aid he provided was always just preamble to the chatter he'd grown feverish to spew about his Christ. In his enthusiasm, however, to gain that Nissan across the way, he darted out onto the blacktop without sufficient premeditation. He didn't glance, that is, to see what might be coming to dispatch him, and he got launched off the hood of a passing vehicle some thirty feet into the air.

That Wade woman in the Nissan across the way was far too busy, as it turned out, lavishing invective upon her child to pay any heed to the racket in the roadway or have much sense of the sort of car that might possibly have streaked by while her boy, for his part, was blubbering and scouring buckle recesses with his tongue. In fact, that woman had shifted back around and was shoving her Nissan into gear by the time that Dunn dropped back onto the pavement, not mangled and torn asunder but pretty well fractured through and dead, and, as best she could tell, that fellow had simply dropped out of the sky.

She screamed and threw open the door of her coupe, climbed out for some open-air shrieking and then looked overhead in a bid to spy the variety of contraption that might have dispatched a gentleman in Malaysian dungarees.

There weren't any skidmarks in the road to indicate that he'd been hit by anybody who'd known or cared he'd hit him, and the wife of that Wade, when the deputies reached her, was hardly prepared to confirm that that Dunn hadn't simply dropped down through the treetops. They inspected him, Carl and Walter did, and discovered a little paint on the front brass closure of his dungarees, a streak of green that was fairly mixed in with the metal, a comely automotive seafoam shade which they recognized straightoff about like any of us would have. So once they'd helped those rescue squad boys parcel up that Dunn, Carl and Walter swung by in their cruiser to pay a call on Ivy Vaughn.

She claimed that if she had killed a fellow she'd have some recall of it, but the woman was graced with such a pure strain of selective obliviousness that we all knew, with the proper irritant to consume and to distract her, she could lay waste to a mastodon and take no heed much of the carnage. Unfortunately, Mrs. Ivy Vaughn's Impala wasn't substantially more forthcoming since, as a '73, it was stout and sturdy and uncorrupted by alloys which meant a man could ricochet off the hood and not leave evidence of it.

Carl did find a piece of a raccoon snagged between the bumper and the grille, but he and Walter never turned up any trace of a collision with that Dunn whose death got classified as a strain of fatal serendipity.

In his capacity as our solitary lawman with a sense of grace about him, it fell to Ray to notify the widow who happened to be sharing at the time with listeners on the Columbus AM dial her unfounded suspicion that her child had been snatched by some wayward parolee, a fellow loosed by simpering bleeding hearts to maraud about the land.

She met Ray at the front doorsill with her handset to her ear and declined to honor his request to terminate her call but instead ridiculed Ray on the Columbus AM airwaves, gave him out to be one of the lawmen about who'd gotten thwarted and stymied, who'd investigated the case of her child to no palpable effect which she declared with adequate contempt to provoke Ray a little. Consequently, he unburdened himself of his news in a Larry sort of way, blurted out how her husband had gotten himself exhaustively fractured and dead.

From there on her front cement stoop with just the doorscreen between them, Ray watched her be shocked and saddened for Columbus radio consumption, witnessed firsthand her exhibition of grief which she managed to vent cleanly between advertising breaks that she would pass soaking Ray for tragic particulars and the sorts of telling details that Dunn seemed to suspect would make for stirring radio. Ray claimed thereafter that he could smell the course her life would take, got a sense she'd carry on like Job but with a booking agent.

Ray came across her boy out in the yard on his way back to his cruiser. He was bathed in gore up to his elbows and had a carcass in his hands. "Look," he said to Ray and showed him what appeared to be a rabbit that he'd managed to turn entirely inside out.

―――

They'd most of them told themselves they'd just swing by to see his eagle with its haughty expression and its wormy reptile in its claws, and some few of them even did just roll past slowly in their cars, but more of them eased up Clayton's steep eroded track of a drive and tried to raise Clayton with a knock on his screen-door rail. He would be singing inside and sketching sometimes on his chimney stack or just sitting in his chair with the greasy headstain and doing nothing at all which was curious for Clayton but was hardly likely to seem to the untrained eye much in the way of eerie prognostication.

So the ones that just came to stand and stare didn't get much out of Clayton but for word they should call him Titus and assurance that he was well which is what, they reasoned, they probably had coming for eavesdropping at the fish house and driving clear out to Clayton's on the strength of Ray's brand of claptrap. Others of them, though, who met with cause to lay their hands upon him, heard from Clayton little cryptic scraps of talk, bits of business that could qualify as authentic prophecy.

Clayton, for instance, informed a Gilley from up along the river just where he would find his misplaced wedding band, not that he made specific mention of that Gilley's missing ring, but when that Gilley reached over and poked Clayton along about his collarbone so as to gain Clayton's notice and tell him he'd not traveled fourteen miles just to watch Clayton sit in his nasty chair and pick at his exposed stuffing, Clayton smiled that Gilley's way and told that Gilley, "Wolverine."

Now that Gilley couldn't say exactly what Clayton intended there at the first which was part of the aggravating beauty of Clayton's prognostications. They all sounded pointless and inconsequential and without conspicuous sense until later on once a fellow had maybe filled his girlfriend's car full of sewage when the penetrating truth of Clayton's remarks would be made apparent to him.

For his part, that Gilley was convinced he'd left his ring in the half bath at home, had laid it like usual in the soapdish on their toothbrush holder. When he didn't find it there, however, he looked for it on the sly about the house and out at the body and paint shop where he worked, and he came across the thing only after his wife had taken his hand one evening and had laid it, by way of invitation, upon her ample chest.

It seems she'd been watching one of those shows on the Fox network out of Staunton, one of those dramas that feature strapping young fellows who traipse around without their shirts, and the sight of all that flawless skin and stark abdominal definition had served to stir that Gilley's wife a little. A sensible woman, she reasoned that since she couldn't have one of those boys the man beside her on the settee would have to do. So as an overture and in the way of matrimonial foreplay, she took up that Gilley's free hand—the one without the beer can in it—and pressed it down upon her cleavage which was when she missed his ring.

Like women will, she assumed straightoff he'd left the thing on some strumpet's nightstand, not that she had any reason to suspect that Gilley of running around on her and not that there were even many available strumpets about. But she screamed at him anyway, that Gilley's wife did, by way of inquiring about his ring, and he assured her he'd left it back at the shop on the ledge of the lavatory, claimed to have taken it off before Gooping his hands clean.

Accordingly, she let on to be prepared to ride with him to fetch the thing which that Gilley proved unenthusiastic at the prospect of and thereby provoked his wife to further contemplation of strumpets, his wife who drove him off the sofa to have him get dressed for a ride.

So he went to the closet after his jacket and after his good brogans, and that Gilley had shoved in a foot and was drawing the laces tight when he felt a foreign item along about his instep and took that boot off to spill onto his palm his wedding band. It all came back to him—how he'd put that ring into his trouser pocket a couple of days before when he was sealing their asphalt drive. He guessed he'd left it in his pants when he hung them up and it fell into his boot which had the logo and the brand name burned into the leather upper. That Gilley ran his finger across the impression and read aloud, "Wolverine."

Chiefly that was the effect Clayton had on people. He'd vent pronouncements that folks usually made poor sense of straight-away or managed to misapply and pretty exhaustively misapprehend until the moment presented itself when they could know just what he meant, all of a sudden and with an attendant chill. So it got to where locals about would show up to lay their hands to Clayton on one of his passably ungrubby spots, and he'd respond with a trifling nugget of erratic commentary that folks would puzzle over and, on occasion, fret actively about until the occasion arrived when they could know what he'd intended.

It wasn't like Clayton had come somehow by the means to spare lives or alter fortunes, would get poked by some fellow in his vacant front room and apprise him of a mole, a grainy little fleck on his derriere that he'd best have gouged away before it got transformed from beauty mark to galloping sarcoma. Clayton simply wasn't the manner of mystic and seer to be useful, but, since we didn't have anything in the way of prognosticators about—most particularly if you didn't count roasting in hell for your sins as a prediction—Clayton did local service as a winning novelty, and folks kept him in saltines and even high-priced deviled ham in exchange for the entertainment that he provided.

He'd been a little off center all along, and we just among us decided that the bar-code scanner at the grocery mart had worked somehow upon Clayton to induce him to swap one manner of odd for another. Unlike Ray, we weren't inclined to worry over Clayton's health, figured a fellow of his vintage who'd passed his days on burly tobacco and pork fat had pretty much earned whatever came his way. We simply knew that Clayton was more entertaining in a family-friendly fashion since he'd left off approximating actorly assets with his forearm.

Accordingly, we allowed for Clayton's occasional forays to the sideboard and the private time he took away from all the poking and the jabbing so as to mark with his hunk of charred wood onto his chimney wall. We all saw him one night endure a massage from a Massey out the ridge who'd come all the way in to extract a bit of commentary from Clayton, was torn at the time between a thirdhand Volare and a secondhand Dodge Colt and had come by the errant notion that, if he pawed at Clayton's shoulder while concentrating upon the quandary he hoped Clayton to address, then Clayton would settle for him what vehicle he should buy.

It happened that Clayton got the bug to draw on his wall just then, so he rose from his ratty upholstered chair and mounted his quartersawn sideboard where he made a mark and then turned and spoke in the direction of that Massey.

"Jimmy Pigg," he said, "Snatcher and Nobby. Victor, Michael, Bones and Snippits. I have shot the ponies. Nine December. Shambles camp."

That Massey, quite naturally, passed on the Colt and dickered for the Volare with its blowby and its fractured block and seepy radiator, and he still swears Clayton with bile and venom whenever that heap fails to start.

THE PLATEAU

An atlas was one of those items that Ray had always intended to buy, like a flashlight for his bedside or a proper oven mitt, one of those things he'd occasionally figure he needed but could never be bothered to get. Come the morning, though, after their visit to Clayton's Kit prevailed upon Ray to ride with her to the local bookstore in order to pick an atlas up, not knowing of course that our bookstore was run by Pentecostal zealots who, when they said "books," meant chiefly Scripture and inspirational doggerel.

That storefront was a beauty shop for years before those zealots rented it out, and the place still has the faint aroma about it of Ultra-perm and Final Net which those bookstore folks have attempted to rout with bayberry scented candles, so just to step in the door of that shop ensures a stifling ordeal. Ray meant to warn Kit, had reasoned that he ought to while she was in the bathroom in his house, but, by the time she'd come out, he'd forgotten what he'd decided he best ought do and didn't, in fact, recall it until he'd opened the bookstore door to permit Kit to pass before him into the stench.

She brayed in the fashion of an irritated mule and fairly bellowed out, "Sweet Christ!" which earned her a chirpy response

from back in the treacly depths of the store as those zealots together informed Kit, "Praise Him." Then they came the both of
them forward to lay siege to Kit and Ray since there weren't any
other customers about.

The mystery and wonder of that place is that there are hardly
ever customers about, and yet those zealots manage somehow to
keep that bookstore open. They don't stock, after all, the sorts of
goods that people are likely to clamor for. Most Christians in
these parts get their embossed Bibles at church confirmations,
and there simply can't be much call for devotional poems lacquered onto cedar plaques which leaves trinkets and sign-of-the-
fish insignias for the trunk flanges of cars, stationery embossed
with uplifting flotsam of talk from the lips of our Lord and calen-
dars featuring soft-focus photographs of assorted earthly splendors accompanied each by syrupy prayerful scraps of verse.

As was their habit, those zealots closed on Ray and Kit together and offered praise and joy for the beauty of the day which
Kit very probably would have been contrary in the face of if the
perfume of the place had not constricted her airways. So Ray
stepped in to be civil and polite and endure from that couple their
blessings before he inquired of them after an actual item of merchandise. Apparently, they'd expected that day to sell but a sateen
bookmark or two along with maybe a packet of note cards and a
praying-hands pewter trivet which constituted the usual volume
of their Saturday business, but here was a fellow at the top of the
morning come to buy a book, and even a book they'd been together divinely inspired to stock.

They were between them, then, full of rejoicing as they led Ray
and Kit along an aisle and put into Ray's hands a copy of the atlas that they carried which Ray failed to examine as thoroughly as
he ordinarily might have due to his fear that Kit would shortly be
recovered enough to speak and was likely to unleash a spot of hea-

then commentary. Accordingly, Ray drove those zealots before him to the checkout counter where he bought that atlas along with a nut cluster log in support of an order of born-again Moravians who had split off from their brethren and were raising funds for a sanctuary.

So they were already back in his Grand Marquis before Ray examined that book and discovered that it was about as detailed as a Disney World place mat. There were maps of the Holy Lands depicting the travels of the Savior and a rendition of Europe radiating from the head of a nail on a German church door. North America was marked and mottled with spots of persecution and triumph along with local religious frequencies on the AM radio dial so that motorists with an appetite for it could get no end of preaching.

Kit had a nibble at the born-again Moravian nut cluster and complained about the waxiness of the chocolate before she directed Ray to make off towards the library in town and shared with him along the way samplings of the talk she would have aired back in that Christian bookstore if she hadn't been plugged up. Kit was railing still as they parked in the library lot and entered the building proper where she got shushed straightaway by that Hartman woman who pretty much runs the place even though there was nobody but the three of them there.

Our local library rivals that Christian bookstore for wholesale desolation, can't raise a crowd even though they're essentially giving the merchandise away. A fellow can even take out a movie with his library card, but Mrs. Hartman chooses the videotapes herself and is partial to saccharine melodramas and nature programs about cats. She won't subscribe to any newspapers that a sensible person would read, and she only takes magazines like *Redbook, Woman's Day* and *Southern Living,* so there are better periodicals about in the waiting room at the muffler shop.

Quite naturally, that Hartman is a magnificent shusher, a prodigious human steam valve, and once Kit failed to leave off talking with sufficient dispatch to suit her, she let go a blast at her again and, in a huffy whisper, informed Kit precisely where she was.

Ray and Kit together took occasion to glance about the place, and Ray prevailed upon Kit to allow him to tell that Hartman, "There's nobody here," which was just the sort of slack-minded shiftless distinction that woman was loath to abide, and she sneered at Ray and saw fit to inform him by way of rejoinder, "Shush!"

Kit was still working over a hunk of Moravian nut cluster which that Hartman had a thing to say about as well, and then she subjected Kit to the strain of pointed and disdainful study which she guessed a creature who was a talker and an eater both deserved. Kit was prevented by a snagged hunk of caramel nougat from speaking as freely as she might have, so Ray took occasion to ask after a secular atlas of the world in about as hushed a voice as he could manage.

Shoving her reshelving cart before her, that Hartman led them into Reference and pointed out a rather handsome book with satellite pictures and maps. She indicated a table where they might consult the thing, and she warned them against attempting to reshelve that book themselves.

"We were hoping to take it out," Ray told her, and while she was still scoffing at him, he informed her that he was a deputy and there was police business afoot which failed somehow to curb her to any palpable degree, and she assured Ray that their reference items simply did not circulate.

Kit was finished grappling with her hunk of candy by then, and she relieved Ray of that atlas and helped herself to a book from the shelves, a collection of thumbnail sketches of adventurers and explorers, and she carried the both of them straight past the checkout desk and into the lot. The audacity of it struck that Hartman speechless for a moment, long enough for Ray to hand her one of the business cards he carried and explain that Kit was not a creature who tolerated scoffing well.

That Hartman was only just recovering her pluck as they rolled into the street, so she spent her irritation on Ailene at the station house who rolled up behind Ray's Pontiac as he parked before the café and who informed Ray and Kit that they were prime suspects in a theft which Ailene allowed a plate of waffles might cause her to forget.

So together in a booth the three of them had breakfast while consulting what turned out to be a youth's guide to explorers and that glossy secular atlas with its maps and photographs. They opened the thing in the vicinity of syrup and jam and margarine, close enough anyway to calamity to have felled that Hartman if she'd seen it, and Kit showed to Ray a detailed map of the continent of Antarctica which looked, in fact, a little like a crab. It was plainly the item Clayton had drawn in soot on his chimney stack, not just generally and by way of vague resemblance and suggestion, but precisely that landmass with its jagged inlets and its bays, its broad lobe of territory that constricted and gave way to the slender whip of peninsula that had seemed to Ray a tail.

Ailene was reminded by the sight of that map of a gentleman she'd dated, an attorney from up by Madison she'd beguiled at a traffic stop back just when she'd graduated from clerical work to authentic patrol and hadn't yet learned to make herself homely for authority's sake. For a woman her age, Ailene is fairly fetching when her hair is hanging free and she's all painted up which was fine enough for filing official papers and answering the station-house phone, but once they took her on board and sent her out in a cruiser weekends mostly, Ailene found it didn't much pay to be alluring.

Our lowlifes about and ne'er-do-wells were prone to think it foreplay when Ailene would break up their drunken scuffles and impose on their larcenies, and she was evermore having to stave them off with her lacquered length of ash. Once she'd gathered up her hair into a bun, however, and dispensed with her face powder, she could usually roll up on most white-trash hoedowns without suffering a spate of grubby handprints on her uniform shirt.

But she was girlish yet and favoring still her lip gloss and eye shadow back when she pulled that Madison attorney for making an unlawful turn. He was lost and polite and failed to favor Ailene with the usual strain of caustic remark but told her instead that he was reminded by her of his late wife who had died—and it seems he grew misty here—in a tragic accident.

Apparently, Ailene exhaled at him with enough of a moan of sympathy to induce that fellow to tell her how he and his wife were out in a boat when a swell came up and pitched her into the water.

"She was chunky," he managed with a dire shake of his head. "Went down like a plug of cement." Then he troubled himself to assure Ailene she reminded him of his wife back in her svelte prechunky days when they had just been married.

Ailene checked that fellow out at the station house, called up Madison way to one of her law-enforcement colleagues and discovered that, as lawyers go, he was rather decent and upstanding but for the fact some folks about figured he had probably shoved his wife.

"And you went out with him anyway?" Ray asked Ailene which Ailene nodded in the wake of.

"He was a fine hunk of meat for these parts, and I'm a pretty fair swimmer myself."

Kit and Ailene exchanged glances and identical tight little smiles which suggested to Ray, as he looked on, that fine hunks of meat were scarce.

"He honeymooned down there," Ailene said and deposited with her foremost fingertip a butter smudge on that map.

"In Antarctica?" Ray asked her.

"Well, on a boat anyway. One of those trips to see the walruses and the seals. Icebergs. Penguins. That kind of thing. He said it was awful cold, told me the food on that boat was richer than he cared for."

"Ah," Ray said which was pretty much what Ray always said when he was stymied by the course of a conversation and couldn't think of anything to say.

"His wife fell in down there too, but they fished her out. Funny, isn't it?"

This time Kit exhibited her pinched little smile at Ray who nodded Ailene's way and told her, "Yeah."

Kit pressed Ailene to tell her what she personally knew of Clayton, and for a spell there Ailene only managed a shrug. "Filthy old son of a gun," she said at length. "Hasn't ever picked up his yard. All he does is watch those nasty movies and talk about them to anybody with ears." Here Ailene hooked her thumb and finger roundabout her forearm in the Clayton style for approximating cinematic talent.

"Heard anything lately?" Ray asked her. "Odd maybe? Out of the way?"

"Funny enough, yeah. You know Russell, don't you? The telephone man?"

Ray nodded.

"He told me he was out working on Clayton's line the other day, splicing it up where the mice had gnawed through it, and Clayton was just sitting in that chair of his, wouldn't say a thing to him until Russell had gone over to shake him once and see if he was OK. Clayton told him 'nine fourteen' and never made a peep otherwise."

"Nine fourteen," Ray said.

Ailene nodded. "Didn't mean much to Russell, not anyway until he'd passed his stone."

"His stone?" Kit said.

Ailene nodded. "He'd been working it through, you know? A few tall boys every evening, trying to sluice the thing on out, and a night or two after he was over at Clayton's, he finally shot it into the bowl. Told me he was standing in his half bath when he heard it clink against the rim, and he could see the face of the radio on the shelf over the tank. Just guess what time it was?" Ailene asked Ray.

"Nine-fourteen?"

Ailene nodded at Ray and, for good measure, nodded at Kit as well who took occasion to declare that Clayton was just a regular Nostradamus. Kit was flipping through the young adults' book of explorers and adventurers by then, and she bowed back the spine to show to Ray a photograph she'd found, a grainy picture of five gentlemen posed against a snowy hummock with a piece of freighted sled and a portion of pony intruding from the right. The wind looked to be up, and those men were bundled in their parkas against it, had raised their hoods, and the floppy rims of the things kept their faces shadowed and dark.

"The polar party," Kit said and then identified each man in turn, tapped with her fingerend upon them and read their names from the caption. "Evans, Edgar. Bowers, Henry. Scott, Robert. Wilson, Edward. Oates," she said. "Titus."

They carried him to a proper doctor clear out at the teaching hospital in Richmond, had to pretty much rip him away from a fellow who'd come to learn from Clayton the name of the miserable bastard who was servicing his wife. His ex-wife actually, and, truth be told, they'd been divorced by then for a year or two longer than they'd managed to stay married.

That gentleman, a Bodine from out beyond the quarry, was a little lit up still from the applejack bender he'd set out on the day before, so he was lurching there in Clayton's parlor between threats of violence against his ex and episodes of blubbering remorse, was mounting in fact such a dazzling exhibition of besotted psychosis that the people who'd come out to gawk at Clayton and maybe consult him a little proved fairly well content to watch that Bodine instead.

Of course, we all of us about well knew that Bodine's ex to be a tramp and were aware that, instead of some manner of cryptic revelation from Clayton, he would probably be better off with a scorecard and a stubby pencil. But for a show of senseless anguish and altogether misplaced betrayal, you couldn't really hope to improve on that Bodine's apple-brandy funk, so he wasn't the only one to object when Ray and Kit showed up intent on hauling Clayton in for a proper examination.

Unfortunately for that Bodine, he was a little too overwrought to talk, so his remonstrating chiefly took the form of grabbing Clayton to hold him and shoving Ray to send him out the door which Ray had managed to announce would surely bring that Bodine to some grief before Kit had actually troubled herself to fell him with kung fu. It was eventually adjudicated that Bodine had been duly warned well in advance of Kit's blow to his face with the meat of her palm and her curled fingers after which she levered him over her hip and upended him onto the floor where the blood from that Bodine's nostrils mixed with what brandy he'd brought up. Naturally, nobody else in Clayton's parlor remonstrated after that, most particularly the male onlookers who were too aroused to bother.

Ray rode with Clayton in the backseat of his Grand Marquis while Kit drove them through the gap and east off the ridge and complained about the handling those occasions when she didn't feel constrained instead to remark on Clayton's stench which, confined in a four-door sedan, was probably tough to tolerate. Even back in his Satin Channel days Clayton had been aromatic, but with the onset of his complaint, he'd scaled new heights of hygienic neglect. So he was musky and greasy and sooty and had the breath of a coyote.

Ray took occasion to show to Clayton there in the back of his sedan the map in the secular atlas that they'd filched from the library which was speckled anymore with biscuit shortening and smudged with butter grease. Clayton greeted the sight of the thing with a lone sharp intake of breath and then dragged his fingerend lightly across the mountains and the snowfields, the jagged undulations of the coast. Ray tried on Clayton the photograph of the polar party as well, and Clayton lifted his filthy hand to his cheek and considered that item wanly, managed to tell Ray with what struck him as wounded melancholy, "Oh."

They stopped first at the old city hospital in Charlottesville downtown, were hoping to hit the emergency ward during a Saturday afternoon lull before the sun went down and the fortified-wine-fueled mayhem set in afresh. The waiting room proved comprehensively populated nonetheless by people with complaints and fidgety relatives with government insurance cards. There were a couple of lacerations and assorted broken bones, but the affliction du jour, apparently, was a ferocious gastric disorder touched off by a batch of tainted chicken from a drive-in up the road.

The waiting-room toilets were getting, consequently, a healthy amount of panicked use, and that room was fairly well steeped in an odor that made Clayton's scent smell like sachet. Ray sat Clayton down in one of the plastic chairs and waited alongside him while Kit approached the counter to check them in with the wiry nurse in charge.

The woman to Ray's immediate right was suffering the wages of bad poultry, and, during intestinal lulls, she saw fit to speak of her condition to Ray. She told about the necks and the wings she had eaten that had tasted "fainty," she called it, and she volunteered a description of the byproduct she was leaving in the bowl which she seemed prepared to speak of in additional detail when she was consumed, of a sudden, by an overwhelming need to rise and dash.

The gentleman alongside Clayton—elderly and coffee-colored—was sort of propped in his chair as he didn't seem much prepared to bend at the waist. He was getting badgered and tended to by a woman Ray took for his wife who would interrupt spells of pouty seething with brief outbursts of talk that were given over largely to the lubricational virtues of mineral oil. She evermore picked lint from that gentleman's cardigan and fussed with his shirt collar as she spoke.

Once she'd caught Ray glancing her way, she addressed him with the news that her husband was plugged and clotted and unforthcoming. "Freddy can't deliver," she told Ray. "Hardly once since Tuesday week."

"Ah," Ray said.

"Tried to grease him, but . . ." Here she paused to glare significantly at Freddy. "Says he don't like the taste."

"Might ought to get some chicken in him," Ray suggested as a patron sprinted past which prompted that woman and Freddy both to contemplate Ray for a time.

Ray just grinned uneasily and listened to Kit across the way whose voice had elevated an octave and a couple of notches in volume which Ray was quick to recognize as prelude to a diatribe and so had Clayton on his feet and his jacket buttoned and was squiring him towards the door by the time that Kit and that nurse were exchanging unflattering assessments of each other. Ray didn't linger at the doorway or pause out on the landing but knew enough to retire into the lot since, once you'd informed an admitting nurse she was a bug-eyed cunt, there wasn't much chance anybody you'd brought was going to see a doctor.

They were in Ray's Grand Marquis already when Kit slipped under the wheel and volunteered into the rearview mirror her customary explanation. That is to say, she turned over the engine and manhandled the gear lever while she barked out, "Fucking people!" and went at a dead yaw out of the lot.

They tried the university hospital on the other end of town, but their walk-in waiting room was thronged as well. There were students about with graver ailments than the infirmary could handle and alumni in amber Wahoo blazers attending a fundraising weekend, doughy balding men for the most part come to town to get bled of cash. Like the students, they'd many of them had too much to drink and were suffering from a surfeit of carousing which failed somehow to prevent them from singing a couple of rousing verses of a school song that had been all the rage back in 1958. In the way of avid alums, they seemed something less than college educated.

This time Kit got left with Clayton, and Ray talked to the admitting nurse, had only just fished his badge from his pocket and settled it on the counter in hopes that it would shore up anything he might say, and he had barely embarked upon the particulars of Clayton's ailment when a gentleman interrupted him—class of 1954—shoved anyway his blazered arm towards that countertop and laid upon it by way of competition his laminated Century Club card which effectively rendered Ray invisible.

They got onto the interstate and headed east towards Richmond once Ray had acquainted Kit with the fact that there was a teaching hospital there which, in its fashion, was the medical equivalent of a barber college. He'd happened once onto a discarded *Star-Ledger* in his booth at the café and had read an article over his cutlet about that hospital in Richmond which tended to welcome curious cases for its students to puzzle over much in the way that beauty schools embraced those patrons with problem hair.

So they raced out through the stunted piney Virginia tidewater scrub and into the creeping sprawl of greater Richmond, and they even found that institution without so very much wandering around, not enough anyway to let Ray and Kit get terribly far past sniping.

They rated a doctor straightaway once they'd established to the receptionist's satisfaction that Clayton's was the most peculiar complaint about, and he showed up with about a half dozen budding physicians in tow. They came crowding into Clayton's quarter of the examination room, and the last of them drew the privacy curtain shut. That actual doctor very nearly brought himself to acknowledge that Ray and Kit were there, managed anyway while considering Clayton to bark out a query or two.

"Name?" he said while, with the aid of a penlight, he peered into Clayton's eyes. So Ray and Kit were a moment or two realizing that they were getting addressed, and even then they weren't entirely sure what name that doctor was after.

"I'm Ray Tatum and this is . . ."

That doctor jiggled his penlight and pointed with the beam by way of clarification.

"Oh," Ray told him. "Clayton."

"Do you know where you are, Mr. Clayton?"

"It's just plain . . ."

"Mr. Clayton." That doctor pocketed his penlight as he spoke. "Do you know where you are?"

Clayton declined to speak.

"Can you tell me what day it is?"

"Touch him," Ray said, and that doctor glared as if Ray had vented a belch. Ray then pointed towards Clayton's shoulder and made sufficient of a dumbshow to induce that doctor to permit his hand to light there and to rest. He was only just training upon Ray a look of curdled skepticism when Clayton dropped his jaw and said, "Myocardial rupture," with what sounded to be brittle and doctorly authority. The students made furious notes while that doctor and Ray considered each other. Kit, for her part, just smiled as she had taken it for a wish.

"How long has he been like this?"

"Can't say. A few weeks maybe?"

"And before?"

Ray shrugged. "About as nasty, but you couldn't shut him up."

"Is he on any medication?"

Ray shook his head. "Nothing going in but crackers and potted meat."

"Alcohol?"

"Not that I've seen."

"So he just . . . what? Stopped talking?"

"Stopped talking sense anyway."

"Tell him about the chimney," Kit said, and the doctor and his charges together turned their attention upon her, the handsome black woman with some manner of library volume in her hands.

"He drew a map on his wall with a chunk of grate ash." The students jotted feverishly as Ray spoke.

"What sort of map."

"A damn fine one, as it turns out." Ray reached for the secular atlas, and Kit put it in his hand. He opened it to the page where the butter grease had bled through and showed it to Clayton who obliged Ray with a fairly violent intake of breath. "He wants us to call him Titus."

"Call him what?"

"Titus," Ray said. "The name of a gentleman who went to the South Pole and very nearly came back."

Ray set in to telling that doctor and telling all of his charges about the skua and the petrel and the cape pigeons, about the first ice and the glass being high which he'd hardly gotten into well enough to be taken for coherent when Clayton reached and made with his thumbnail a mark on that atlas page. He left a lone indentation in the glossy paper a bit south of the Beardmore Glacier, Graphite Peak and the Dominion Range.

"Searching wind," he said. "Three-degree depot. Pressure and sastrugi."

There was a regular riot of scribbling on the part of the medical students, and that doctor even muttered, "Sastrugi?" as if by way of authentic inquiry which Kit seemed armed with knowledge enough to take on and address and was describing with her hand the effect of prevailing winds upon a snowfield when that doctor declared his intention to scan Clayton and to bleed him, turned to tell his charges exclusively how they would plumb him for imbalances, measure his gases and his chemicals, gauge impulses to his brain. Then he directed a pair of particularly brawny enrollees to pluck Clayton from his metal table and settle him in a wheelchair, and that physician led the pack of them into the bowels of that place.

He left behind a female student to speak to Kit and Ray and rehearse on them her doctorly condescension. She displayed a ready talent for patronizing chat, ended up instructing Ray and Kit to retire to the waiting room where they'd find magazines, a snack bar, insurance questionnaires and a TV set with horizontal roll tuned to *Headline News*.

So Ray and Kit settled into a couple of molded plastic chairs where they sat in peace for very nearly a quarter of a minute before the girl at the registration desk began to plague them to provide her with pertinent details about Clayton. She called them over and offered to them a printed form to complete which Ray tried to tell her they weren't remotely between them equipped to do, had no notion of the date of Clayton's birth or the maiden name of Clayton's mother, couldn't conjure his Social Security number, say what diseases he'd had as a child or so much as hope to identify Clayton's working status since there was no box to tick for abject sloth.

So they sat, Ray and Kit, unengaged in that hospital waiting room, or rather Kit sat unengaged while Ray watched a segment on the television that featured a brace of supermodels, lanky sisters who surfed in thong bikinis by way of distraction, they told it, from the appreciable pulls and pressures of their glamorous careers.

Forty minutes later Ray got to watch that same report again on account of how there is, in fact, no news anymore to speak of, just movie stars waxing rhapsodically over their latest roles, farflung foreign devastation from earthquakes and monsoons, domestic political sniping and professional sports scores along with supermodel siblings surfing in brief swimsuits to cope. About the only thing worse than having to wait in a hospital or an airport, in having to sit for hours in hopes that the dawning will find you somewhere else, is having to do it in the nattering ceaseless presence of *Headline News*.

Ray went, he told it later, a little batty from the ordeal and rose from his molded plastic chair in an agitated state. "I'm going to go find him," Ray informed Kit and, once she'd asked him, "Find him where?" Ray pointed towards the double doorway that led into the hospital proper, back along a corridor that was cluttered with gurneys and laundry hoppers, that was teeming with interns and orderlies and had that care-facility stink—a blend evermore of human excrement and uneaten pudding cup.

And Ray had very nearly even worked up the actual nerve to go, the pluck to charge along that hallway and seek out Clayton, when he spied that doctor approaching with his straggling brood and Clayton in among them getting pushed along in a chair.

"A curious case," that doctor informed Ray and Kit, and his students nodded in such a fashion as to confirm that they found Clayton's condition curious as well. Then that doctor named for Ray and Kit the various tests and scans they'd run and set about visiting upon them the assorted results in vaguely disdainful fashion as if Kit and Ray were wanting together in medical expertise through an unfortunate lack of gumption on their part.

The long and the short of it was that Clayton had proved essentially normal. No tumors or encrusted vessels, no blood abnormalities but for a touch of elevated sugar and a suggestion of altitude edema which that doctor, as was his habit, caused Ray to ask him to define. He indicated subsequently to Ray and Kit some swelling in Clayton's hands and asked if Clayton had lately exerted himself in any strenuous manner, had been perhaps out flying or scaling Alpine peaks.

"He's been sitting in a chair for a month and a half," Ray told him.

"Odd," that doctor observed, and his chorus of enrollees shook their heads and muttered "Odd" among themselves as well.

That doctor consulted his test results further before apprising Ray and Kit that Clayton had presented, particularly on his fingertips and ears, with possible signs of pernio as well. A layman's lull ensued, of course, and Ray permitted Kit to ask of that doctor what pernio might be.

"Chilblains," he told them and laid his finger to a darkened bit of Clayton's ear which prompted Clayton to recoil and to flinch. "Frostnipped, I'd guess."

"He won't pay for the fuel oil to run his furnace," Ray said, "and his cousins stole his kerosene heater."

That doctor nodded and made a notation which prompted his students to scribble as well. "Naturally, this would all be a lot easier if he would talk to us."

"He didn't say anything?" Kit asked. "Nothing at all?"

"He did speak to Mr. . . . ."—that doctor paused to consider his charges and fixed on a young man at the back of the group— ". . .Watson."

"Williams," that fellow volunteered and so earned from his instructor a spot of icy diagnostic perusal. Mr. Williams informed his notepad primarily, "I was helping him out of his shirt, and he told me, 'Rick engine.'"

Kit repeated it to Ray who said it to that doctor who turned towards Mr. Williams and asked him if he was prepared, in fact, to be sure.

"Yes sir. 'Rick engine,' that's what he said."

"Mean anything?" that doctor asked Ray and turned an inquiring eye on Kit as well, an inquiring eye that wandered a bit up and down her length in the first display of that doctor's helpless ordinary urges.

"No," Ray told him, "but, funny thing," he added and then paused so as contemplate how he'd be best served to proceed. "Ever since he's been sick," Ray called it for want of anything more suitable, "Clayton's sort of known what's going to happen before it does."

A regular riot of scribbling ensued in the wake of Ray's scrap of talk, and the doctor shifted from Kit to look Ray up and down a little as preamble to inquiring of him, "What?"

"There was this family from Wilkes-Barre," Ray set in, "going down to Florida somewhere," and then Ray left off to consider all of the details he would have to marshal and the strain of humorless doctorly skepticism he'd be obliged to thwart with little more in his quiver than Clayton's ambiguous manner of pronouncement. "Somehow he just seemed," Ray chose to say, "to know they were coming through."

That doctor made a conspicuous show of jotting a note in Clayton's file and then he lifted his head and responded to Ray, told to him simply, "Ah."

He claimed to not have much idea how to go about treating Clayton since, in all of his tests and scans, no grave ailments had turned up. Accordingly, he had decided—in consultation with his students—to refer Clayton to a doctor of psychology he knew, a gentleman attached to that teaching hospital with an office in Petersburg who'd probably be happy to analyze Clayton once they'd tidied him a little.

"Excuse me?" Ray managed.

And that doctor told Ray and Kit, "He's filthy," which his gaggle of students all saw fit to nod vigorously about.

"You can't wash him here?" Ray asked, and that doctor was just beginning to sneer when a nurse came scampering towards them from back along the corridor and apprised that doctor how a lady

he'd treated was arresting and convulsing and just generally doing that doctor the disservice of expiring which he and his students went dashing off to be convenient to watch her at.

Ray gave the admitting nurse one of his embossed deputy
business cards so that they could home in with the bill once they
had tabulated the charges, and then he pushed Clayton out and
spilled him onto the backseat of his sedan where Ray joined him
and let Kit drive in the gathering darkness west towards home.
By then Kit and Ray were a little too weary to have terribly much
to say, so she just steered and tuned the radio while Ray sat alongside Clayton and laid from time to time his hand on parts of Clayton's person in hopes of tempting from Clayton, Kit decided,
some little lost Dunn child talk.

She saw Ray in the mirror jabbing at Clayton like he was test-
ing a melon, and she endured it halfway to Charlottesville before
she finally told him, "Stop."

———

They never spoke between them about what they'd do and where
they would carry Clayton, but Kit just drove straight to Ray's
shabby bungalow out past the gravel quarry where they fished
Clayton out of the cavernous backseat of Ray's Pontiac sedan and
negotiated, with Clayton between them, Ray's frost-blasted cement walk. Monroe was still lifting herself from the doormat by
the time they had mounted the porch, was struggling to stand
fully upright on her balky arthritic hinges, and she lurched over
to greet Ray by poking, as was her custom, his thigh once with
her snout.

"Back at you," Ray told her, and as he searched out his doorkey,
Monroe greeted Kit with a thrust of her nose and then applied the
thing to Clayton who rewarded her with a whiff of his heady
road-kill bouquet.

Monroe sniffed Clayton's inseam straight through the front room and into the kitchen proper where Kit and Ray had figured they'd best settle Clayton onto a dinette chair, had reasoned that the vinyl upholstery on the back and on the seat wouldn't soak up scent like the chintz on Ray's settee. Monroe hovered and sniffed and savored while Ray and Kit retired to have a confab by the sink.

"Wash him or feed him?" Kit asked.

"Wash him, I guess," Ray told her and considered Clayton across the way with a blend of resignation and disgust while Kit opened up Ray's Coldspot and rummaged about the meat drawer as if she had ideas about cooking supper while Ray scoured Clayton clean.

"Uh uh," Ray said.

Kit looked his way with a pound of ground chuck in hand.

"*We* wash him. *We* feed him," Ray told her, and he was sufficiently emphatic to prompt Kit to put that ground meat back, swing shut the icebox door and join Ray in contemplation of Clayton who looked to be studying his reflection in the kitchen windowglass while Monroe conducted a nasal survey of his filthy trouser legs.

Kit and Ray both seemed to know instinctively that stripping Clayton naked and soaping him up together in Ray's tub was just the sort of enterprise to bind them to each other. Not romantically or in any sentimental sort of way, but they'd simply have bathing Clayton as the strain of undertaking they weren't likely in other company to repeat, a grubby little interlude peculiar to just them, very probably indelible and so passably momentous, significant enough anyway to give them pause there in Ray's kitchen to decide each if the other was the sort they'd like to wash a stranger with.

They ran Clayton a tub with a healthy squirt of kitchen dish soap in it and then walked him into the bathroom where they showed him the steaming water and put a laundered washcloth in his hand before retiring, the pair of them, into the hallway and shutting the bathroom door. They waited hopefully there at first for the sound of Clayton's brogans hitting the floor and the slap maybe of his belt buckle on the porcelain, and, when they didn't hear anything but the drip from Ray's seepy bathtub spout, they lingered in silence a few minutes further with little to no hope much.

"I won't touch a thing south of his armpits," Kit assured Ray as she laid her weight against the bathroom door.

They all washed him, even Monroe who wandered in to lick him a little, peered in the over the tub rim and swabbed Clayton's upper arm before watching forlornly while Kit collected Clayton's clothes and shoved them into a plastic garbage sack. Ray made a bid to clean Clayton's nether parts by agitating the water, but Kit was that sort of creature ungiven to leaving things half done.

So Ray suffered instruction to go at Clayton's privates with a rag, and he soaped up that terry cloth and closed his eyes and made a sounding which failed to prompt from Clayton even an involuntary twitch. He just sat at his ease in the water with his hands floating out before him while Ray winced in something other than his sad little way as he scoured Clayton's privates with main force which Ray had to figure he'd be fairly levitating about.

Ray announced once he'd finished, consequently, "The man's sicker than I thought."

They dressed him in the fat clothes Ray had bought himself a couple of winters back when he was working in the hills down south of Roanoke and had passed a season surviving on Tater Tots and greasy icebox eggrolls that he'd been prone as not to sluice down with a cocktail of his own devising—bourbon and Wink with a spoonful or two of maraschino cherry juice.

The corduroys he pulled out still barely spanned the girth of Clayton's gut as Clayton had one of those bellies like an outsized knotty cyst which was ledgy enough across the top where his ribcage yielded to it to accommodate maybe a tallboy or a couple of candlesticks. Otherwise, Clayton was bone and sinew, was quite lavishly mole speckled and variously asprout with wiry unbecoming tufts of hair. There was even, Ray noticed, lush prickly growth on the tops of Clayton's feet, an opportunity he met with once Kit had declined to pull on Clayton's socks.

It was probably Clayton's corrugated toenails that put her off. Untrimmed and amber and about as delicate as tusks, they were a little too revolting for Kit to be tempted to put her own hands near. So Ray got enlisted to figure a way to slip some tube socks past them without suffering a laceration or getting himself contaminated by one of the various funguses Clayton was hosting on his feet. Kit and Monroe together watched from the safety of the doorway, and Clayton even paid a little notice from his perch on the toilet lid while Ray labored to work a scaly untautened foot into a sock as he informed Kit he'd rather be picking clean a catbox with his teeth.

Ray persuaded Kit that, as a matter chiefly of proper sanitation, she'd have to feed Clayton dinner on her own since it hardly seemed sound and fitting for a fellow who'd swabbed clean Clayton's privates and had touched with his actual fingers both of Clayton's scaly feet to bring his tainted flesh in the vicinity of dinner.

"So I'll be feeding you too?" Kit asked him, but Ray was fairly quick to allow that he didn't suspect he'd ever be eating again.

Kit cooked a meatloaf, was famous in fact roundabout for her recipe as Ray had made once a sandwich from the leavings that

Ailene had up and eaten, had taken it (she'd insisted) from the station-house refrigerator by mistake, though she'd quite plainly managed to polish it off on purpose and had been struck by the fact that the meat between Ray's bread had flavor to it, and not that sort that arises when salt substitute and tomato ketchup get mixed. Kit's meatloaf was vaguely hot and ever so exotically spiced, and Ray got charged to track Kit down on the phone and learn the ingredients from her while he ate for lunch the sandwich that Ailene had overlooked—turkey ham and yellow cheesefood between fractured melba toasts.

Ailene had worked overtime accommodations on Kit's recipe, had drained some taste out of it to better suit her upland palate and had carried that meatloaf to potluck suppers across the breadth of the county in her ongoing quest to meet and snare a man. Unfortunately for her, most men worth snaring didn't frequent potluck suppers, so Ailene passed the bulk of those evenings giving Kit's adjusted recipe out to those women who'd been, like Ailene, struck by the spices and the savor, and that dish became pretty widely known in these parts as colored meatloaf.

However, as that recipe traveled among the face powder and blue rinse crowd, it got tamed and integrated and largely routed of its bite which Ray suggested, once he'd watched Kit dump that chuck into a bowl, might be the variety of loaf best suited for Clayton.

"We wouldn't want to feed him anything that might disagree with him." Ray managed, by way of enlargement, an articulately anguished expression that went a ways, in fact, towards suggesting that while he'd soaped up Clayton's scrotum and had touched with his bare hands Clayton's revolting feet, there wasn't much chance he'd see clear to wipe clean Clayton's bunghole, so Ray wanted everything that went in Clayton bland enough to stay.

Kit spilled out a teaspoon's worth of ground cayenne into her cupped palm. "My colored meatloaf's colored," she told him. "Period."

And it was, Ray noticed, might even have been a little extra colored since it was all he could do, while he ate the stuff, to keep from tearing up. Furthermore, it didn't help that Kit had lavished pepper flakes on the greens she'd cooked.

"Fruit of Islam kale," she'd informed Ray as she shoved the bowl his way.

The appreciable spice, however, in the food just seemed to qualify for Clayton as something else he wasn't obliged to pay any notice to. That went for his flatware as well which he failed to trouble himself to use. He instead dragged his fingers about his plate and scooped up morsels of food, and he'd raise to his mouth and eat whatever he'd not rained on his shirtfront or dribbled onto his corduroy pants or dropped onto the floor where Monroe would scarf it up and then lovingly lick the linoleum.

"Now what?" Kit asked Ray as she laid her fork across her plate and shoved the thing towards the center of the table. "Doesn't the man have relatives somewhere?" Kit eyed Clayton as she spoke. She reached across the dinette and flicked a scrap of garlic from his shirt.

"Who do you think emptied out his house?"

"They can't all be trash."

"Look at him, for Godsakes. Sure they can." And even though Kit was ordinarily the sort to take direction poorly, she did pass a moment or two in steady contemplation of Clayton who was rheumy-eyed and passably toothless, was receding at both his hairline and his chin and did look to Kit the sort who just might be cursed with relations given to the moral refinement of buccaneers.

"No Astors in that woodpile," Ray assured Kit which Clayton saw fit to punctuate with a ripping eructation.

"So," Kit said and then asked Ray again, "now what?"

Ray hadn't planned, as it turned out, so terribly far ahead, and, beyond letting Clayton pass the night on his fold-out davenport, Ray hadn't yet quite figured just what he'd do. "Get him some fuel oil for his furnace. A keeper maybe—some kind of nurse."

"Does he have any money?"

"I doubt it."

"Insurance?"

"Probably not. Just that house of his and maybe some thirty or forty acres that runs back into the woods."

"Which around here is worth about squat."

"About."

"So no money, no coverage, no blood kin worth a happy god-damn," which Ray weighed and figured for a fair and accurate assessment that he was nodding his assent about when Clayton chimed in with a wholly unmuted vaporish discharge, a violent burst of unadulterated methane that Ray and Kit together must have half expected to lift Clayton off his seat.

Monroe crowded Clayton's chair and laid her chin upon his thigh. She gazed up at Clayton thunderstruck, Ray guessed, with admiration and contented herself with doting on Clayton well into the night.

By the time they put him to bed, Clayton had unfreighted himself of sufficient perfume to have made additional glorious advancements in Monroe's esteem. She ignored Kit, which was nothing exceptional, but she neglected Ray as well so as to expend her full devotion upon Clayton who didn't seem to notice her gentle nudges at his inseam or her long slow greasy licks upon his hands. In fact, Clayton didn't register anything much throughout the course of the evening but just sat by oblivious to talk about him, insensible to his gas and numb against the ceaseless fawning notice of Ray's dog until there at the last when Ray was touring the house and switching off lights.

He paused at the hallway door with the floorlamp pullchain pinched between his fingers. "Come on," he told Monroe who'd settled her chin on the davenport mattress well in the orbit of Clayton's scent and in the vicinity of his hand. She rolled her eyes in Ray's direction in that fashion that she favored to let Ray know that, while she'd heard him, she meant to make as if she'd not.

So Ray called her by name, as was his practice, in a less agreeable tone, and Monroe was huffing already and warbling a little wanly in her throat in her customary show of slow reluctant canine resignation when Clayton shifted to look upon her and laid his hand atop her head.

"Wildcat," he told her. "Rimfire. Forty grain," which Clayton supplemented with a low discharge of breath that impressed Ray as positively mournful.

Kit by then had stepped from the toilet and had come upon them all—Clayton stretched out on the fold-a-bed with his hand upon Ray's dog and Ray hard beside the doorway with the pullchain in his fingers and his jaw, she noticed, unhinged just a bit.

Kit watched Ray shift from considering Clayton so as to consider Monroe before she troubled herself to inquire of him, "What?"

———

Apparently, it was that selfsame night when one of those fledgling Richmond doctors, that Mr. Williams who'd helped Clayton from his shirt, got involved in a fender bender that gave way to a throttling. It seems he'd stopped in at a gas mart for his usual burrito, that brand made to go from its freezer packet straight into the microwave, and he'd bought as well a half-gallon pail of

cola which he was obliged to balance and wrangle once he'd settled back into his car.

That fellow drove a cruddy little Datsun that he'd come by
from a cousin since, like most interns, he'd taken the long view of
personal prosperity and was satisfied that he'd have gaudy gobs of
money after a while. And, naturally enough, he behaved in that
car like the owner of a cruddy Datsun which is to say he wasn't so
awfully scrupulous behind the wheel. He was a little more attentive to the bucket of soda between his legs and the molten burrito
he was permitting to cool off on his dash than all of the possible
hazards in the gas mart lot behind him as he started that coupe of
his and whipped it back out of his space.

To Mr. Williams's misfortune, a boy had lately pulled up to
the pump island in an ever so meticulously kept and garishly
chrome-encrusted Monterey. He was the sort who even Armor
Alled his radiator hoses, and him and his girl were well into their
usual Saturday night tour of Henrico County and had need of a
couple of dollars' worth of additional high-test gas. He watched,
that boy did, in horror as a ratty little import rolled back from the
storefront and into the quarter panel of his sedan which prompted
him to dart over and inquire of that intern just what in the name
of merciful Jesus he thought he was about.

For his part, that fledgling doctor had gotten steeped in Clas-
sic Coke, was saturated pretty much from his sternum to his
knees which caused him to swear and leap from that coupe in a
fashion, understandably enough, that boy with the dented Monterey took for a further provocation, and he responded by knocking that intern to the ground.

Mr. Williams saw fit to loose upon that fellow a doctorly snort
which served to suggest he thought himself a bit too good for
quarreling over vehicular misadventures in gas mart parking lots.
That boy with the Mercury responded by kicking that intern in

the ribs which had the effect of laying him out with a view of that Monterey front tag, a personalized plate embossed across its breadth with "Rick-n-June."

That fellow with the dent invited that intern to share with him a reason why he didn't deserve to get the holy living shit stomped from him, and, apparently, Mr. Williams did indulge in a remark.

"Rick engine," he said, by all accounts, which failed somehow to spare him.

THE POLE

"Just handing them out like candy, aren't you?" As he spoke, the
chief gestured with a trio of Ray's embossed deputy business
cards.

"I thought maybe . . . ," Ray told the chief and then trailed off
with a shrug as Ray had neglected to work up the manner of
plucky rationale that would have much chance of holding sway
with a fellow like the chief.

The chief grunted and collapsed into the chair behind his desk,
dropped hard onto the seat as if he'd plummeted from on high
and thereby jarred from the coiled spring pivot a sharp metallic
complaint. He then pointed towards a stool against the opposite
wall like he meant for Ray to perch there, but the seat was stacked
with three years' worth of quarterly police gazettes, a few file fold-
ers and telephone directories, a sweat-salted Pennzoil cap. Ray
elected to stay where he was.

The chief gazed sourly at Ray's business cards between his
thumb and his curled finger until he'd seen clear to pluck one free
and show it to Ray. "Give that woman back her books."

"Yes sir," Ray told him with a largely persuasive touch of

shame just as the chief brought those last two embossed cards to Ray's notice both at once.

"Clayton can buy his own goddamn fuel oil like everybody else, and he can be sick on his own stinking dime." Then he dropped the both of them into his wastebasket as well and canted back loudly in his squeaky desk chair to swivel and rock and wait for Ray to say whatever he might.

"I thought maybe we'd have a little petty cash we could shift Clayton's way. He's in a hard spot just now."

The chief lurched forward and rose from his chair, steered his bulk across the office to a freighted set of shelves where he plucked a strongbox from beneath a heap of dusty copy paper and brought the thing back by its dainty little handle like some manner of ungainly purse. He set it on his desk and opened it, shoved the thing at Ray.

"Take whatever you need," he said, and Ray peered inside to find, in with the lint and the grit on the rust-puckered strongbox bottom, a note from Walter in the form of a fifty-cent IOU, a ballpoint pen, a rather dingy nickel and six pennies, two dollars' worth of Confederate script and a eucalyptus lozenge.

The chief informed Ray he wasn't paid to see after Clayton's affairs, no matter what sort of mystical nonsense folks thought Clayton was talking.

"So you heard?"

"I guess so," the chief said, and he shared with Ray the news of how Ailene's friend Russell, the telephone man—which he troubled himself to shout so as to ensure that Ailene could hear him from where she was sitting in the squadroom proper—had come to Bible study with a kidney stone in a celery salt jar.

"I didn't know Russell was a Baptist."

"He's loud heathen trash," the chief told Ray by way of clarification. "But it seems that Clayton," and here the chief shouted again for the benefit of Ailene, "had prophesied that stone away and shaken Russell up a little. So he fished the damned thing out of the commode and carried it to church."

"Nine-fourteen?"

The chief glared at Ray, broke off briefly to step towards his doorway and glare a bit at Ailene instead, but he wandered back soon enough to visit again on Ray his stern regard. "That Clayton's no prophet," the chief told Ray, "and his troubles aren't our business." The chief offered Ray a slip of pink paper from his message pad. "Stick to police work why don't you."

Ray took the sheet and read the name scrawled on it. "Which Tuttle?" Ray asked, and the chief winked at him and smiled as he said, "Myra Jean."

So Ray drove out from town past the rolling mill and over the creaky iron bridge that gives onto the Lynchburg Pike about a quarter mile shy of where Grover customarily sits on the shoulder of the road in his shabby lawn chair and waves at passing traffic. It had begun to rain by the time Ray had gained the four-lane proper, so he eased his cruiser off into the cinders and climbed out to acquaint Grover with the fact that he was getting immoderately wet. Ray coaxed Grover out of his lawn chair. He folded the thing and packed it into the trunk and permitted Grover to ride, like he'd grown to prefer, in the backseat of the cruiser where Grover shoved his fingers through the holes in the metal divider along Ray's seatback and set about listing for Ray the sundry vehicles he'd seen.

After about every third or fourth car, Grover would interrupt his progress in order to inform Ray, "Got dropped on my head when I wasn't but a child."

His mother, as it turned out, had taught him to say it instead of his telephone number or his name as she'd wanted him to let people know up front that he was dim. And because he was dim, he tended to air it with that touch of boastful pride most common to motel lounges where fellows with little to recommend them will tell with a wink to females, "I'm a Sagittarius," as if they'd become one through earnest study and by dint of advanced degrees.

Grover anymore is in his sixties and still lives with his mother who dresses him in green twill trousers and matching green twill shirts that she insists he wear buttoned clean up to his Adam's apple. He wears cordovan wingtips and a tartan plaid cap with earflaps, for Godsakes, so if he hadn't ever actually gotten dropped on his head, he would certainly look a suitable candidate for it. Grover's mother has to be ninety-five if she's a day, a shriveled old thing who camps on her settee in a housedress and a tattered cardigan and dribbles her Tube Rose juices into a nasty Luck's bean can which she changes out for a fresh bean can about every other year.

"How's your mom getting on?" Ray asked of Grover like he evermore asked it of him, and Grover wiggled his fingers in the seatback divider holes.

"Misses Daddy something awful," Grover told him, pretty much like he evermore did, even though by then Grover's father had been dead in the ground for going on thirty-five years.

Then Grover went back to cataloging for Ray the vehicles he'd seen which included a National Guard convoy and a big lumbering construction crane that Grover was describing down to the lugnuts and the fender skirts as they crested the ridge and rolled south on the spine to the Tuttle homeplace which is a sort of a jack-leg split-level with a single wide inside. Harold Tuttle, Myra Jean's husband, added the back deck and the parlor, and he's that ilk who should never be allowed to have a hammer in his hand.

Harold had retired, as was usually the case, to the safety of the yard and had been joined there by his neighbor, a Crowder woman from across the road, who stood in the quilted bathrobe and the sneakers she always wore and smoked a Chesterfield as she pitied Harold's matrimonial misstep and reminded him of the cousin she had who'd cherish a fellow like him.

Myra Jean, for her part, was raging about the trailer home and flinging the odd gewgaw and piece of stoneware out the door. She'd claimed for years by then to be passing through the change of life and suffering, as a consequence, a grievous hormonal imbalance that caused her, every now and again, to become entirely unhinged. She'd start out beating on Harold and, when she could manage it, pitching cats, and, once she'd routed them all from the trailer, she'd set about throwing those items that would usually shatter to pieces on the rocks out in the yard.

Myra Jean flung out a pickle dish that busted violently on the steps, and she paused in the doorway to inform Harold and Ray and Grover as well that men were nothing but a pack of sons of bitches and unholy bastards. Then she disappeared for about a half a minute down the length of that single wide and showed up again with a ginger-jar lamp that she tossed into the yard where the shade went to pieces and the jug cracked a little and the cord whipped around at the plugend to leave a welt on Grover's shin which he leapt and jigged and openly wept for a minute or two on account of.

A Reavis from just up the road who happened to be passing by with his wife stopped off in order to advise Harold how he would handle a woman who ventured to drive him out of his house and break his lamps in his yard. That Reavis is a pretty frequent witness to Myra Jean's tirades due to how he and his wife are together the sorts of people who tend to shop at the grocery mart for one or two items at a time. They go for a loaf of bread or a pack of chicken parts, a jug of milk or a box of coffee filters, and it just never seems to occur to them to draw up a proper list and buy everything they're low on all at once.

So that Reavis will come stalking from his kitchen with an empty jar in hand. "Out of chow-chow," he'll say, and it's on with the coats and out into the pickup.

He's that sort who's overburdened with opinions about what other people should do and is prone to be freer with them than is decorous and seemly. So he was laying out for Harold a course of action with Myra Jean while his own wife was barking at him from his truck down by the ditch, reminding him of the merchandise they'd set out from home to fetch. The Crowder woman from across the street made mention once more of her cousin and issued a guarantee to Harold that he'd get doted on with her while Myra Jean located a cat who'd made a grave miscalculation and inflicted upon that creature a spot of air travel.

Ray fished from his uniform pocket the pink sheet from the chief's message pad. He showed it to Grover and told him, with one of his winces, "Police work," which prompted Grover to remind Ray of how, as a child, he'd been dropped on his head.

———

Most evenings Ray would stop in at Clayton's on his way home from his shift, would carry him sometimes fresh saltines or West Virginia Chinese takeout and would usually run up on a caller or two who'd dropped by for prophecy. It was early in June by then but still crisp sometimes at night, so Ray would switch on Clayton's floor furnace and check to see what if any additions Clayton had made to his chimney-stack map. Ray would touch him, of course, would find occasion to poke and prod Clayton a bit in hopes of provoking from him some scrap of little Dunn girl talk.

Clayton, however, hadn't said much to Ray since that night on

Ray's settee when most of his talking had been, in fact, directed at Ray's dog. He did still manage to visit on townsfolk the odd glancing prognostication and had come to be known about for the sort of curious attraction that we tend to be a little short on in these parts. Year in and year out, we're likely to see a few barnyard deformities—five-legged calves, carbuncled chickens, misshapen geese and ducks, and a Gillum out the pike had a few years back a nanny goat with a handle, a loop of cartilage you could shoot your fingers through and hold her by.

We've got a rock out towards the reservoir that looks, for all the world, like a Parkerhouse roll, a waterfall on the edge of the National Forest that folks with no girth much to them can walk, if they see fit, altogether behind. There's an abandoned lead mine up a hollow from the river that's haunted, people say, by a fellow who got brained a hundred years ago by an errant chunk of slag.

The story goes that if you sprawl beside what anymore is a weedy hole in the ground, only under the dark of the moon and around the witching hour, you're likely to hear that miner whistle a snatch of "My Country 'Tis of Thee" which we prefer to think a touch more eerie than your standard ghostly manifestation since it's uncommon for a gentleman to be both dead and patriotic at once.

As it turned out, Clayton's gift for prophecy came upon him at a favorable time since we had nothing much to distract and divert us at that particular juncture but for the carcass of a creature our ophthalmologist's wife had hit with her car, a young buck with a strangely tapered snout and an odd nap to its fur that turned out to be the mongrel offspring of a llama and a doe and earned that woman a ticket from Larry with a suitably discounted fine for having killed some strain of diluted deer out of season.

Furthermore, Clayton's ilk of prognostication aroused wider interest than a goat with a handle or a rock in the shape of a dinner roll ever might. Even given the usual sweeping appeal of ghosts and spooky places, the weedy opening to that lead mine wasn't a pleasant spot to sprawl, and you can listen to a dead fellow whistle the same scrap of melody only so much.

Clayton, then, had novelty going for him and variety as well, and he was hardly hurt by the fact that he actually seemed to foretell the future even if only in trifling and useless sorts of ways. He'd also secured by his talents an inexhaustible advertisement in the form of Russell the loud-talking telephone man with his kidney stone in a celery salt jar. Russell was hardly the sort that people were given to trying to hear, like Kit, but was that ilk instead we were comprehensively helpless against.

So we pretty much all of us had gotten exposed to Russell's kidney stone story along with other examples of Clayton's gift that lineman would shore up that kidney stone with. If anything, then, the traffic out to Clayton's had appreciated over time and hardly seemed likely to flag and wane as long as Clayton could deliver the strain of commentary folks were likely, at length, to find themselves dazzled by. Clayton even had the potential, as best as any of us could tell, to outperform in the long run that little Dunn girl shrine which had left off bringing in the bouquets and transient well-wishers in near the volume it had managed at the first. Some grievers, of course, had returned with the improved weather of the spring but hardly so many as to clot up the blacktop and make for a gaudy floral hummock like before.

Consequently, that Dunn girl shrine had become pretty much a forlorn spot on the roadside by the time that Clayton had fled the grocery mart without waiting for his change. Part of the problem was that there weren't any live Dunns left by then among us, just the spirit of that little blonde one in the Homer Blaine Park woods and the carcass of her daddy in the Presbyterian churchyard. Her mother had retreated with her brother clean back to Ohio by then, had sold off her husband's dairy farm to a guy from out Richmond way, a fellow in loafers and chinos and a pale yellow shirt who drove a black Range Rover and had about him a pronounced air of shiftless real estate speculation.

Boyd, his name was, and, as he lingered among us to file for his various permits, we came to learn that Boyd was a Realtor and a contractor both which made him a particularly curious species of thoroughgoing ignoramus since he was obliged to pretend to competence in two different fields at once. Like most Realtors, Boyd didn't know anything about residential construction, and, like most contractors, he was chiefly gifted at getting the roofer on the phone and fixing into place, when the time came for it, switchplates and outlet covers with the little screwdriver that served him as a key fob.

Naturally, he was squirrelly and unforthcoming in his talk, seemed to think every little scrap of chat was overture to a negotiation, so we were obliged to hear from the girl who notarizes deeds at the county seat that Boyd intended to put nearly sixty houses out on that Dunn farm, each centered upon its own luxurious quarter-acre lot. Locally, this was pretty good news for most of us about since it meant work for the tradesmen and steady business at the lumberyard, the hardware store and the electrical supply. People, of course, like the bird lady who wandered Homer Blaine State Park complained about the threat to the upland quail and goldfinch habitat, and she and her ilk made all sorts of racket over environmental studies which they even extracted from Boyd his earnest personal oath to conduct.

As it turned out, though, that fellow was a gifted human lubricant, and he disarmed that bird lady and her friends with his sympathetic palaver, made out to be both an incurable treehugger and the manner of bird enthusiast who couldn't even eat a Cornish hen without a vague twinge of guilt. At the same time he was easing the way for the permits he required by cultivating that girl at the county seat who processed the applications. He made out to find her intriguing until his paperwork came through when he hired on a motorgrader driver and a bulldozer operator who knocked down the farmhouse the Dunns had lived in and set about cutting roads.

Lanes, rather, and rambles and courts and circles as the developments Boyd tended to build were that sort with scant measurable quality to them but no end of baseless pretension. Those roads even got curbing and gutters that drained into the old cow pond, little bits of stacked rail fencing at the turnings and Parisian style lightposts. The houses, however, were all constructed on the same boxy two-story plan. Several of them got garages, a few got wraparound porches, and the one built down at the old homeplace with authentic trees in the yard was dressed up with a fieldstone walk and a weathercock on the roof.

It sold first since the rest of those houses were scattered about the unshaded pastureside, and around town we uniformly agreed that Boyd was likely to lose his pastel piqué shirt since we couldn't really figure where a fellow and his wife would have to be living at present in order to mine some allure from the prospect of a house out in a field, most particularly a slapped-together eyesore of a place in a cow lot full of slapped-together eyesores with the wind whipping through in the winter and the sun beating down in the summer and the neighborhood touched the whole year through with near perfect hideousness.

We were foolish enough, as it turned out, to undervalue Boyd's slimy marketing savvy and to discount what must be the painful ordeal of a winter in the upper Midwest. All Boyd did was to build a little guardhouse at his turn in and set up one of those gates that block the road with a length of painted plank. Then he hired a Yokely, the one with the teeth still and the personal gumption to shave, and he dressed him up in a uniform that resembled Grover's outfit but for the clip-on tie that Yokely wore and the sharply creased garrison cap.

The way the thing worked was that Boyd would meet up with his prospects in town and yacht them out to his development—Cotswold Hills—in the snug comfort of his Range Rover. Boyd would draw up at the security gate where that Yokely would greet him with a smile and request of Boyd his laminated identification card. As that Yokely returned the thing, he would apologize for the delay to whoever Boyd had ridden over with him and remark that a fellow couldn't stand to be too careful in this world. Then up with the gate, and in they would roll along an impeccably tended stretch of Wordsworth Way to a knob that gave onto a view of those houses littered across the hillside which were touched by then with the golden glow of exclusivity.

Essentially, Boyd was selling that Yokely and his guardhouse and the opportunity for folks to live on the proper side of that painted plank, so it didn't much matter that he'd built a slew of rubbishy drafty homes with crawl spaces instead of basements and aluminum trailerpark windows, linoleum everywhere that they could get the stuff to stick, cheesy wood-grained vinyl cladding and electric heat-pump furnaces, a few spindly saplings in each yard by way of horticulture.

Boyd had put azaleas around the guardhouse and proper cypress mulch, a stout rail fence to keep out interlopers, and he'd gotten his Cotswold Hills sign made for him in Williamsburg with more taste and craftsmanship than all of his houses put together. Unlike the rest of us, Boyd knew going in that he wasn't selling homes which was why it didn't matter how he made them, and he'd show off those shabby houses with untempered shamelessness, would let his prospects wander freely through and imbibe all the frailties before he'd apprise them of how he'd gotten just lately an offer on the place.

Consequently, our dire predictions for that enterprise of Boyd's proved to run entirely contrary to how the thing played out. He filled up that housing development with snowbirds down from the upper plains and retirees fleeing the heat of the Gulf for the summer. A few locals even bought in, folks with cause to know their guardhouse Yokely had come by the scar on his chin and the serpent tattooed on his forearm in prison once he'd gotten convicted of being a thieving lout. And we'd most of us heard from the tradesmen Boyd had put to work about the corners he'd cut and the chiseling he'd done and the code infractions he'd bribed away, so we weren't inclined to sympathy for that sort from around here who allowed themselves to get seduced and smitten by the place.

Naturally, that Yokely had made a few unsavory chums in prison, and he'd soon enough discovered, after a month on guardhouse duty, that the little controller he used to raise that painted plank also opened all of the garage doors in the place. One of that Yokely's buddies had a pickup truck and an ongoing appetite for criminal misadventure, so he'd lurk in the vicinity two or three days a week, and that Yokely would wave him in once he knew a house was empty.

They were cagey, those two, in the way that ne'er-do-wells are often cagey which is to say that, instead of getting caught and found out straightaway, they were scooped up and charged by Carl and Walter only after a month or two. It was January by then, and that Yokely and his buddy had been stealing nothing but lawnmowers on account of how they'd reasoned they were out of mowing season, so a fellow wasn't likely to miss his Snapper for two or three months at least. The trouble was those garages were so awfully tight that Cotswold Hillians had grown accustomed to barking their cars against their mowers, so they noticed a shortage of clattering collisions whenever they pulled in to park.

The Cotswold Hillians fell into immediate dissension over whether or not they should go to the expense of hiring another guard. The ones with garage door controllers didn't among them see the point since they'd found they could raise that painted plank from the comfort of their cars while the rest of them wanted to hire some fellow to press his button for them which became a moot issue once the meter reader had wheeled in off the blacktop and had failed to stop before he had bumped that plank and snapped it cleanly off.

Of course, a number of Cotswold Hillians were preoccupied by then with frozen water lines and overloaded electrical circuits, with asphalt drives that the frost had cracked and fissured like parched earth. Then a storm came through and made off with most of the shingles in the place, and, accordingly, it got to where we rarely thought of the Dunns anymore when we drove past that vacant guardhouse and that busted painted plank, could hardly hope to conjure that dairy farm and the Daytonians who'd worked it with the little blonde child who'd gone into the woods and had never come out again. By that time, they'd gotten supplanted by Boyd's gated community where the houses were falling to pieces and all of our class-action litigants lived.

Even the Dunn left for us to tend and tidy in the Presbyterian churchyard failed to do much service as a reminder of all that he'd been through. He'd gotten laid in a rooty piece of ground beneath a white oak tree, and the shade and the nuts and the windfall leaves all kept his sod from thriving, so one good clipping could last him almost a year.

He was situated pretty snugly alongside a Grissom from out the gap on account of how far more Presbyterians had been claimed by the Maker than the church elders had planned for when they'd laid that cemetery out. Those members who'd passed, consequently, were forced to be more chummy in decomposition than they'd ever elected to be in actual life. So that expired Dunn was as close to that Grissom on the white oak side as that Grissom's wife would be on the downslope once she'd finally expired. In the meantime, she was obliged to conduct confabs with her late husband in the interloping presence of that Dunn crowding in upon them.

She probably would have been less bothered but for the topic of their chats which was evermore and without variation personal finance. The wife of that Grissom had been raised to speak only discreetly of money, and it was a subject that she and her husband had touched upon all too infrequently which was why she came twice a week to the graveyard to beg that Grissom for some kind of sign that might cause her to know just where he'd hidden away his treasury bonds.

That a Dunn from Dayton was always lurking close enough to hear her functioned as a nagging irritant for that Grissom's wife who, when out among the living and presented with a pretext, tended to speak uncharitably of those Dunns, most particularly the dead one in the Presbyterian churchyard who, by all rights, should have been beyond contempt.

The most of the rest of us far preferred to carp about his wife who we saw on TV and heard on syndicated radio. She'd put that farm of theirs up for sale almost before her husband was cold and had rid herself of it to Boyd for something south of a princely sum on account of how she had insurance money and an itch to be elsewhere. Dayton at first, but apparently Dayton was no longer big enough to hold her, and she moved to Cincinnati where she set herself up in business as a suffering victimized woman with an inordinate store of pluck. She'd had a daughter up and vanish on her, had had a husband get killed and was trying alone to raise a boy who seemed a bit touched with psychosis, who tormented and dispatched most every creature that wandered into his reach.

Personal tragedy, though, had failed somehow to make that woman soft, and she'd come through the punishing tumult of her vicissitudes without professional counseling or government subsidized intervention, had elected instead just to grab onto her bootstraps and to jerk. That was her version anyway, and she even let on to have been strengthened by her ordeals while invariably failing to mention that she'd been callous from the getgo and pretty well suited to sloughing off her troubles like a husk.

Like most everybody else on talk radio and palaver TV at the time, that Dunn woman wasn't called upon to marshal any facts or supply specific answers to pointed and considered queries but was expected to unfreight herself, when she got called on for that purpose, of a lively uninformed and nonresponsive diatribe which suited her well because she always knew just what she thought but not necessarily why she'd come to think it. Moreover, her voice was pleasantly pitched for TV and radio. Even in full dudgeon, it was never prone to grate upon the ears, and she'd submitted herself to a makeover since her dairy farming days, so her hair had been styled to hide her jowly unbecoming places and her face powder made her look a little ruddy from the sun.

Most significantly, that Dunn was a walking bundle of confounded expectations. Given her disappointments and her personal tragedies as a mother and a wife and a helpmeet in a failing family farm, people naturally expected from her tenderness for the downtrodden and compassionate understanding where it came to the put upon, but instead she was always prescribing that folks stop whining and stiffen up. She was like that fellow on the Fox news channel with the bolo and the eye patch who'd been shot and yet was still a gun enthusiast, or the brunette on the

News Hour with the beauty mark and the twitch who'd been throttled by a convict on work release and chose still to champion parole. In short, that Dunn was as close to a provocative surprise as we get anymore on the airwaves which she enhanced and supplemented with a knack for the manner of scornful abuse that tends to pass these days for debate.

That Dunn was chiefly a case of years of telephone chatter paying off as she was glib and ever so rarely at a loss for a cutting remark which kept her in demand until sheer exposure had brought her the sort of fame that sheer exposure anymore is capable of bringing. Our movie stars get by on dimples and comely overbites. Our singers make do with sculpted midriffs and choreography. Why, then, shouldn't a TV commentator get ahead with nothing but agile rancor to recommend her?

Soon enough she got invited to fill in for the weatherman on the national morning news show that aired over the Staunton station. Then the perky hostess, who that Dunn knew from back when her daughter disappeared, came down with a virus and that Dunn got enlisted to move over to the desk where she demonstrated a talent for frothy congenial bickering with the cohost. She proved readily capable of conducting the sorts of trifling interviews they feature on that national morning news show, chats mostly with presidential candidates and that strain of celebrity author who has overcome an addiction or developed a protein diet, has embraced a newfound faith in the Lord Christ or survived a flirtation with death, has done, in fact, virtually anything short of writing his book himself.

One holiday weekend when everybody else must have been otherwise occupied, that Dunn even filled in as the anchor on the national evening newscast.

So the one Dunn was dead, and the other seemed to us acutely content with her fame while her remaining child was packed away somewhere for our protection. Accordingly, there wasn't detectable clamor any longer over the Dunn who'd strayed up into the woods and disappeared. That girl's mother never troubled the chief for news on the status of their inquiry, and the fact was that they didn't really have an inquiry anymore. The flyers were all weathered and covered over, and the national alerts had long since been sent. Her picture had even gotten replaced on the bulletin board at the warehouse grocery in Staunton where they display photos of missing children alongside the film drop.

There wasn't, then, anyone prodding and poking and demanding results from Ray, nothing to drive him but for what hunger he mustered on his own which he tried to have us believe was inspired by his ardor for the law and his native sense of civic indignation, attempted to let on that he was just a helpless snoop at heart. Of course, we all of us knew better. Even those among us uninclined to pry had come by then of word that Ray had lost a daughter to drowning, and we tended to sense without troubling ourselves to say it to each other that he'd replaced, in a fashion, the child he'd surrendered with the one he hoped to get back.

Naturally, we didn't any of us share our views with Ray but only analyzed him out of his hearing. It seems even Kit didn't trouble herself to joust with him about it those occasions when Ray would volunteer talk of that missing Dunn, would suggest that he felt a compelling professional duty to root her out and would welcome even clairvoyant aid from Clayton.

Ray would remind Kit he'd sworn an oath and had professional obligations, and Kit would only ever tell him, "Uh huh," tell him, "Right."

She went for a month or more without coming around there in the shank of the spring. The way we heard it, she got called in to work on a couple of grisly homicides where the carcasses both turned up on National Park land. They found the leavings of a woman in a pillowcase out by Mammoth Cave in Kentucky. A couple of local teens had come across her on a ramble through the woods, a boy and girl on their way in to a spot—as it turned out—where they were given to spreading a quilt on a patch of moss and fornicating. It was their special place, and they hiked to it with scrupulous regularity as they lived with their parents and drove each imported subcompact coupes, so they didn't have anywhere they could both be naked and stretch out except for their mossy patch of ground well off the trail back in those woods.

They tried to let on that they'd been out taking the air on an innocent stroll until Kit had pressed them sufficiently about their quilt and their Lancer's rosé when they offered a fuller accounting of their activities—owned up to a dazzling frequency of fornicating alfresco—which permitted Kit to pin down almost the hour that pillowcase got left, and, as it turned out, by a gentleman who'd bought a ticket to the cave and had toured through it in his slacks and his blazer and tie with an emerald green shopping bag.

It was a stout bag, sizeable and crisply creased and printed with the name of a Paducah men's store, a large enough sack to accommodate that pillowcase full of pieces which were wrapped in foil, they came to discover, and labeled each with freezer tape.

That fellow had been filmed by a surveillance camera in the Mammoth Cave parking lot, by a camera above the ticket window at the Mammoth Cave entranceway, by a camera at the mouth of the cave itself where he had paused to adjust his tie knot and cinch his blazer shut deftly with one hand alone against the subterranean chill. Kit had that footage spliced together and carried it over to Paducah where she played it for the chief of police who'd seen that gentleman before.

"Claude," he told her and then shook his head and informed her behind it, "Huh."

As it turned out, Claude was an officer at the last remaining local bank where the checking was free and they gave out suckers at the drive-thru window. Claude chiefly authorized loans and signed off on charge-card applications, had a desk out on the floor where he served as a visible symbol of rectitude. Claude was known in Paducah to be upstanding, was a deacon in the Baptist Church, had only lately stepped down from his city council seat and lived in a fine old section of town in an impeccably maintained house where Claude and his wife had raised a son and married off a daughter.

Claude had a grinding wheel out in his garage where he sharpened tools for his neighbors, and he was famous about for how he scoured his lawn and shrubbery of leaves in the fall.

Claude had always, apparently, liked things just so but had grown feverishly particular over the past few years while Dorothy, his wife, had largely lost interest in housework and in cooking and had set about taking the sorts of courses mornings at the community center that had the effect of bringing clutter into the house—stalks and seedpods for flower arranging, cotton string for macramé, paraffin that got on everything in the kitchen when she batiked and pins and scraps of tissuey patterns for the jumpers that she made.

Claude had stifled his irritation for as long as he could manage. That anyway is how he told it back at the station house, and he allowed that he had seen fit to remonstrate with his wife while she was shoving spindly lavender stalks into a quiver of a basket that she'd woven from strips of dampened beech tree bark. Apparently she was not in a mood to endure a remonstration with anything approaching wifely grace, and she ignored Claude as she rained lavender seeds all over their wall-to-wall carpet which prompted Claude to bring to bear upon her a little hooked hand scythe that he'd ground to a razor's edge out on his wheel.

As for the trip over to Mammoth Cave, they'd neither of them ever been which had struck Claude as a shame since they lived hard by in Paducah.

Kit told Ray all about the house with its meticulously edged walk and its mulch beneath the hollies and the azaleas in the front that looked piece by piece and scrap by scrap to have been laid into proper place. She told him about the front stoop with its bleached concrete as slick as glass and described how Claude drew open the door in his trousers and shirt and tie, with a dishtowel tucked in at his belt to serve him as an apron.

He'd only just let them into his tidy antiseptic front room when he noticed the dirt that Kit had picked up tromping through the woods, a crust of it anyway on the outsole of her shoe which induced him to pull from a sidetable drawer a square of stout brown packing paper that Kit obliged him and stood upon as she inquired about his wife.

Then it was off for Kit to Hatteras where a boy had washed up on the seashore with a barbecue fork shoved well into his neck. He'd gotten, she learned at length, into a heated dispute with a buddy in Morehead City, a buddy who'd let his carcass get disposed of by the tide.

The thing that Ray and Kit shared together was a sense between them of what was veneer, of what was froth and dressing and civil confection laid onto the meat of this life, that feral and treacherous core that we, the most of us, rein in except for odd moments behind the wheel while traveling the roadways when even the mildest among us can wish vicious death on some fool for clotting his route. They'd simply both seen the consequences of far too many unchecked impulses to entertain much faith between them in our assorted national lies, our dewy conviction that we're more decent and honest than anybody else, freer and harder working, more God-fearing and elect. So there was a regular world of piffle they never spoke about, knew both for a kind of social meringue that wasn't worth their notice.

Accordingly, they always seemed to us a trifle short with each other, never indulged between them in our local brand of courtly insincerity but tended to have at each other in a way that struck us as unsheathed and abrupt.

Ray was reading one evening that book on explorers he'd not returned to the library notwithstanding the chief's directive and uncharitable talk from Mrs. Hartman who tended to take book-borrowing habits as the measure of a man. Consequently, she was down on Ray and thought poorly of Kit as well which she passed her days in the library communicating in a whisper to anybody who wandered in and looked the least conducive to chat. So chiefly, that is to say, she talked to the Hoyt who carried the mail. He'd drop by in the shank of the morning and try to leave it on the desk, but she would invariably spy him and corral that Hoyt into a conversation which concerned exclusively Ray's deplorable morals for a time.

So he was sitting there reading that stolen book one night out at his house probably with that dog of his atomizing the air from the settee, and he was likely listening—the way he did—to that saxophone player he favored who Ray approved of because he played no tune precisely the same way twice. In fact, he sounded lucky, from what Ray had inflicted on a few of us about, if he strayed across the actual melody so much as one time proper. Ray, then, was there with his dog and his music and likely a cupful of mash reading in that young adults' book of explorers and adventurers and pausing every now and again to flip back to the antique photograph of those five men in their parkas posed against a snowy hummock with their portion of sled and their piece of pony, their whiskers dusted with frost.

Kit called him from maybe Paducah or maybe her Morehead City motel which afforded Ray occasion to ask what exactly had become of those five fellows. "It just says here they perished, and that can cover a world of misery."

"Don't you know anything?"

"Well, yeah, but . . ."

"They died. All of them."

"What? Froze?"

"Scurvy. Exhaustion. Disorientation. Four months of Antarctic winter in a tent. Yeah, I guess you could say they froze."

"Who found them?"

"A search party went out in the spring. Saw the top of the tent somehow. Three of them were in it and all their journals and papers. It turned out they'd lost one just off the glacier. Evans, I think. Died in his sleep. Oates stepped out of the tent one morning into a blizzard, and they never saw him again."

"Titus?" Ray asked.

"Titus," Kit told him, and then, before she cradled the receiver and as a means of signing off, she offered up a strain of suggestion to Ray. "For Chrissakes, Tatum, read a book sometime."

And because her fuse was shorter and she was quicker to fire than Ray, Kit was long gone off the line before Ray had managed to muster a response which he visited upon Monroe who'd rolled up onto her elbows to be vaporish while she gnawed at a hair mat.

Ray shook his plundered volume at her. "I'm reading a book," he said.

———

Only the laundryman saw him, that Everhart from over in the valley who drives the big yellow paneled Martinizing truck and delivers bedsheets mostly and window sheers. He wears a khaki uniform and a waist-length zippered jacket, shiny black oxfords and a kelly green clip-on tie, and he'd made a detour between deliveries to put himself on Clayton's road as he was suffering just then through a thorny spot of smoldering romantic intrigue, the type of trouble he felt prognostication might unknot and improve.

That Everhart had a wife he was not so fond of as he once had been. They'd married right out of high school when they were both still incomplete, adolescents really with a feverish hormonal attachment that was marked chiefly by incendiary jealousy. They liked all of the same movies and the same sorts of food and were compatible where it came to romance, mustered mutual urges about twice a week or so when that Everhart's wife would put on her husband's Martinizing hat and jacket and make out to be the sort of dry-cleaning temptress a fellow could win with the proper starch.

The trouble was that they weren't either one quite fully formulated and had been married four or five years before they became both authentic adults which was along about when their plans and enthusiasms began to diverge. That Everhart's wife worked for Dr. Lowery answering his phones. She took appointments and endured from his patients sundry complaints about their bills and, being convenient, tolerated a wealth of Dr. Lowery's blather which was what probably helped make the woman eager to have a child.

Those Everharts had discussed children the way young couples often do—the wife with her biological itches and the husband with his bankbook—and that Everhart thought, like men usually will, that they'd agreed together to wait. His doubts, however, were hardly a match for Dr. Lowery's wearing prattle, and that Everhart's wife saw maternity leave as her only form of escape.

As the prime breadwinner, her husband harbored misgivings about the expense of a child, tried to tell himself anyway that he was worried about the cost of feeding and clothing and just generally keeping a hardy son or daughter which became even more of a burden with a sickly afflicted sort. Of course, he was actually troubled by all of the stuff he'd no longer be able to buy, the power tools for his shop in the basement and the senseless implements for the yard, the plasma TV and the laser disc player, the goatskin topcoat he'd had his eye on. Furthermore, he guessed a child in the house would pretty much guarantee that him and his wife would never again indulge in congress on the dinette which was just the sort of thing, he had to figure, they probably discouraged in baby books.

Naturally, like most men, he never up and said anything outright but just went around being mysteriously peevish. He would occasionally make vague mention of his personal concerns about bringing an innocent baby into this world which his wife, understandably, thought had to do with the coarseness of the place—the violence, the despots, the toxins leaking out of sewer pipes—when instead that Everhart feared they would produce the sort of offspring who never quite sees clear to move out of the house.

He sometimes ran across that ilk as he delivered laundry, actual adult children content to live still in their old bedrooms, that sort with nothing to recommend them but car payments and appetites. So when that Everhart carped and groused about bringing an infant into this world, it was chiefly because he'd looked some twenty-odd years down the road to the day when he'd have a son he couldn't drive out of the yard, that sort who'd wolf down all of his Poppycock, sticky up his remote control and sprawl evenings on his settee harvesting lint from between his toes.

Of course, that Everhart couldn't say anything concrete to his wife since even he knew he'd come off like a jackass, that species of heathen ingrate prepared to take the miracle of birth for little

more than a cramping lifestyle imposition. Worse still, it turned
out that Everhart's wife enjoyed her pregnancy. Even the chafing
and the bloating and the hemorrhoids failed to compromise her
glow, and she got a little free with talk about the next child they
might have well before she'd bothered even to drop the first one.

Just along about then, a girl came to work for that Everhart's
Martinizer, an exotic variety of female for these parts. She'd lived
all over but, most recently, out in New Mexico where she'd passed
a year or so tinkering with her aura and supporting herself selling
jewelry she'd made out of feathers and polished rocks. Before that
she'd bottled her own bath oils over in San Francisco, had passed
six months in Iowa in a blank-verse writing workshop, had been
employed as a hair-tint model—she called it—in the East Village
of New York and had served for a while as a cabana girl at an Antigua nudist resort.

She'd been on her way out to the Chesapeake where she'd
hoped to work crab pots, but in passing through, she'd gotten
waylaid by our upland vibe. That's what she told that Everhart
anyway her first day on the job when he was riding her around in
his laundry truck to acquaint her with the county and show her
the route she'd be taking over for that Everhart's colleague who'd
quit. She failed to pay much notice to anything that Everhart had
to say but just stood in his panel truck's doorwell admiring the
rolling terrain and inquiring of that Everhart after the various
birds and vermin they'd see—groundhogs and tree squirrels
mostly, goldfinches and turkey buzzards.

She spoke little of her personal history until once they'd
stopped for lunch. That Everhart carried her out to the cafeteria
by the freeway where that girl shrieked when she recognized a
couple of people she knew—the Ritchies who'd retired into our
uplands from Wisconsin. That Everhart delivered bedsheets to

them about every other week, and he'd once helped them move a hall tree and relocate a corner cupboard as they were both a little frail and aged for furniture shifting.

He left that girl to catch up with them and then join him at the table, and once she fetched up with her molded Jell-O and her succotash, that Everhart idly asked her how she'd come to know the Ritchies which brought about talk of her cabana girl duties at that nudist Antigua resort.

"Me and Sarah," she said and indicated Mrs. Ritchie across the way who was poking at her chiffon pie with her fork, "we got pierced together." With that she unzipped her Martinizing jacket and unbuttoned her khaki shirt that she tugged open just far enough to expose her lefthand nipple which that Everhart saw was skewered through by a braided platinum ring.

By then, of course, he was a little too spit-deficient for commentary, so that Everhart passed a silent moment in further contemplation of, most particularly, Mrs. Ritchie who was drumming her dessert. She plunked it with the back of her fork and then borrowed her husband's glasses for a detailed examination of her meringue topography.

For her part, that girl ate her succotash and picked at that Everhart's biscuit, acted like everything was normal and ordinary between them, like she wasn't sitting across from a man she'd shown her nipple to, and not just a regular unornamented female nipple but one shot through with jewelry and so more seductive and stirring than most.

She'd gone, then, and muddied up that Everhart's opinion of her. He'd surely already checked her off as the sort of woman he would bed, but that was in keeping with that Everhart's routine personal process which he applied to starlets, models, family friends and strangers on the street. However, in showing him her bare chest she'd raised the possibility that he was the stripe of man she might bed back which served to shake that Everhart up since, like the bulk of fellows, he'd chiefly known lust to travel but one way.

He demonstrated thereafter an unnatural interest in most everything she said and encouraged talk from her throughout the afternoon. He admired that girl's name—Skye with an *e* which was her personal contraction for Stacy. He pretended to a rampant curiosity about druids and a feverish interest in the healthful effects of blended Asian teas. He pressed her tirelessly on the details of her vagabond existence, lied to her about his politics and his humanitarian leanings, gave himself out as an authority on accumulated blue-crab lore and interjected every now and again a comment about piercing in hopes that she might draw open her shirt and show him her nipple again.

In short, that Everhart rode that girl around and courted her in his truck in as best as a married man with no intent to get caught courting can insinuate his mind is on romance. So maybe she knew she was getting wooed, but just as likely she didn't since that Everhart cranked up to full allure probably seemed just unduly polite. Anyway, she hardly turned out the type to pay much heed to men, not to say that she didn't eventually accommodate a few around, but she proved that strain of woman who could take a man or leave him, was prone to yield with a shrug to her suitors as if to say, "Aw hell, why not?"

So that Everhart likely could have had a dalliance with that girl without running the threat of her becoming clingy, but the thought of his expectant wife made do to stop and stay him, inflicted upon him anyway enough moral agitation to put an appreciable dent in his sexual appetite. In as much as he had the capacity for it, that Everhart was tormented since Skye was precisely the manner of girl to seem magnetic to him, a wanderer with pierced parts and very probably tattoos who'd shown up just as he was getting cemented into place by a wife who joined him anymore in the bathroom mornings so as to spew bile in the toilet while he shaved.

He'd been wrestling with his misgivings before that girl had come along to tug open her shirt and heighten the pitch of his quandary, but with Skye to do service for him as a nagging workweek temptation—sort of the human version of a floor-length goatskin coat—that Everhart went for a month or two not knowing any peace. His wife got on a jag about how their house would be too small to hold them just along about as the weather warmed and Skye shed her khaki jacket and took to tying the tails of her shirt up to air her navel as she worked. It proved to be both pierced as well and agonizingly downy and so ratcheted up that Everhart's turmoil a couple of notches more until he divided the bulk of his time between picturing his colleague naked and wondering which particular item among her assorted cutlery his wife would see fit to plunge into his chest.

If he'd had a preacher and been one of the practicing faithful, that Everhart would have consulted him or, at the very least, would have prayed. As a heathen, however, who passed his Sunday mornings watching the Hoakie's coaches show, he didn't know where exactly to turn for advice. He had a couple of buddies about he'd known pretty much since middle school, but he was obliged to figure that they'd tell him to follow his unfurled organ since that's the sort of instruction in crisis that buddies always give.

That Everhart instead elected to go on stewing for a time, and his wife hardly remarked the advancement in her husband's irritation since she was thoroughly preoccupied with her belly and her glow. For her part, Skye failed to pick up on that Everhart's mopey hints that he was more than a little smitten with her and in a state about it, so he got left alone to wonder what he'd do and how he'd do it. He took to having lunch most days at Ruth and

Glenola's café in town which made do for that Everhart as a strain of culinary mortification. He thought if he ate at the cafeteria or out at Little Earl's, where the food usually came with a smattering of flavor, he wouldn't mull his troubles like he could afford to at the café where he was assured of going largely undistracted by the cuisine.

He tended to trade off between the breaded veal cutlet and what they call barbecue which comes atop a soggy bun and looks fairly predigested, and but for Ruthie stopping by every now and again to natter at him and refill his tea, that Everhart could usually count upon getting left alone with his troubles as the other customers tended not to be of the intrusive chattering sort.

Ray would read his local paper and push his beans about his plate. The Dover brothers, who were both acutely prone to intestinal ulcerations, had found they could eat the bland café chili without any ill effects and would sit at the counter with their bowls and their slices of white bread sopping up what looked essentially like café barbecue underwater.

The customers otherwise tended to be in the throes of miscalculations. They had most of them either forgotten how bad the food was at the café—had assumed anyway that likely it had improved over time—or they'd strayed in off the interstate fueled by the faulty notion that the best local cuisine could probably be found right in the heart of town.

So the café tends to have a mausoleum serenity to recommend it along with food that's retained somehow the flavor of the boxes it came packed in. It's not, then, the sort of eating spot given to talk or helpless eructations which made it agreeable for that Everhart who had personal choices to mull and inviting, at length, for Russell the telephone man and his kidney stone.

Russell had been pitched out of the fish house and had lost his privileges at Little Earl's, so the café was about the only spot left for Russell the phone man to go, and he took to showing up daily for lunch, would have the pickleloaf sandwich and soup, and had been working the café a couple of weeks before that Everhart came. Russell had made of himself a regular imposition on the diners who were suffering without him one form or another of culinary disappointment and so hardly had need of a fellow shaking a kidney stone in their faces and acquainting them with the mystical circumstances of its discharge. Accordingly, Ray had seen fit to put Russell the telephone man on notice that the next bother he gave a customer got him pitched into the street which had served to mute Russell a bit and had managed to constipate his fervor.

Russell failed, as a consequence, to approach that Everhart straightaway but just slipped up on him over the course of a solid week at the café until he perched one day on the stool at the counter right next to that Everhart and set his celery salt jar on the Formica without getting a rise out of Ray who must have been otherwise engaged with the "Heard on the Grapevine" column.

Russell elected to wait for some sort of overture from that Everhart beside him, that Everhart whose gaze did fall upon that celery salt jar at length with the kidney stone on the bottom about the size of a spring pea.

"What is that?" he asked Russell the phone man who took up that jar and said to him, "This?"

It seems Ray had scolded Russell into something like a vampire's ethics and standards in that Russell could say what he wished about his stone only once invited to speak. So that Everhart endured the whole story and took it as timely and intriguing, shook Russell the phone man's celery salt jar and marveled over Clayton's powers, was personally at a point where he guessed he could make fit use of a prophet, could work backwards and figure out what he'd done from how his future had turned out.

That Everhart drove his Martinizing truck directly out to Clayton's and attempted to formulate and hone an apt inquiry along the way. He'd come away somehow from his conversation with Russell the telephone man thinking Clayton a manner of Appalachian swami who required that his seekers and pilgrims probe him formally for a response. So even out in Clayton's rutted drive, long after that Everhart had shut off his truck, he lingered to improve upon his query in an effort to make conspicuously plain that he was torn between a girl with a nipple ring and his wife of seven years who was fully freighted at the moment with their child. That Everhart essentially wanted to know which female he'd best choose and how hot exactly the fires of hell might be.

So he worked up his question in sundry versions and was polishing one to a sheen as a woman came charging from Clayton's house, stomped down his steps and stalked into his yard where she paused to indulge in a violent undergarment adjustment before continuing towards her ratty little Cavalier in the ditch. She was that Combs from past the airfield who occupies her time with melodramas on afternoon TV. She's a raging hypochondriac evermore prepared to believe that she has contracted whatever her favorite soap opera characters have come down with which are not even usually authentic diseases and actual complaints.

That Combs, consequently, is prone to amnesia—the intermittent temporary sort—sleeping sickness and coma, sub-Saharan parasites, and she was down once for a solid week with an intergalactic stomach virus that Dr. Lowery tried to tell her was some strain of Hong Kong bug. Dr. Lowery, in fact, had served to provoke that Combs to Clayton's house once she'd shown up at his office with a touch of river blindness which she claimed to have caught at a boat launch by the James.

An heiress on one of her TV shows who'd vacationed on the Nile had just at that time returned to her Greer's Cove mansion and lost her sight which permitted her domestic help to pilfer from her freely, and that Combs had people—blood relations mostly—she didn't want around her blind.

Dr. Lowery went in instead for sympathetic conjunctivitis and laughed that way he does with his whole big blubbery self ajiggle as he told that Combs about the only thing she'd catch in the James was carp. Straightaway, she grew indignant and went fiery on Dr. Lowery in afternoon actress fashion, apprised him she'd heard of a fellow about with the power to inform her if she, in fact, was destined to go blind.

And with that she swept out of the office and drove directly over to Clayton's as he'd by then predicted a vapor lock for that Combs's aunt by marriage. Clayton had told her anyway, "Wholesome goodness," and then not even a week thereafter—when her Corsica had bucked and sputtered and she'd wheeled it into a ditch—she'd found herself stopped beneath a billboard advertising loafbread, that brand with the shock of wheat on the bag and the child with the slice in his mouth.

That Combs's aunt by marriage had popped open her hood and, in lifting her face from the noxious updraft, she'd seen on that breadsack "Wholesome Goodness!" in letters the color of chaff.

Apparently, Clayton was on his way to his sideboard as that Combs let herself into his house, and she had heard enough to know to poke and prod him as he passed, but Clayton just climbed up the drawers and mounted that quartersawn top without remark. He took up from the mantelpiece a chunk of charred wood and improved upon the outer rim of his sketch upon the wall. She talked at him, that Combs did, acquainted him with her complaint and informed him of everything she'd done down at that James River landing, told how she'd rinsed her gritty hands off in a silty eddy, told how she might have touched her nasty fingers to her eyes.

Clayton, for his part, struck that Combs as wholly inattentive which she took for a rather poor quality in a prophet and a seer since she guessed a fellow like Clayton would be best advised to listen if he hoped to have any notion of what to predict. She told him as much, of course. Those Combses are inclined to speak their minds, not the sort given to fretting over social delicacies, so she visited upon Clayton her dire opinion of his mystical technique, and while she was at it, she complained about the general filth and stink of his house. Then she told him she felt a touch of river blindness coming on and jabbed Clayton in the thigh by way of inviting from him confirmation, but Clayton ignored her soundly enough to earn a dose of scalding wrath.

That Combs went stomping out of the house and down the steps to the rubbishy yard where she paused to resituate the silken panties she'd purchased at the recommendation of a starlet on a cable shopping show, that redhead who plays the conniving third wife of a sheet-steel mogul and often wears beneath her slicker some strain of plunging undergarment by way of an assignation uniform. As it turned out, that Combs wasn't quite built for the cut of panties that redhead had been hawking. They tended to creep and migrate on her, and we'd all of us seen her about town performing her fashion of vigorous extraction, precisely the stripe of undertaking that Everhart witnessed from his truck.

He was not, as a type, so forthright and insistent as that Combs and so tapped on the doorscreen and waited a fruitless few minutes for Clayton to answer. He could hear him inside, the wheeze and rustle of Clayton at his chimney, and he kept knocking and calling until he'd determined it seemly to go in. Clayton failed to pay that Everhart measurable notice as well, but that Everhart tolerated neglect far better than that Combs had and went about airing his inquiry pretty much like he'd composed it, though he did see cause to ornament the thing with a spontaneous enlargement or two in a bid to provide Clayton with the fullest flavor of his dilemma.

He forgot, however, to lay hands on Clayton the way Russell had advised him, and when Clayton failed to offer response, that Everhart put his query again just as Clayton made a significant mark upon his chimney stack, ground the knobby tip of his charred hunk of wood into the heart of his continent.

"Great God," Clayton said as he grimly shifted his head from side to side. "Saint Olaf," he told that Everhart. "Great God."

Now that was a little bit more in the way of oblique and unhelpful than that Everhart had bargained on, but then he'd never actually gotten prognosticated at before and didn't feel qualified to judge the worth of Clayton's talk until he'd known ample occasion to chew it over a little. So he thanked Clayton and offered him a coupon for complimentary Martinizing before returning to his truck and wheeling out the drive to travel the rest of his route.

In the course of the afternoon, that boy distilled sufficient sense from what little Clayton had suffered himself to say to prompt him to tell his wife that they would name their firstborn Olaf even before he'd shucked his uniform jacket and set his thermos in the sink. His wife was sitting at the dinette, was occupying a couple of chairs—was ponderous enough by then to have need of a brace of chairseats—and she looked up from the child-rearing book she was studying at the time to assure her husband that no child of theirs would go by the name of Olaf.

That Everhart informed her, like men will occasionally, that he'd already made up his mind which prompted his wife to snort in a way that Everhart found belittling, and they got in a shouting match that seemed condemned to yield to violence. That Everhart anyway stalked towards his wife at the dinette with his hand upraised and a sufficient glint of bloodlust in his eyes to make of himself an incendiary allurement. It seems that, early on, they were the sort of couple inclined to battle and fight as a manner, more often than not, of strenuous foreplay, so in the grip of nostalgia, that Everhart's wife threw her muumuu up over her head, slouched back in her dinette chairs and yanked her husband to her which that Everhart couldn't help but feel had been divined and foretold.

Ray had passed that boy on the road as he was coming away from Clayton's, had overheard everything the phone man had told him at Ruth and Glenola's in town and had drifted on out towards Clayton's on his afternoon tour of the county just to satisfy himself that fellow had tolerated Clayton's strain of predicting with grace. Ray found the parlor empty but for Clayton in his chair with the headgrease stain and the ruptured armrests, and Ray took note straightoff of the alteration to Clayton's sketch on the wall.

"Plant your flag, did you?" he said to Clayton who just shivered at him back, sat there in his filthy upholstered chair with his amber teeth clapping together, and he was quaking still as he reached for his sleeve of Zestas even though it was mild outside by then and Clayton's floor furnace was cranked up somewhere between simmer and fricassee.

Ray gathered up the tattered quilt that Clayton had let drop to the floor with its exposed stuffing and its hanging threads and its encrustations and stains, and he draped it over Clayton and tucked it well enough to keep it from sliding off before he drew

Clayton's arms out to free them for cracker and potted meat consumption which was along about when Clayton turned out to have a thing to say.

"Joyce and Stumpy," he told Ray. "Dale and Hank. Missy and Abilene."

"Texas?" Ray asked him, but he knew even as he spoke that it was fruitless to bother, had finally noticed how Clayton's remarks were all unbidden and unforeseen, how you couldn't get from Clayton much of anything you wanted but only instead could get just what you got.

Ray refilled Clayton's water tumbler at the kitchen sink and carried out with him a fresh sleeve of saltines to leave on Clayton's table. Clayton ignored everything Ray told him by way of leave-taking and adieu, just sat there in his filthy chair beneath his tattered quilt while Ray let himself out of the house and descended to the yard where he met a fellow and his wife fresh out of their truck in Clayton's rutted drive.

They were Sapps from down the pike. You can hardly hope to mistake a Sapp around here as they are, all of them, impossibly hairy and given to moles and chinlessness. The females have sideburns and brush mustaches. The men all sport eyebrows that meet. So Ray had no need to be acquainted with those two outright to recognize the husband for a Sapp by blood and his wife for the manner of backhollow female barren enough of personal prospects to take a Sapp for a mate.

"Hold on," Ray said and put himself between Clayton's house and those Sapps since Ray'd been around long enough to know that Sapps didn't think much of lawmen, resented authority and were down in a general fashion on people with jobs. "I don't know what you heard or where you heard it, but he can't do a thing for you." Ray jabbed a thumb in the direction of Clayton's dilapidating house as he spoke.

The husband spat by way of response. Those full-blooded Sapps are awfully prodigious spitters, and then he glanced at his wife who had dropped her gaze already to the ground. She considered the weeds and the rocks there with sufficient desolation to cause Ray to figure that she was the one who'd prompted them to come, had hoped to hear from Clayton how some thorny business might transpire or, more likely, had been keen to learn something she'd feared would happen wouldn't.

Ray dropped his jaw as if he intended to stave off those Sapps again, but that fellow forestalled him with surgical placement of a stream of saliva, shot it cleanly between Ray's oxfords so as to make Ray understand that Sapps never needed to hear a thing but once.

"Come on here," that Sapp told his wife and steered her by her sleeve back to his pickup, an old green Dodge with a quarter panel cobbled entirely out of gutter tin.

He got the thing started eventually and went sputtering out of the drive, glaring all the while at Ray until he'd passed behind a hedgerow, and Ray knew they'd motor up the road in deliberate Sapp fashion. He knew that Sapp would cuss him soundly as far as the junction at least where he'd pull off the blacktop and sit with his wife in silence on the cinders. Ray knew they'd wait for him to pass. Ray knew they would come back.

☙❧

THE DASH

Those Everharts had moved on to afterglow and butter almond ice milk by the time that Ray's shift had ended and he'd passed through his hedgerow into his yard. He had a sack in his arms from the grocery mart with a couple of tallboys in it and a frozen chicken dinner with whipped potatoes and apple crumble. Ray's bag was paper even though he'd asked for the plastic sort with handles once the Tiffany in the express lane—the one who looks like a Delores—had shoved Ray's change his way and interrogated him about his sacking. Ray was having, consequently, some trouble wrangling his groceries up his walk along with the bulk-rate rubbish he'd fished from his P.O. box and his unslung gunbelt.

So he wasn't entirely free to notice there was anything amiss until he'd all but gained the porch steps and had paused for an adjustment, permitted those catalogs slipping from his fingers to drop altogether to the ground—the one with the brushed nickel kitchen sink fixtures, the one with the shearling hammock for cats, the one with the double-stitched gusseted trousers like the Gurkhas used to wear. As Ray kicked at them, he loosed a corrosive remark and glanced up towards his dog—or up anyway towards the vacant porch planking where he had cause to think her to be.

It seems Monroe's custom was to nap afternoons on the bristly mat before Ray's front door. The thing had come with the house and was gritty and treadworn, had a couple of snow geese on it that had gotten napped over by sprigs and tufts of Monroe's discarded hair. Ray's porch faced west, and his overgrown shrubbery effectively blocked out the wind, so Monroe could take to that doormat in the shank of the day and get her balky joints roasted while she slept.

Ordinarily she'd hear Ray's Grand Marquis roll in off the road as his struts were squeaky and his tailpipe rattled where he'd hung it with grounding wire, and she'd labor to her feet and travel out to the lip of the porch planking to welcome Ray home by gazing at him in a fashion that seemed to say, "Where in the name of sweet Christ have you been?"

So Ray assumed that she'd be handy to share in his aggravation, and he had a foot on the lowermost step before he'd spied her on the mat which proved to be enough of a sight somehow to stun Ray and to stop him since he knew Monroe for a regular creature, a dog of impeccable habits, who might have been ill and vaporish but was rarely out of place.

"Hey," he said to her and then watched her stay precisely where she was with her feet stretched out before her and her snout against the sill. "Hey!" Ray shouted and was dropping already his groceries as he spoke.

He didn't rush to her straightaway but just lingered there on that lower step, glanced down towards Lyle's and then up the street towards the cow lot just above him. Ray was suffering that itch we most of us get for blessed ignorance, that nostalgia for the moment before we knew whatever we've found out.

"Hey!" he managed one time further just as he saw the clotted blood and so set about trying to bring himself to hew to the proposition that the creature before him on his bristly doormat was only, after all, a dog.

She was warm from the sun and loose still in the joints, and the blood she'd spilled on the planking was wet still where it had lapped into cuppy depressions. Ray stroked her a little, worked his arms beneath her and lifted her off the mat, spoke to her as he carried her down the steps and over to his sedan. "Come on," he said. "Let's go for a ride. Come on."

He laid her out up front because she'd never much cared for traveling the roads in the back, settled her onto her grungy beach towel with seahorses and sand dollars in the weave and left a hand to rest upon her as he wheeled up to the junction.

Doyle's wife answered the door, had plainly been expecting somebody otherwise as she was talking already before the stile had barely cleared the stop. "I can't think what in this world happened to ours unless Doyle carried it out to the . . . oh," she told Ray once she had spied him on the landing, and she passed a moment in contemplation of the creature in Ray's arms before she reached her fingers out to touch Ray's sleeve and to console him, before she turned her head and called along the front hallway for Doyle.

Ray passed in through the foyer that was still only about half hung with paper and followed Doyle back to his laundry room where they laid Monroe out on a table once Doyle had shifted it clear of bath towels and two empty price-club washsoap jugs. Doyle is, far and away, the best dead pet veterinarian we have, isn't afflicted with a callous bone in his body and has no use, as a general rule, for patronizing platitudes. So he didn't tell Ray what a glorious gift Monroe's vaporish life had been, didn't try to

suggest that it was somehow a blessing that she'd gone quickly—
that she'd been peeved and alive in the morning but mercifully
dispatched and bled out by night.

Doyle didn't, in fact, see need to tell Ray anything at all but
just made the sort of necknoise Ray was personally geared to savor, and he and Doyle passed a moment together in solemn study
of Monroe.

"She was a good girl," Ray offered at length.

"Yeah."

"Windy," he added by way of qualification.

"Oh yeah."

"But a good girl."

Doyle's wife drew up in the doorway and knew to say nothing
from there which was probably how she and Doyle had found
each other in the first place as they were given together to a similar pitch of grace.

"What happened to her?" Ray asked Doyle and then conveyed
by his expression that he'd not inquired and examined yet sufficiently to know which ordinarily would have been a little odd for
a sheriff's deputy. Ray had investigated, after all, more deaths by
misadventure than he could probably count, had seen about every
possible manner of bloody human carnage, had poked at gashes
and fractures and exit wounds with but a pencil end. He struck
Doyle, however, as squeamish where it came to his own dog, so
Doyle laid back a conspicuous clump of sticky matted fir and
pointed out to Ray the wound beneath it.

"Shot, I'd say," Doyle told him and had Ray help to turn her
over so together they could see the pulpy tear where the bullet
had punched out. "Probably pretty quick."

"She made it home." And Ray indulged in one of his winces as
he spoke, seemed to be conjuring all the trifling business that

he'd been about while his dog was dragging herself up through the yard to expire on Ray's front porch.

"Couldn't have come far," Doyle told Ray, and Ray told him back, "I know."

Then they neglected between them to speak further for about a half a minute while they digested the evidence and settled each upon the culprit, the fellow they'd both been sure had shot her once they'd seen that she'd been shot.

"Want me to talk to him?" Doyle asked.

Ray shook his head. "I'll do it."

"But not today, right? Not just now."

And when Ray nodded to allow that he would surely hold off until he'd cooled, he was even in actual earnest as best he could be, but still Ray failed to wheel his Grand Marquis up through his hedgerow and only stopped down past the cow lot once he'd gained his neighbor's yard.

Ray left Monroe on her grungy towel, straightened it up a little beneath her, and made his way through the rubbish and the rusting junk that littered that Gullick's front lawn. That Gullick comes from a long and, even for these parts, remarkably sorry line of kin. His grandfather got throttled to death one day by a fellow whose cattle he'd stolen, and that Gullick's own father had been cooked through by a jolt from a transformer while attempting to splice his house to town power without the benefit of an account.

That Gullick used to have an uncle in prison who'd shot and killed a state patrolman so as to spare himself from explaining just how he'd come by the car he was driving, and that Gullick's own sister was fully intending to poison her second husband— had mixed a box of squirrel bait into a pot of tapioca—but a spell of faulty recall and a grievous weakness for pudding had induced that woman to bag herself instead.

Ray's Gullick had been married for maybe thirty years, and the institution had served to civilize him a little. He'd attracted and wed somehow a Butner who'd come from lawful people and who'd refused to share with her husband in his sense of persecution, wasn't prepared to believe that this world had been the Gullicks' for the having until conniving sorts had come along to snatch it for themselves. Accordingly, she'd served to dampen and temper that Gullick's resentments, and she'd likely been the one to prompt her husband to pick up the yard since, once she died, the place went to rubbishy pot in a hurry.

In his widowed years, that Gullick had begun to hate again and loathe and despise and seethe and rail in place, quite apparently, of bathing. He grew cantankerous and contrary and gloriously profane, would routinely lavish abuse upon the mailman and the meter reader, once made some sort of vile display to a female census taker that she could never quite bring herself to speak in telling detail about. So he was already a bit of a problem before he started shooting cats, was one of those sorts the chief is fond of calling "independent" and dismissing as just a cranky old uplander hopelessly set in his ways.

At first that Gullick only shot those felines that happened to wander into his yard which he numbered among his unassailable rights in this great land, but then he took to shooting cats in the street and cats in the trees across the road, trees in the yard of that Gullick's unfortunate neighbor, a Dwyer from down South Boston way whose view of his own unassailable rights conflicted with that Gullick's.

They most particularly fell out once that Gullick had up and shot a calico that was sunning itself at the time on the roof of that Dwyer's refurbished Gold Duster. Miraculously, the bullet only came across that creature after passing through the windshield first, after ricocheting off the mirror stem and up through the tufted headliner. That Dwyer called the chief, and the chief sent out Larry who went about writing citations which did little to defuse that Dwyer and just set that Gullick against the police.

So by the time Ray had moved into his shabby bungalow there was a history of friction already on his street, and Ray used to walk over and iron out disputes because he was handy for it, most particularly once that Gullick had graduated from cats to dogs, had wounded anyway a hound once that had come through after a rabbit and had shot at a Schnauzer a girl from up the street had been walking on a leash at the time.

Pretty much from the beginning, Ray had been for locking that fellow up as Ray was hardly the sort to subscribe to the chief's personal theory of independence. A man equipped with both baseless festering antagonisms and a gun simply struck Ray as a threat to life and limb and civic harmony. The chief resisted Ray, though, and that Gullick never got properly hauled in, was issued a time or two citations he failed to bother to pay and got a visit once from the chief himself who bought that Gullick's bullets from him for five or six times the actual going rate which merely supplied that Gullick with funds for both fresh ordnance and malt liquor.

Mostly Ray got enlisted to talk to him, and he'd stopped by a half dozen occasions or more, would fetch up on that Gullick's front porch after word of his latest enormity and would speak to that Gullick through the rusty doorscreen that Gullick would never open. He'd just stand there glaring, would hear Ray out and inquire if he was finished, would step back into the murk of his filthy house and swing shut his paneled door.

Ray had to figure Monroe had been lured up the street by some strain of decomposition, roadkill out on the asphalt or expired vermin in the ditch. He suspected she'd probably been dining when that Gullick found her out, and Ray recalled an occasion or two Monroe had trailed him to that Gullick's, recollected the savor that Gullick had troubled himself to lavish her with.

That Gullick drew open the door and, as was his unvarying custom, dredged phlegm by way of greeting and salute. Ray had yet, as it turned out, to settle by then on just what he might say, so the pair of them stood in bald silence for a time contemplating each other until that Gullick saw fit at length to inquire of Ray sharply, "What!?"

It seems Ray was meaning to hold forth on the general topic of pets, explain to that Gullick how what he was prone to take for targets with fur were companions, more often than not, with various sterling qualities, creatures given to inspiring sufficient affection and adequate emotional attachment to mean that Gullick could just as well be shooting toddlers in the street.

Then Ray had intended, apparently, to ply that Gullick with talk of his own dog who Ray had taken in as a gangly vaporish greasy adolescent and had fed and cared for, had bathed occasionally and endured noxious gases from for what was, by then, the best part of a decade. Ray wanted that Gullick to know she'd broken a tooth on a bone in the yard, had a scar on her snout where a thorn had snagged her, a limp from a fracture she'd suffered and a little knob of flesh on her right foreleg where her dew claw had torn off.

Ray meant to tell that Gullick that she'd been fond of watermelon, had liked to sleep on her back on the settee with her legs all in the air, had detested the voice of that Richmond news anchor—the woman with the scarves and the brooches—and had poked Ray with her snout whenever she felt emphatic about a thing. Ray wanted, in short, that Gullick to know that she had been somebody to him, so he passed a moment there on that Gullick's front porch organizing just what he'd say, kept at it even a little after that Gullick had asked him "What!?" before Ray elected instead to shove his hand through that Gullick's rotten screenwire and lift that Gullick's doorhook from its eye.

That Gullick hardly had time to whine about his rights and privileges before Ray knocked him over and pretty much kicked him entirely across the room which was hardly Ray's style and not remotely his personal manner of practice. Carl, by all accounts, is the official station-house thug. He's been known to settle disputes by rendering all of the participants senseless and almost dispatched a boy who'd mouthed off at a traffic stop by tapping him, Carl insisted, on the head with his flashlight. Larry had once run a Blacksburg dentist over with his car, but Larry was off duty at the time and driving his own Ambassador coupe, and that dentist, who'd lured away Larry's wife, had irked and irritated him.

Ray, for his part, had shown himself to be cast in the mold of the chief. He was slow to peeve and could endure all manner of raw insulting talk without resorting, in most cases, to his lacquered stick or his lawman's gift for leverage. So it wouldn't quite be apt to say that Ray got touched off by that Gullick, got incensed by his glare through the screenwire or the tone of what little he'd said. It's more likely that Ray got fed up in a general sort of way by the fact that he lived in the manner of place where a fellow would shoot his dog, a fellow so callous and contrary as to never have bothered to wonder if maybe Ray might prefer his dog unshot.

That Gullick was merely a type that Ray had seen too awful much of by then—a citizen in the sorry latter-day American vein. He was staunchly opinionated and pretty exhaustively misinformed, got all of his news off the television where they'd rather be first than right and don't so much own up to mistakes anymore as rework and improve them until, in any given moment, almost anything might be true.

So that Gullick could believe whatever he wished about dogs

and the people who owned them, could mount a case from all
he'd heard on TV about the scope of his liberties, could be content that he was well within his personal rights to bear his arms
and shoot, whenever the urge came on him, most anything he
pleased. What Ray offered with the toe of his brogan was a counter-
supposition, and he contradicted that Gullick clear across his
front room and into his short back hall, made his own view
known in a fashion he felt that Gullick might understand since
even a blinkered old cuss with no conscience to plague him can't
misconstrue a throttling. A man's likely to decipher the set of
your mind while you're stomping him half to death.

Now Ray had been in the army once, was stationed out in the
wilds of Texas, and he'd managed to pick up a skill or two while
he was on the government's dime. He'd learned to type passably
well, had taken instruction from a sergeant on how best to tuck
his flat sheet so his corners didn't pucker, and Ray'd developed a
talent for stripping the skin off of russets with a jackknife. He'd
been schooled in the niceties of carburetor reconstruction and the
handling of recoil-less sniper rifles, had learned how to disarm an
assortment of anti-personnel devices, and Ray had become acquainted with a hand-to-hand technique that allowed him to render a fellow's windpipe flatter than was useful for admitting air
enough to sustain life.

Ray, as he kicked that Gullick, must have happened to recall
that he'd been trained to kill Communist insurgents with his bare
unaided hands, and he had to figure even the most committed
Maoist stooge was built pretty much on the order of an upland
Gullick. So Ray reached a little experimentally towards that Gullick's throat which essentially marked the moment of Ray's personal graduation out of the field of local law enforcement.

Though Ray would stay on for a couple of months thereafter as
a deputy, he was done in just about every way that counted once

he'd noticed that he was actively strangling the life out of a fellow which Ray had to think was hardly in the spirit of his employment. So he saw clear to turn that Gullick loose and smacked him across the face to prompt that Gullick to suck air like a newborn. Then Ray rose to his feet and eyed that Gullick squirming on the floor, a man he'd failed to dispatch but pretty readily could have which proved enough for Ray to know the time was ripe to move along.

Ray collected that Gullick's pistol off the highboy by the door, shoved the barrel of that Gullick's rifle into a knothole and crimped it over. Then he took up the box of shells that Gullick kept out to be handy and turned to tell that Gullick how with the next creature that he shot, Ray'd see clear to let him keep not breathing, but Ray had hardly started talking before he got stayed and distracted by four words in bold print on that bullet box.

Wildcat. Rimfire. Forty Grain.

Lyle noticed Ray digging the hole in his yard and came over to quiz him about it, and Ray invited him through the ditch and past the autumn-olive hedgerow since he knew Lyle for the sort who wouldn't be remotely tempted to inform him Monroe had only been a dog. Lyle's Queenie had run off and vanished probably twenty-odd years back and Lyle still troubled himself to call for her sometimes there at the edge of the woods, carried a picture of her in his billfold, kept her water bowl scrupulously full.

"Ohhh," Lyle said when he saw Monroe expired upon her towel, loosing it as if it had been wrung from him. Then he stooped and ran his hand the length of Monroe's greasy pelt, looked up at Ray and shook his head, said one time further, "Ohhh."

They swaddled her as best they could in her grungy car-seat

towel with its seahorses and its sand dollars worked into the weave, and Lyle, because he was geared that way, cited a verse or two of Scripture while Ray shoved dirt in to cover her and tamped it with his shovel blade. They put rocks on top to discourage the ghoulish scavengers about, and Ray fished a splintered picket from under the porch steps to serve as a marker which he and Lyle admired together in respectful silence for a time.

"Guess you can't leave now," Lyle said at length while considering still the grave.

Ray offered Lyle one of his sad little winces and told him, "Or can't stay."

Ray carried his shovel up onto the porch and leaned it against the clapboards, fished for his keys as he eyed his doormat clotted with dog fur. Lyle watched him into the house before he departed from Ray's yard, before he slipped through a gap in the autumn olive and crossed the ditch to the road where, on the way home, he lingered by a stand of clammy locusts and shouted up towards the wooded hillside, "Queenie! Queenie girl!"

———

We most of us heard about it, of course, and were interested in our way, not that we're widely given to Lyle's strain of tenderness. There are plenty of fellows in these parts who'd likely dispatch their own dogs if they caught them rooting through their gardens or nosing around in their trash. So chiefly we were keen on the throttling Ray had visited on that Gullick which we'd heard about indirectly from a brace of that Gullick's nephews, twin boys of that Gullick's sister who made out to be bent on revenge.

They're not bright boys, those nephews, and there's precious little about them that truly had much need of duplication. They got their looks from their daddy primarily, a homely auto-body man who died a few years back in an acetylene explosion, and

they're both of them nearly as tall as their mother who's bordering on stunted herself. So they can fit still into husky clothes in
adolescent sizes which those nephews never require much prodding to speak at length about because of all the money they save
on trousers just by being runts. Their passions run to gruesome
horror movies and that manner of video game which calls for
them to dispatch savage intergalactic assassins whose puce bodily
fluids and tissuey pulp spray gaily from their wounds.

They stay still at home in the basement bedroom that they
shared as children, live with their mother on the settlement
money the acetylene people paid and talk about businesses they
mean to start and fortunes they mean to make, talk about girls
they've seen in magazines—the airbrushed improved sort—they'd
like sometime to run across and pleasure. In the spring, when the
water is prone to get up in the creek below their house, their bedroom floods and they live for a month or two in the attic where
they mean to do pretty much everything they meant to do down-
stairs.

Naturally, those nephews share between them a native dislike
of lawmen, harbor together the common white-trash suspicion
that the police somehow serve to keep them down with their niggling commonwealth statutes and sundry civil proprieties. They
were predisposed, accordingly, to detest Ray already even before
he showed up at their uncle's and nearly choked the life out of
him, so it wasn't much of a leap for those boys to plot to bump
Ray off.

They couldn't, however, decide if they would prefer to cut Ray
or shoot him, hang him, poison him, stomp him or maybe just
blow him entirely up. They were, though, sufficiently savvy and
watched more than enough TV to know that they needed to lay a
little public relations groundwork before they dispatched Ray by
whatever method they settled on at last. So they gave Ray out as

dastardly and a danger to folks about, little more than a uniformed hoodlum with a yen for crushing windpipes and a taste for kicking civilians down the back halls of their homes. They spoke freely of the throttling Ray had seen fit to visit on their uncle without troubling themselves to touch upon the provocation for it, and those nephews allowed how it wouldn't surprise either one of them terribly much if Ray were to stave in one day soon the wrong set of ribs about and find himself on the mortal end of a spot of retribution.

Of course, we figured out what they were scheming and made it known to Ray. For a week or two it came up as a coda to heyhowdies around town. We'd trade the usual palaver with Ray— moan about the weather, complain about the Congress, air what half-digested statistics we had picked up off the news—and then, by way of parting, we'd suggest he watch himself on account of that Gullick's nephews seemed inclined to do him mischief.

It was a topic that looked to pain Ray, invariably raised from him a wince, partly because he wasn't the sort who liked his business public and partly because, we had to figure, he was saddled with regrets, wasn't equipped to thrash a man and then let himself off unchastened. As for those nephews, Ray did about them what any of us would have done which was absolutely nothing whatsoever since we all knew that they needed Ray as a source of indignation, as an ongoing local example of how this life was stacked against them which excused them for passing the bulk of their days planted on their mother's couch.

For our part, we decided Ray had more fire about him than we'd figured and given the circumstances, guessed we would have stomped that Gullick ourselves since even those fellows about who might be prone to shoot their own dogs wouldn't have taken well to that Gullick doing the job unbidden.

A few of us even got a firsthand dose of the lively forthright

Ray by happenstance in the hardware store one Saturday afternoon. We were some of us sitting around the woodstove over by
the nail bins which we do in the winter for warmth, but in the
summer—like it was then—we make use of that stove as a sheet-
steel ottoman.

Now it was along about then that Clayton had left off with
prognostications. He'd gone a week or two with nothing whatsoever to say and so was losing his luster as a local curiosity, had
probably dropped a little south of our whistling ghost you had to
sprawl in the weeds to hear since nobody much had the stomach
for standing in Clayton's squalid house just to watch him sit in
his ratty chair and shiver.

Ray came into the store with Kit, was after a porcelain fixture.
That he was irritated upon arrival is plain to us anymore, but
none of us paid much notice to Ray or gauged his mood at the
time since we were busy instead with our usual sidelong glances
over Kit by which we routinely conveyed to each other our wholesale willingness to get grievously kung fued by the likes of her. So
we were paying among us precious little heed to Ray who'd carried in for comparison's sake the broken socket from his bathroom. It had a pullchain on a rocker and threads for a single bulb,
and Kit, apparently, had fractured the works by jerking on the
cord.

As it turned out, Ray had warned her about the fixture over his
lavatory, had asked her to tug the pullcord with what tenderness
she could muster on account of that thing was not so hardy as it
had once been. Ray, you see, was not the sort to up and replace a
failing item but preferred instead to nurse it along until, at some
inconvenient moment, it finally jammed or broke or simply quit.
Then he could know both the aggravation and the nagging regret
that he'd not gotten around to fixing it beforehand.

Kit followed him back to electrical and watched Ray fish

through a heap of porcelain pullchain fixtures until he found one that suited him somehow. He held it up and, by way of demonstration, gave the chain a tug and told Kit, "Can't just yank on it," which she responded to straightoff by parting her lips and showing Ray her tongue which touched off a fresh spot of sidelong glancing among us.

Ray was almost to the counter before Russell called out to him, or spoke anyway in that voice of his that carries like a shot. "What do you figure's up with Clayton?"

Ray stopped and turned towards us. Kit eyed us a little herself.

"Not saying nothing to nobody. With a gift like that man's got, it don't hardly seem fair." Then Russell shook his celery-salt jar in a punctuational sort of way.

Ray passed a moment in contemplation of his shoetops, and we some of us figured we were in for a shrug and one of Ray's pinched winces, but once he'd lifted his head he didn't look to us in much of a wincing mood. "I'll tell you what's up with Clayton," Ray informed Russell in a tone Ray didn't oftentimes employ. "He's disappointed."

"How's that?" Russell asked him and spiced his inquiry with a calypso kidney-stone beat.

"Let's say you were going to the South Pole, going to be the first man ever to get there."

Russell let his stone fall silent. "All right," he told Ray.

"So you get on a ship and you sail all the way down to Antarctica, build a little hut on the shore and spend months dragging supplies up your route. Then the summer comes and you set off, walking. You've got ponies pulling your sleds. You're living on oatmeal and suet stew. You're sleeping in a tent at fifty below. It takes you an hour every morning just to get your boots on. Your clothes stay frozen. You're half blind from the snow."

"Ray," she said to him.

"But you walk. Every day. Eight miles. Ten miles. Twelve miles. Six miles. South you go, up the shelf from the coast and into the mountains, through a pass atop a glacier. One by one, you shoot your ponies. Butcher them. Throw nuggets into your stew. Chew raw chunks as you walk, dragging your own sled now, harnessed up like a mule."

"Ray."

"You reach the polar plateau. Ten thousand feet. You're sick from the altitude. From the cold. From thirst. From hunger. But you walk. And walk. And walk some more. A thousand miles altogether just to stand on a spot of this earth where no man has stood. And then you see it, miles away yet, but you see it. A stick plunged into the ice. A flag in the breeze. Scarlet and blue. Saint Olaf's cross."

"Come on," she said and even tugged at him but with likely less force than she'd seen fit to use on his light pull.

"After all that, you're beaten and by a month at most. Second to a Norwegian with dogs and skis and luck, you think. In his route. In his weather. More luck than you—weak, sick, cold and with a thousand miles yet to go. How do you think *you'd* feel?" Ray said to Russell who glanced about at the pack of us there before grinning at Ray, before telling him, "Disappointed?"

"Leave Clayton alone, why don't you," Ray advised Russell the phone man who snorted with laughter and informed Ray that Clayton had never been south of Lynchburg, and Russell shook, as was his custom, his celery-salt jar for emphasis as he spoke which Ray elected to take for a provocation.

Ray grabbed it from Russell and pitched the thing—that Dunn woman would have called it—across the breadth of the store towards the garden implements hanging on the far wall where it struck the blade of a posthole digger and shattered into slivers.

Russell groaned and grunted like a man rendered breathless by grief and then shot from his chair and dashed off to hunt up his precious stone while Kit told Ray, "Come on, now," and managed to lead Ray past the jackknife rack and the dowel carousel and up along to the checkout counter proper.

"He ain't talking to you either, is he?" Russell shouted towards Ray from his hands and knees in among his spice jar leavings, and Kit had herded Ray fully out the door and into the hardware store lot by the time Russell called out, "Find her now, why don't you."

———

We knew he'd been looking, authentically searching, out touring in his car and not just visiting Homer Blaine State Park to wander down along the trailhead and ruminate in the trees. Ray had decided somehow that child had been snatched away to orchard country, claimed to have come by a sense that she'd been carried off from the lot in that van, the one that had been green if it had not been blue instead with the urinating husband and the wife off in the woods. Ray felt anymore she was alive still and told as much to Kit who had grace enough to let him merely feel it.

So they'd ride weekends, Ray and Kit, south into apple country seeking out Winesaps and Mutsus, orchards with children about—Joyce and Stumpy. Dale and Hank. Missy and Abilene. And they didn't tour haphazardly with just Ray's pitch of certitude to guide them but with routes and recommendations from those Meechams up the pike who mounted yearly pilfering forays into apple country.

They were three-season plunderers, those Meechams were, and industrious for trash. They stole berries from a fellow down in the valley come the shank of spring, would descend upon his fields in the dark of the moon with their empty joint-compound buckets and creep through all of his berry patches picking his bushes nearly clean. He had strawberries and boysenberries and black and blue berries both, even a little raspberry hedge up by his tractor shed where it was sheltered from wind and frigid mists but vulnerable still to Meechams.

Of course, those Meechams had their neighbor's nectarines in the height of summer and peaches they stole from groves down in the sheltered hollows nearby along with what produce they could spirit off of garden plots or fish out of the Dumpster behind the grocery mart in town. In the fall of the year, they featured apples almost exclusively in addition to what trinkets they'd shoplifted from the Rexall, and those Meechams liked to offer more than yellow or red Delicious which is just about all that orchard keepers grow up in these parts.

Accordingly, those Meechams would load up a couple of evenings a week in their truck and drive south down the Lynchburg Pike to where the groves are far more plentiful and the varieties of apples run towards the exotic. They could gather up Empires and Granny Smiths, Fujis and Northern Spies, Mutsus, two kinds of McIntosh and three different strains of Winesaps. Those Meechams would sift through the orchards collecting fruit in old feed sacks or, if the trees had been picked already, they'd pay a visit to the cold house where they'd make off with an orchard box or two.

So they'd dropped by probably all of the apple orchards down the pike and had lurked enough around most of the orchard keepers' houses to have a sense of whose yards were littered with toys and evidence of wee ones and whose yards instead were only littered with rusting adult junk. Ray was fairly shrewd, then, to see clear to consult those thieving Meechams, drove out to pick up a peck of freestone peaches at their produce stand and engaged a couple of specimens there in general talk of apples which Ray managed to steer and focus until he'd come around to Mutsus that Ray made out to fairly dote on when he snacked. He made mention as well of Winesaps that he claimed to favor for baking and wondered of those Meechams manning that stand what sort of land precisely a man might need to grow a healthy blended grove of Mutsus and of Winesaps both together.

That pair of Meechams, like Meechams will, contested with each other straightaway as they both of them had experience enough in plundering orchard fruit to have developed decided preferences as to blossom set and globe. One of them insisted that Mutsus most particularly liked a crease, a little fold of ground where the frost might lay but the wind was blocked and shunted which ran counter to the opinion of that Meecham's thieving colleague who was prepared to allow that, while Winesaps might be improved by a hollow, your Mutsus preferred the upflung brow of a hill.

As they were loath to reconcile their views or brook much contradiction those Meechams indulged together in a spot of blistering profanation that seemed pretty much guaranteed to erode into blows. Consequently, Ray stepped in to quiz those Meechams on sundry orchards they had seen, groves with maybe Mutsus and Winesaps growing both together which those Meechams saw fit to temper their blaspheming and mull about, and shortly they both recollected a place out along the banks of the James though they couldn't agree as to where exactly or how precisely to get there.

"Eighty acres maybe," one of them proposed, but the other cut it in half and seemed to recall the orchard keeper's house was brick and squat and boxy which his cousin contradicted with a snort.

So they disputed and swore and insulted each other until they'd more or less agreed there'd been some manner of barn all

caved in and overgrown with climbing roses and a couple of tractor carcasses tumbled together into a ditch.

"House was yellow," that Meecham offered, the one who'd
dredged phlegm over brick.

"Right," his cousin allowed and nodded. "Them people on the
James. The ones with the chickens. The ones with the three-
legged dog."

The other Meecham jerked his head and snorted again but con-
vivially this time while Ray, for his part, inquired of those
Meechams, "What people exactly and where?" Ray had reasoned,
you see, that folks in these parts—given the general set of their
minds—were likely to call most three-legged yard pets "Stumpy."

Even still, he couldn't find that orchard straightaway due to
discord among Meechams. Ray and Kit toured one weekend a
healthy run of territory along the James and came across countless
cattle farms and a few refurbished estates, the sort with painted
plank fencing and horses by way of cosmetics. They failed, however, to run across even the first grove of fruit trees, so Ray went
back to that Meecham stand and interviewed fresh Meechams
who proved equipped to relocate for Ray the orchard with the
three-legged dog.

They shifted it down off Bent Creek near the Buckingham
slate quarry—that orchard, they allowed, with the yellow house
and the tractors in the ditch. Ray even came across a Meecham
who drew up a pantleg for him and showed to Ray the scar he'd
gotten from a run-in with that dog.

"Wouldn't think he could run much," that Meecham suggested as he rolled his pantleg down. Then him and his crew of
relations about all shook their heads and spat, and the unbit
Meechams permitted the bit one to say, "Could goddamn fly."

It was a Friday when they found her, and they'd been listening to her mother on the radio. Kit had strayed across her while she was tuning up the dial and had loosed the knob and sat back so that she and Ray together might soak in a spot of lively syndicated vitriol. That Dunn woman was in the throes of a dudgeon over a White House aide who'd been discovered in the embrace of a starlet. She was the daughter of a fellow who'd played a cowboy on TV—the one with the chintz eyepatch and the engraved derringer up his sleeve—and she specialized in shucking her blouse and parading around in just her panties while some homicidal mutant or another watched her through her closet louvers.

She was almost invariably reaching in for her robe when she'd get killed.

Now it seems that starlet had grown agitated over mollusks, some West Coast strain of the creature threatened by an ilk of toxin at docks in a harbor where, most particularly, Liberian freighters called. Those mollusks, apparently, were tainted and failing, and the mollusk gatherers were suffering along with that starlet's personal kaiseki chef who couldn't find hale ones to serve. Since, aside from silicone and collagen, that starlet was deeply opposed to impurities, she spoke out about the Liberian toxic threat to those harbor mollusks, held a press conference on a knobby bluff above the water which attracted authentic newspeople who squandered actual videotape.

Shortly she'd made of herself on the magazine shows a manner of mollusk spokesmodel and had improved her general standing by seeming to have a worldly concern to the extent that she got interviewed on public television by their homely correspondent with the wandering eye and the acne pocks who most usually extracts nonresponsive palaver from scholars and diplomats.

That starlet even got called in for a session before Congress, sat between her lawyer and her martial arts instructor and read a prepared statement in a modest high-cut frock that covered her tattoos almost entirely. She came out in stout opposition to toxins, recommended legislation and didn't seem to have much earthly notion of where Liberia was.

The trouble started for her at the state dinner she attended that same night where she chatted up some senators, met a trio of marquises and a swarthy little prime minister with palm oil in his hair before she went off with an aide on a personally guided White House tour. He was the aide with the bangs and the dimples and the ready gift for mendacity which is likely as not to pass anymore for charm, and he squired that starlet down a vaulted West Wing corridor where great men, he told her, had struggled with thorny crises of their times.

He pointed out the spot where Reagan had finalized invasion plans and had signed off on the storming of Grenada, showed her the windowsill Nixon had perched on while deciding to resign, the huntboard where Khrushchev and Kennedy had shared some claret and a cheese log. He indicated the doorway to the room where Truman had retired for prayer after giving the order to drop the atomic bomb.

Then he led her up to a table in a shallow alcove off that hall, an ancient thing with stout legs and a distressed mahogany top where Lincoln had signed, he told her, the Emancipation Proclamation which jolted and stirred that starlet in a profound sort of way since Lincoln was on the folding money she employed for tipping valets and so was known to her as some strain of politician.

Something about being in a White House corridor steeped in history in the company of that aide with the bangs and the dimples and the knack for prevarication prompted that starlet to forget for a moment her mollusk obligations and the sober selfless purpose of her trip out from the coast. She became instead a creature titillated by the fact that a fellow who knew the president and spoke with him probably daily had, while pointing out a bust of Hoover, laid his hand upon her thigh. He'd then backed her into the alcove with the Emancipation table and lifted her onto the mahogany top as he probed her ear channel with his tongue.

So she had ample incentive to forget her proper purpose in D.C. since that aide was cute and powerful and that girl was slightly tipsy on a combination of vintage sparkling wine and her customary amphetamine. She permitted, consequently, that fellow to pretty much peel her gown off of her, and he worked his way down her torso lavishing praise on her sundry parts, had just in fact given her navel stud a tug between his teeth and was shoving his fingers under the band of her panties when the young son of a senator's chief of staff wandered into that White House hallway looking, he told it later, for the gentlemen's lavatory which hardly explained how he happened to have his disposable camera in hand.

Fortunately for him, his mother had bought him the model with the flash, so he proved able to illuminate that darkened hallway alcove where, by the time he snapped his picture, that largely uncloaked starlet looked to be trying to crush that aide's skull with her thighs like a pecan. As snapshots go, it was a fine one, was well framed and highly detailed and just the sort of picture that, back twenty years ago, a boy might have kept in his drawer for evenings when his parents were out. But that modern-day son of a senator's chief of staff contacted a lawyer who negotiated terms for that picture with news outlets all over the world, and though things were at first a little rocky for that aide and for that starlet, it was the mollusks probably that suffered the most in the end.

The president's detractors tried to let on that they were scandalized by that chief of staff's son's exposure to such debauchery in the White House, and they went about wringing their hands over that child's compromised innocence, but it turned out he was appreciably more of a hellion than a cherub, the sort of kid who probably watched the Satin Channel through the snow and was as degraded as some adults are only shorter.

That White House aide, for his part, insisted that he'd been in France and was not anyway the sort to swab a starlet in an alcove since he was fairly completely convinced that he was maybe a little bit gay. He made that disclosure in the White House briefing room with a touch of moist indignation and then made it again on a Sunday morning tour of the network political shows. He let on to be stung and offended and managed it with such mendacious flair that the hosts let him hold forth on tax incentives with hardly an interruption.

That starlet, of course, appeared nude in a national magazine, was featured on the cover with her private parts obscured by assorted mollusks, and she began to go unbutchered in the movie roles she took, played usually the type of girl the leading man saw fit to romance before the leading lady had come into his life. So instead of getting murdered that starlet anymore got dumped and humiliated while the mollusks in the harbor enjoyed untempered Liberian toxin baths.

Now most of us did little more than shake our heads over this sort of business, came across it in the paper and on the TV and aired our opinions about it. We men invariably figured that, were we feeling mildly gay, we could get reoriented by a creature like that starlet while the women were prone to catalog those portions of her person that failed to impress them as unimproved and real.

We didn't elect to detest them and revile what they had done, couldn't see fit to condemn the president for his associate's indiscretion or get much wrought up over the flagging moral standards of the nation since we all of us knew, the men anyway, that given the occasion and a suitable piece of furniture Lincoln had signed virtually anything on we surely would have had a go at that starlet ourselves.

On those TV channels, however, where the programming consists of people haranguing each other over thorny social issues and hotly debating the specious depravity of contending political views, they chewed on this matter of the aide and starlet long after we'd let it drop, but even they'd moved on before the radio hosts could turn it entirely loose, folks like that Dunn who with her special knack for bilious resentment kept her listeners agitated to a fairly corrosive pitch.

While she could be cloying and presentable on morning television, that Dunn was at her incendiary best on syndicated radio, and, as they scoured about for that orchard with the tractors in the ditch and the ill-humored three-legged canine with four-legged velocity, Ray and Kit listened to that Dunn tolerate comments from her callers who couldn't say much she didn't see clear to augment and improve.

As radio audiences go, hers sounded the "independent" sort, vinegary and wholly unencumbered by actual facts, and they proved keen to join with that Dunn in her assorted condemnations, detested with her that presidential aide who was maybe a little bit gay, dismissed that starlet as a surgically augmented mollusk hugger, and proved prepared to think them guilty both of wanton bigotry for having indulged their sexual appetites in the selfsame mahogany spot where Lincoln had inked his name to free the slaves.

Then they all got to moan together, led and directed by that Dunn, over the sorry moral erosion and liberal softening of our nation, a state of affairs that had served to bring such as that starlet into the White House where only God-fearing and unaugmented patriots belonged. The whole episode functioned as a further disappointment for that Dunn whose practice it was to claim to have been rendered wise by suffering as she'd lost, after all, a child and a mate and had sold off a family farm which she liked to say had hardened her when it came to human interaction, had given her license to be indelicate and traffic in unvarnished truths.

So she lapsed into what she usually lapsed into on her radio show—a pageant, that is, of unbridled excoriation with that aide and that starlet and our morally flaccid president to launch her and all manner of offenses against good sense to fuel her along her way. That Dunn spoke with no trace much of delicacy, was scaldingly blunt and impolite which she was permitted because of her travails and stinging disappointments and never because, Ray noticed, she was simply the sort of creature likely to hurl a chunk of cabbage as a conversational gambit and knock a produce man unconscious over a shortage of frisée.

We figure anymore that, by that time, Ray detested the woman outright, surely in part on account of her politics but largely due to her claim that her brace of personal tragedies had translated for her somehow into something other than nagging static grief. Ray, after all, had lost a child of his own, had lost a mate as well in a fashion, and he was afflicted still with the pitch of anguish he'd known right from the start, had failed to be rendered anything much but rootless and unsettled which had led in its way to dogless and so, but for Kit, adrift. So Ray got reminded why he was down on that Dunn as they traveled through orchard country looking for a couple of rusting tractors heaped up in a ditch which Kit spied essentially where those Meechams had promised they would be, and there was even a three-legged terrier peeing on one at the time.

The place didn't look terribly prosperous as working orchards go. The trees were a bit dry and bug-eaten, the orchard grass was high, and the yard around that frame house had run to hardpan chiefly but for the flowerbeds up by the footings which featured assorted leggy weeds. Ray and Kit were hardly out of the car before they heard the children and had attracted the rigorous notice of that short-haired three-legged dog who orbited the pair of them headlong as he snarled and barked and kept at it even after a fellow had wandered out of one of the sheds with a corroded sprayer nozzle in hand and pouch chew juice to spit.

He let go a stream. He dabbed himself. He told that dog, "Shut up!"

Ray had his khakis on, his badge, his tarnished bright brass name tag, and Kit hadn't changed out of her green twill Park Service shirt and pants which, doubtless, caused the pair of them to look like trouble to that fellow who wasn't straightoff so jolly and helpful as otherwise he might have been.

Ray plied the man with pleasantries in as much as he was equipped to, told him anyway, " 'Lo," and mounted a bid to smile and nod agreeably, and Ray was even on the verge of inquiring of that gentleman what his canine's name might be, had joined Kit in watching it bark and snarl and race flat out around them, when that fellow took a rock up and shouted, "For shit's sake, Stumpy, shut up!"

That dog just ran a little faster and barked a little louder. That rock missed him by eight feet.

Before Ray could even ask that gentleman after a little blonde girl child, a whole pack of children scampered around the house and into view—a trio, as it turned out, from the neighbor's orchard up the way along with the four that fellow and his wife were raising on their own. They were laughing and screaming, the most of them, and served as lively bait for the dog who chased them across the hardpacked yard and into the orchard proper— the four boys in their filthy dungarees and their nasty shirts, the three girls behind them each in a proper jumper. Two brunettes, Ray noticed, one of them wholly toothless in the front, and a blonde girl who didn't chatter like the others were chattering, who didn't shout the way they shouted as they ran.

That fellow with the nozzle and the burly chew turned partway towards the house and called out, "Joyce!" which served to bring a woman to the doorscreen, a thick woman in a housecoat and a pair of fuzzy mules who considered dully Ray and Kit, who asked her husband, "What?"

Ray was dodgy with her once she'd come into the yard, let on that him and Kit were working some strain of niggling civil matter and had a few harmless questions that they needed clearing up.

"Is your dog licensed?" Ray asked and while that woman was glaring at her husband by way of reminding him how she'd tried to send him to the hardware for the tag, Ray glanced out through the orchard and set to quizzing her on the children—the boys who turned out to be the neighbor's, the boy who turned out to be hers along with the two little dark-headed girls who proved to be twin sisters. That woman opened her robe and lifted her top to show Ray where they'd been pulled out.

"Cut me wide open." She glared at her husband as if he'd wielded the knife.

"And the blonde one?" Ray asked.

"My sister's girl," Joyce told him as she cinched her housecoat shut.

"Is your sister around? Think I could talk to her?"

"You can try."

She led Ray and Kit off between the house and the rickety shed her husband had come from, left him in the yard with his rusty nozzle and told him to watch the kids which freed her to march Ray and Kit out across the back of the lot and up through an

231

overgrown pasture to a knob that was planted with cedars which were all of them corralled inside an unsightly chain-link fence.

Kit noticed the headstones before Ray saw them and pointed one out to Ray, a cross of granite that was stained and weathered and a little ice-pocked in its creases. Next to it a stone had pitched full over where the ground had given way, and the lamb of Christ draped along the top of the marker just down from it had suffered an ear to drop off and a leg to break at the haunch.

Joyce fixed herself before she swung open the gate and entered the graveyard, laid flat anyway the lapels of her housecoat and ran a hand once or twice through her hair in the best show she could muster, Ray figured, of respect and reverence for the dead.

The newer markers, some of them, had pictures on them in keeping with local custom, photographs that had been reproduced on oval enameled plaques and were affixed to the headstones in shallow ornamented recesses. They weren't any of them proper portraits but only casual snapshots instead of elderly men and women chiefly enjoying their golden years—standing in ill-fitting suits in their front rooms, plopped on their settees with their cats.

Joyce's sister's stone was plain and low and about the size of a shoe box, was polished and engraved on top and rough hewn on the sides. Lois, her name had been, and she had passed at thirty-six.

"Awful young," Ray said. "Sick?"

Joyce nodded after a fashion, not like Lois had been diseased and incurably afflicted but a little more vaguely ill. "She used to get these headaches," Joyce told Ray and drummed on her forehead with her fingerend. "Took one night her medicine all at once."

"Sorry," Ray told her and then wondered of Joyce if her sister had seen fit to wed which prompted that woman to wag her head and snort.

"Randy," she told him and visited on Ray an utterly curdled expression.

"He around?"

She shook her head. "Took off. Might be any Goddamn where." Joyce then considered Ray and Kit baldly and at length so as to cause them both to know that they were being contemplated. "I thought you come about the dog."

From there upon that hilltop, Ray looked out across the orchard to where that pack of children was playing among the trees. He pointed towards the blonde one. "Missy?" he said.

"Woman from the county sent you, didn't she?"

Ray didn't say she hadn't.

"Like I told her, she'll talk when she talks. They all do. She don't need any help from them. Hell, if I'd gotten shipped clear from Russia as hardly more than a baby girl, I might be a little stoppered up myself."

"Russia?" Kit asked her.

Joyce nodded. "Somewhere over there." She turned to join Ray, gazed out over the orchard a little herself. "No telling where that child would be but for Lois. No telling."

And Ray and Kit neither one chimed in to offer contradiction.

Kit loitered by the shed with Joyce and her husband while Ray ventured into the orchard, passed up a row and crossed to the spot where the children were playing between gnarled trees. They were all of them squatted together jabbing branches into the grass in a bid to turn up bugs to fling at each other. Once Ray had hunkered down among them on his shoeheels and asked them what they were about, the charm of the enterprise seemed to drain away, and those boys and those girls jumped up and scur-

ried through the orchard grass but for that Dunn's child who occupied herself in study of a leaf.

Nobody can say exactly when Ray decided what he'd do. He
watched that child run her finger along the veins and down the
stem of her leaf, glanced every now and again towards that three-
legged dog that was ranging swiftly about them, orbiting in
upon Ray and that girl and grumbling in its throat.

"Pretty," Ray said to her, pointing towards her leaf. "Angela,"
he added, and that girl lifted her head and looked upon him but
not in such a way to suggest he'd told her anything that meant
much to her at all.

She reached out her hand and offered Ray her leaf, and he held
on to her fingers as he took it which must, somehow, have been
sufficient for Ray to satisfy him, Ray who'd lost a child of his own
through some strain of careless neglect and now had found one by
way of Clayton's ilk of upland mysticism and devoted persever-
ance on his own part. Ray was just the sort who could appreciate
the balance of the thing which was probably why he turned her
loose and chose to let her go.

She ran off across the orchard, but that terrier stayed behind to
close on Ray, hobbled towards him and proved ungainly when he
walked. He sniffed Ray's trousers, reared up and poked Ray
firmly with his snout.

"Hey!" Ray shouted down across the orchard towards that
hovel of a shed where Kit and Joyce and Joyce's husband stood together on the hardpan. "What'll you take for this dog?"

Kit watched Joyce and her husband exchange the strain of
glances that suggested they weren't between them terribly tender
about pets. Joyce's husband spat and scratched his temple with
his rusty nozzle. He drew in breath enough to serve him and
yelled back, "What have you got?"

The way we figure it anymore, it was along about then that Clayton slipped away. He was in the company of a fellow who'd driven all the way down from Caledonia in hopes of a prognostication, a Brewer who'd come by some money from the estate of an aunt who'd died and who'd decided to enlist Clayton to help him sort through investment options.

That fellow had gotten from a boy he knew a faulty impression of Clayton's talents, had been led to understand that Clayton was a regular sort of seer but far more penetrating and reliable than that palmist on 29 who burned sandalwood incense, claimed to have a Gypsy in her woodpile and treated most everybody's life line as if it were Methuselah's own.

That Brewer had a buddy who was starting up a business, was planning to market a miracle snoring elixir on line, a concoction his wife had cooked up in a saucepan in their kitchen, nose drops she'd made from tea and mint and mustard oil and scallions that had cured her husband entirely of his tendency to snore. That Brewer's buddy laid the success of the stuff to capillary action which served to open nasal byways to near twice their normal girth and so made them more inviting for respiration.

Now that buddy had need of capital to market his elixir, and he'd visited on that Brewer his rather delirious business plan which charted the fabulous growth of his miracle snoring elixir company that he intended to take public in little more than two years' time. As a charter investor, that Brewer was promised a trip to the stock exchange, and his buddy seemed half inclined to let that Brewer ring the bell.

That Brewer's wife was campaigning instead for a certificate of deposit that would grow and compound and make at length for a healthy college fund by the time their five-year-old had graduated high school—that Brewer's son and namesake who that Brewer felt persuaded would be enrolled on a football scholarship instead. That Brewer, apparently, accounted himself a bit of a seer as well.

So he wasn't torn exactly by the time he sought out Clayton but was looking instead for miracle snoring elixir confirmation, any suggestion on Clayton's part that nose drops were the way to go which that Brewer was prepared to construe as apt counsel and advice. He allowed in time that he was a little put off by the squalor. At least that palmist on 29 was fragrant and agreeably neat, but Clayton was sitting there glumly in his nasty clothes in his greasy upholstered chair in a room that, but for the grit and dust, was pretty nearly vacant.

Being from all the way up in Caledonia, that Brewer had yet to learn that Clayton had left off with prognostications, didn't even know that Clayton was the sort of grubby upland mystic a fellow wouldn't hear from anyway if Clayton never got handled and touched. That Brewer just stood there and talked to Clayton from the opposite side of his doorscreen, only worked up the temerity to step into the house at length where he repeated pretty much everything he'd intoned through the screenwire, told Clayton all about his investment dilemma with the same effect he'd produced from outside.

Clayton failed to do that Brewer even the courtesy to nod and instead rose from his chair and stepped to the hearth where he climbed onto his sideboard, and that Brewer endeavored to take instruction from the mark Clayton made on the wall.

Clayton dropped his chunk of charred wood back onto the mantel. He told that Brewer, "I'm going outside and may be some time."

Then he climbed back down and crossed the parlor, passed into the kitchen where that Brewer heard him wrangle open the swollen paneled door.

"Hey mister," he shouted, but Clayton didn't trouble himself to answer, walked up across the back lot and out across a brambly field to where it yielded to the woods. Without pausing or turning or glancing back in response to that Brewer's shout, Clayton stepped into the leafy forest proper and disappeared.

That Brewer waited for probably half an hour to see if he'd come back and presently got joined in Clayton's front room by Russell the telephone man who'd stopped off to see if Clayton had taken up with talk again.

"Where'd he go?" Russell asked that Brewer who walked him to the kitchen door and pointed out across the property to the scrubby woodland border.

"Said he'd be a while."

They stood there together the pair of them in silence for a time until that Brewer decided he might improve the wait with an inquiry and so nudged Russell to gain his notice.

"Snore much?" that Brewer asked.

⁂

GLORY

We had to learn how to tell it, how to milk the whole business for proper dramatic effect which proved, where it came to Clayton, largely a matter of omission. We don't, that is to say, much dwell upon the life that Clayton led before the morning of his transformation in the grocery mart, aren't inclined to dredge up Clayton's satellite enthusiasms, speak of what trash he came from especially on his mother's side or make even passing mention of the dustups that he knew back before—there in the presence of our most appropriate Tiffany—Clayton got somehow entirely overhauled.

Naturally, in the telling we improve upon Clayton's talents and make him out to be more useful to us than he ever was. We let on that Clayton healed a couple of fellows of their complaints and foretold events in such a way as to prevent some of us from having the sorts of misadventures that we otherwise might have had. It's when we get to the story, however, of Clayton's disappearance that, as prattlers, we are prone to shine and excel, especially those among us who've boned up on the history of the thing—dug out *National Geographic*s from our attics and garages and so can spice our chatter with the odd authentic fact.

As runs of country go, this place is haunted territory. They've got Jefferson and all of his leavings off to the east towards Charlottesville. West of here in the valley are groves where Ashby and Stuart rode and fought, shade trees where General Jackson paused to pray and eat his lemons. Aside, though, from our whistling ghost of a miner in a weedy hole in the ground, we were a little short of attractions here on the ridge, had just our sweeping panoramas and cool upland summer air until Clayton introduced us to Antarctic exploration which we like to think makes us worldlier than the lowland natives about.

We've gotten, most of us, to where we can give a pretty full accounting of exactly what became of the Titus Clayton thought he was. We'll haul folks out to Clayton's house to stand before his chimney stack, draw maps of our own on napkins at the café or at home and wonder of whoever we've managed to rope into a dissertation what they know of the race for the South Pole, of Amundsen, of Scott.

We acquaint them with the particulars. "Nineteen and eleven," we tell them, back before anybody had troubled himself to get to the South Pole yet. Then we point out on the chimney or on our dinner napkins where the Norwegians set out from with their dog teams, with their skis and savvy—the spot where Scott and his men departed with their ponies and their sleds.

"A thousand miles in," we tell them. "A thousand miles back." Ice. Wind. Cold. Eating the dogs. Eating the ponies. Starving, as it turned out, anyway.

It's proven a wonderful story to tell, stark and simple, unambiguous at heart. The Norwegians, with their skis and dogs, got back before they died. The Brits, in harness and walking, died before they could get back. From cold. From scurvy. From the galling sight of the planted Norwegian flag. They found the most of them in their tent come spring, brittle and frosted through, but for Titus Oates who'd seen fit to stray into a blizzard.

"I'm going outside," he'd told his mates, "and I may be a while."

Then we reveal how Clayton said the same thing to a boy, a fellow come all the way from Caledonia for snoring elixir advice which provides us usually with apt occasion to pause for eerie effect before we add how, just like with that Titus, we've yet to turn up Clayton. And for very nearly an entire year that was even actually true.

We'd looked for him, of course. Russell had raised the alarm at the station house once he'd pumped that boy from Caledonia for the particulars of Clayton's route after he'd taken his leave and stepped into the yard. Ray organized us, naturally, and had us sweep up through the woods and clean over the ridge and out through the hollows and into the National Forest where there was hardly any end of woodland for Clayton to wander through.

We found the carcass of a black bear, killed a pair of beefy rattlers, pulled ticks off each other and ate untold gnats but failed to turn up Clayton. As this is a piece of the world that tends to be more forest than not, we couldn't do much but wander about and shout out Clayton's name and hope that he knew he'd gone astray and wanted to be discovered. After a month, however, there hardly seemed much point in looking anymore, and we all told each other—by way of collective absolution—that Clayton would either turn up or he wouldn't.

Even Ray wore out at last, though we'd see him for a time out in the reaches of Clayton's back lot on the fringes of Clayton's woods not shouting or searching or doing really anything much at all but just standing the way he used to stand in Homer Blaine State Park, down by the springhead off of the trail in the unsettling half light.

The chief is equipped with a fairly reliable sense about people and had been keyed in on Ray ever since that Gullick shot his dog. So it couldn't have been much of a surprise to the chief when Ray stepped into his office there in the middle of a shift one afternoon.

The way we heard it, Ray just stood there, looked to be conjuring what to say and finally could only manage to pluck his badge off of his shirt. He studied the thing on his palm for a moment and looked still passably lost for words, so the chief did what he could to help Ray along, asked of him, "Had enough?"

Ray hadn't brought anything much with him which meant there was precious little to move. The furniture and dishes had come with his rental house, and Ray was severely knickknack deficient, so he just had his service revolver and belt, some clothes, a few pairs of shoes. Kit helped him pack in as much as there was any packing to do, and Doyle and his wife sent the pair of them off with a festive dinner at their house which was about all the leave-taking Ray saw fit to partake of and conduct. He didn't tell even the postmaster just where he might be going, and we figure anymore it could have been that he didn't actually know.

Ray's house got let out straightaway to a family of untempered trash that had escaped somehow from the trailerpark down on the branch below the quarry, but they defaulted on the rent and junked up the yard and got evicted by main force which opened the way for a batch of fresh tenants who proved only marginally shiftless—threw windowscreens onto the shingled roof and let the grass grow up knee-high. So the place was a bit of an eyesore but for that corner of the lot where Lyle had taken upon himself the chore of tending to the gravesite. He kept the grass trimmed and installed at his own expense an engraved granite marker, put up galvanized staubs at the four plot corners that he joined with chain-link swags.

We noticed in time that Lyle didn't call for Queenie much anymore, didn't stand in the ditch and shout up into the woods in a bid to raise her on account of he'd assumed the lasting care of Ray's greasy vaporish mongrel, a dog that Lyle could cross the road and be sure he could find.

A fellow out hunting came across Clayton a year or so after he'd vanished, and even still he failed to report it straightaway on account of how he was both out of season and hunting on federal land which he had to think Larry, in particular, would frown upon and cite him about. So he told a buddy who told a cousin who told a neighbor of his who felt himself far enough removed from the original transgression to drop by the station house and tell Carl, as it turned out, where he'd come by word that Clayton's carcass was.

And it was just a carcass with bones poking through and teeth and tufts of hair, little bits of flannel and scraps of twill and dried out brogan leather. The thing was facedown in the leaves and so well entwined with brambles that they had to take Clayton apart before they could get him entirely loose. He was almost out of the county, had apparently walked the full breadth of it before he'd finally laid down on the forest floor to expire.

They brought a doctor out to look at him, a pediatrician from the office park who pronounces for the county, and he poked at Clayton a little with a length of hickory branch until the chief had squatted beside him and had asked him, "How'd he pass?"

"What are you hoping for?"

The chief looked around at nothing but hardwoods as far as he could see. They were a good mile and a half off of the nearest road. "Quit maybe," the chief suggested. "Went as far as he cared to go."

"Fine then," that doctor said as he flung his branch aside and stood.

Clayton's people, most especially those trashy relations on his mother's side, set about quarreling straightaway over Clayton's meager holdings, and they detested each other enough to ensure that they'd never sell his place since nobody could agree who'd get which portion of the proceeds. So we were left with the house and the chimney stack with its continent upon it, the scrubby little treeline that Clayton had crossed his field to slip into, and, by way of editorial discretion, we chose to omit Clayton's carcass along with the visit, apparently, Ray saw fit to pay where Clayton fell.

He probably heard they'd found him from Doyle or read about it in the Richmond paper where Clayton had rated a dozen lines beneath the story of an Afton roadhouse tiff. Nobody saw him but Grover, and Ray had visited by then the woods, had hiked in probably to stand there with his various nagging regrets as near to where Clayton had fallen as he could get without a guide.

Rain had started in by the time Ray had gained the pike which was why he'd troubled himself to stop for Grover. He pulled off into the cinders, folded Grover's lawn chair and packed it into his trunk, settled Grover onto the backseat and drove him down to his mother's house, a ten-minute trip that permitted Grover occasion to place Ray at last.

"I knew you," he said to Ray as they wheeled into the drive. "You was the law around here or something. Wasn't that you?"

Ray fished Grover's lawn chair out of the trunk, helped Grover out of the car and squired him up under his mother's porch awning where Ray rapped on the stormdoor rail. We like to think anymore Ray visited on Grover his sad little wince of a grin as he nodded and told him, "Yes sir. I guess it was."